Drifting Like the Waves

Patricia Montana

CONTENTS

1

CHAPTER 1

There were only three people in the kitchen, but still I felt suffocated.

Saying this, the head count did kind of depend on whether you counted Nora as a single person; as she leaned back in her chair, stomach jutting out alarmingly over her jeans, this was certainly debatable. Hitting the eighth month of pregnancy seemed to have triggered a growth spurt for my sister's unborn baby, as if it had suddenly realised it better get a move on if it had any hope of being born normal-sized. Nowadays, she looked as if she'd swallowed a beach ball, and most people had taken to eyeing her with a constant wariness, extremely aware of the risk of her popping at any moment.

The abundance of clutter in Gram's tiny kitchen wasn't exactly helping matters. Recipe books were stacked in the most random places – on top of the microwave, in the gap between the fridge and the worktop, even a couple functioning as a doorstop – which made no sense at all. Gram was what you might call an experimental chef; she relied more on her own instinct than printed instructions. Usually, this meant throwing odd combinations of ingredients together and hoping for the best.

And, as if that wasn't enough, she seemed to harbour a strange fetish for post-it notes. Masses were stuck all over the kitchen, most of them concentrated onto the fridge door, but the words scrawled across them were barely legible. I was in the middle of trying to work out what egg red oon meant when I noticed Gram had placed a steaming mug right under my nose.

Tea. Clearly, she'd not only missed the morning forecast that said we were in for highs of twenty-five, but had also failed to look out of the window and notice the sun shining over the town of Walden-on-Sea.

"Isn't this exciting?"

Looking up, I caught sight of Nora smiling wildly at the both of us. Her grin stretched so far across her face I thought it might split it clean in half; she seemed to be having trouble controlling her glee.

On the contrary, there was no danger of me having the same problem.

"I just can't believe it's finally happening, you know? Lenny and I getting our own place, Flo coming to live right by the sea! Won't it be lovely? Everything's just turning out to be so perfect."

Perfect was not the word I would've used to describe the situation, but I wasn't about to ruin Nora's good mood. Besides, I knew all too well that her crazy hormones could have that covered in three seconds flat. I'd spent the whole journey here listening to her nonstop chatter – detailing how wonderful it was going to be, how lucky I was to be able to step right out of the house and onto the beach, what colours she and Lenny were going to paint the baby's nursery (leaf green was looking their best option at the moment). The problem was I just didn't share her enthusiasm. I felt bad, really I did, but I just couldn't bring myself to be excited about the prospect of relocating from busy north London to the spectacularly boring seaside town of Walden-on-Sea to live with my grandmother.

It all started somewhere around the start of Nora's second trimester – a point at which she'd suddenly decided it'd be a good idea to sell the cosy London flat we'd shared forever and shack up with her hippie boyfriend Lenny.

Lenny, a guy who liked to refer to himself as an 'eco-warrior' was, hands down, the most bonkers person I knew. Long straggly hair – which was known to sometimes not see shampoo for weeks at a time – and a fashion sense only to be described as eccentric made up his normal appearance, while his time was divided between spending time with Nora and handing out flyers in the shopping centre to promote his world peace campaign.

A campaign which, I had to add, didn't seem to have achieved much more peace than putting Lenny on good terms with his downstairs neighbour.

He wasn't exactly most girls' dream guy, but then when was Nora ever like most girls? I didn't know what my older sister saw in him, but it had to be something. And something was enough to turn her into a total convert; before long, she'd gone full-on hippie, braiding her hair, recycling like a madwoman and obsessively checking the label of any non-organic item that found its way into our house.

She was in love.

And, shortly afterwards, knocked up.

I wouldn't have minded so much if we'd been able to stay put. Sure, a newborn baby would've been an inconvenience, but I could brace myself for the loss of a few hours' sleep. Though it wouldn't have made for the greatest living arrangement, I could've coped. But instead, Nora decided the only way she could give her baby the so-called 'stable family environment' it needed was to move into Lenny's flat.

And with no parents to speak of, where did that leave me?

The sleepy seaside town on the south coast, known as Walden-on-Sea, with a population of eighty per cent pensioners and one hundred per cent nutters. Home to my grandmother, who'd bought a cottage there ten years ago.

"Don't you think so, Flo?"

My head snapped upwards, an automatic reaction at the mention of my name. "What?"

"You can just smell that sea air, can't you?" She inhaled exaggeratedly, even though the kitchen windows were closed. "Bet it could cure anything. I'd probably consider moving down here myself if it wasn't for Lenny's job and all."

I wasn't sure occasionally using the 100 for a pound deal at the print shop to churn out a few flyers counted as a job, but I kept quiet.

"Yeah," I said instead, "what a shame."

Glancing back down at my mug, a closer inspection revealed it wasn't just tea at all, but instead some strange herbal concoction with a strange smell. Across the table, Nora had already started on hers – and by the looks of things, she was actually enjoying it. Knocking the drink back like water, she seemed relatively unconcerned by its questionable odour. Barely two minutes had passed before her mug hit the table again, and she looked over at Gram. "You haven't got any more of this stuff, have you?"

"Plenty," Gram answered, her worn slippers shuffling on the linoleum as she scuttled over to the kettle. "Do you want any more, Flo?"

"Oh, um…" My eyes shifted guiltily downward. "I'm okay for now, thanks."

Really, I should've been used to Nora's erratic cravings; they were here, there and everywhere as often as her mood. Just the other week I'd caught her in the kitchen at three a.m., poised to have a twenty-jar order of blueberry jam shipped to our door, special delivery. It was only luck that I'd been able to get to the laptop in the nick of time and cancel the order.

"But I love blueberry!" she'd protested.

She's allergic to blueberry.

"So, have you girls seen the town yet?" Gram asked. Her tone was bright, much like the outdoor sunshine, but I knew that the term 'town' was being used in its loosest sense. Walden-on-Sea was nothing more than a tiny village, adored by tourists for its quaint atmosphere and dinky little shops. It was one of the reasons Gram had been so drawn to it in the first place. My gaze swept over her – across the tight ringlet curls she swore were all natural, the pearly lipstick that wasn't quite neat at the edges, the thick lenses that made her eyes look slightly disproportionate. She was unchanged from the last couple of times we'd seen her. Still the same Gram. Maybe that was partly why I felt so apprehensive about moving in.

Before I'd even opened my mouth to speak, Nora cut in. "Not really. Only what we saw on the way down here."

"Oh, it's beautiful. You're going to love it, Flo."

She was looking at me now, the attention momentarily migrating away from Nora. I knew she could sense my lack of enthusiasm – anybody with half a brain could – but even for Gram, I couldn't pretend I was happy about moving away from London. It'd been home my entire life; I couldn't imagine living in a place where heavy passing vehicles didn't make the windows hum all hours of the day. Here, the faint calling of seagulls overhead seemed likely the only disturbance.

"Here's an idea – why don't you girls go and have a look around? Get to know the place a little bit. It's got a really great charm if you just give it a chance." She looked out into the hallway where my two unopened suitcases sat. "I've got to sort the spare room out before you can move in, so you might as well."

"Sounds great!"

Though the scraping of Nora's chair was almost instant, rising to her feet took considerably longer. She gripped the side of the table for support, tongue sticking out in concentration, finally managing to haul herself upwards. Physical exhaustion seemed to follow the ordeal, and she blew a strand of wavy blonde hair from her face. "Let's go."

I couldn't delay it any longer. Bringing the mug to my lips, I braced myself and took a swig. It was as bad as I expected: some foul-tasting herbal mix that could only be stomached with a hearty dose of pregnancy hormones. Trying my best not to splutter, I discreetly tipped the rest into the sink and hoped Gram had other types of teabag in her cupboard.

As it turned out, exploring the wonders of Walden-on-Sea took all of fifteen minutes. I knew the place was small, but I didn't realise just how tiny. It almost reminded me of that miniature town at Legoland, where everything was both reduced dramatically in size and oddly colourful. Even just passing through, I could sense the close-knit community; everyone and their dogs seemed to know each other, smiling like everybody was their oldest friend. In a way, it was nice, but my inner pessimist couldn't help but wonder how kindly they'd take to outsiders.

We trekked up the stony beach toward the rickety pier, but all that lay at the end was a set of ancient amusements that looked as if they'd been at their prime sometime in the eighties. The seafront housed a disappointing parade of shops, each painted a different shade of pastel, but none of them caught our interest either. Unless you happened to be looking for a laundrette, twenty-four-hour minimart or a fish 'n' chip shop, the shopping facilities of Walden-on-Sea were significantly lacking.

One that we did stop in front of, however, was a small whitewashed building sandwiched between a dinky little gift shop and the laundrette. Or rather Nora stopped, peering right into its window, which sort of blocked the entire path and left me with not much choice but to do the same.

"Look at that!" she exclaimed, pointing at a canvas which stood on an easel at the front of the display. It was a landscape, an intricate oil painting so delicate it showed almost every pebble of Walden-on-Sea's beach. "Isn't that one amazing? It looks just like a photo!"

Murmuring an agreement, my gaze trailed upwards to the shop sign – Walden Arts, it read, amateur art gallery. The painting in question was surrounded by a whole host of others making up a window display, an array that stretched from self-portraits to charcoal sketches to a sculpture made of a peculiar prickly wire. It looked somewhat like a dog, but I couldn't be sure.

"You know, your stuff should be in here too. Those sketches you keep in your bedroom are way better than some of this lot."

I shook my head vehemently, although I could feel myself glowing a little from the compliment. It didn't matter that it was from my sister: the most biased opinion I could get. "They're really not," I said. "And plus, I couldn't handle them being on show for everyone. It's bad enough you snooping through them in my room."

"Maybe you shouldn't leave them lying around."

"They were in my sketchbook!" I said. "Which I keep under my bed!"

Nora merely waved her hand dismissively. "Seriously, Flo," she began, turning to me with a rare undertone of sincerity to her expression, "you're talented. You could really get somewhere if you showed your work to other people. Nobody's going to see it underneath your bed."

"I don't want to."

It was true. To me, drawing was private: my personal equivalent of a diary. Nora only saw the end result because she was nosy, but that I could deal with. She was my closest friend, the only person I fully trusted. It hadn't always been that way, but out of the accident had sprung an intangible bond, pulling us closer together. Our relationship went well beyond the regular sisterly connection; in the past three years, she'd become two parents and an older sister, all rolled into one. Secrets were nonexistent between us.

And now we were being separated. Voluntarily.

I didn't know whether that made it better or worse.

"You are okay with this, though, aren't you?" Nora said, breaking me from my thoughts. "Moving down here with Gram, I mean. You'd tell me if you were really worried about it, wouldn't you?"

"Of course," I said immediately. I didn't even need to think about my response; it was automatic, the same way it had been every other time she'd asked over the past few months. "I'm fine."

Because how on earth was I supposed to tell Nora, who was on the brink of starting her new life and over the moon about it, anything different? She was moving in with Lenny, having the first child of the big family she'd dreamed of since she was a little girl. I couldn't stand in the way, just for the sake of staying in familiar surroundings, where I'd gained more stability than I'd ever thought possible after the accident.

She'd given up three years of her life to take care of me; I couldn't ask for more.

"Honestly, Flo, all it'll take is a bit of time and you'll love it here," she assured me. "I know it'll be strange at first, but you'll get used to it. We both will."

I forced myself to nod. "I know."

Part of me worried the conversation would continue, but it didn't need to. Within moments, Nora's attention had been diverted elsewhere: a location further along the street we were standing on. "Now, come on," she said, tugging at my arm. "I'm starving, and I think I saw an ice cream shop further down the road."

I sighed. "Nora, I'm really not that hungry..."

Looking back at me, she shook her head, determined not to take no for an answer. "Uh-uh. Ice cream makes everything better, and you, my friend, are in dire need of a double scoop."

She was right, of course. She always was. So I didn't pull away from the grip she had on my wrist, instead letting her drag me up the street, her insistent tugging something for me to follow as we headed toward the ice cream shop.

The ice cream shop that, although I didn't know it yet, was going to change my life.

2

—— ❧ ——

CHAPTER 2

Had it not been for her balloon-sized stomach, Nora probably would've skipped all the way down the street.

Realising this actually made me kind of thankful for the eight-pound baby growing inside her – if nothing else, it saved me from being embarrassed by my sister's immaturity. Still, I couldn't deny that the prospect of ice cream was growing more appealing by the second; it'd only just occurred to me that I'd skipped lunch, and it had only been the excitement – ha – of my arrival in Walden that had distracted me from thoughts of food.

I let her drag me the street, dodging the oncoming stream of people with a slightly embarrassing lack of agility and dignity. Passers-by tended to make way for Nora, for obvious reasons, but without the advantage of an obstacle-repelling balloon for a stomach, I had it significantly harder.

True to her word, at the end of the row of seafront shops sat a miniature ice cream parlour. Its outer walls shone a sunny yellow, setting it well apart from its pastel neighbours. To call it small would be a major understatement; ducking under the striped awning and pushing through the door, I almost went face-first into Nora's back. She'd come to an abrupt halt, pulling up the rear in a queue of tourists that wound all the way up to the counter and took up almost all of the shop's available floor space.

"So what do you think I should get?"

I'd barely adjusted to the dimmer light of the shop's interior, but Nora was already scanning the menu eagerly, her eyes glued to a large blackboard that covered the entire back wall.. On it was a long list of flavours, scrawled messily in chalk, but in a way that made the hurried scrawl seem intentional. Cartoon ice creams constituted the border, but my inner perfectionist was quick to pick up on how their cones were slightly too large to be proportionate, the hatched markings lacking the elements of a proper texture.

"What do you reckon – chocolate fudge brownie or mango swirl?"

"Um..." I blinked, momentarily struggling to find my sister's whereabouts on the menu we were reading from. "Well, I guess mango sounds—"

"Chocolate, yeah," she interjected, robbing me of the chance to finish my sentence. Leaning forward, she continued squinting at the board, while I hoped in doing so her bump wouldn't touch the back of the people in front of us. Said group was a family of four, their tourist status made obvious by their cheap beach shop flip-flops, huge bags and inflatable shark the dad had tucked under his armpit. "You can't go wrong with chocolate."

"Whatever you want," I told her, as the queue shifted forward a few paces. "Go wild."

She threw her arms up in the air. "See, but then there's caramel. And I like that too."

By now, she'd begun shaking her head, submerged in thought inside her ice cream centred world. Had Nora not been eight months pregnant, her indecisiveness might've been irritating, but I'd grown used to it. The thing was, my sister liked anything as long as her hormones told her to, and I knew firsthand how bi-polar those things could be, One moment she'd have a hankering for peanut butter; the next she'd be gagging, claiming the taste made her feel sick.

Needless to say, we hadn't eaten a normal meal in months.

Leaving her to it, my eyes began to wander around the shop, losing myself in its small details, the things I always seemed to pick up on. The walls, contrary to their exterior counterparts, were painted sky blue, while the tiles beneath our feet gleamed with fresh polish. Behind the counter was a little less organised; there seemed to be about ten different things happening simultaneously, unhindered by the fact there was only one member of staff in sight.

And when my eyes landed on him, my heart did a somersault.

Call me shallow, but he was cute, and that's all I noticed from a distance. The customer at the front of the queue appeared to crack a joke, because he laughed – and genuinely, too. A warm grin stretched the length of his face as he dug his scoop into the tub below him, slopping two hearty scoops of raspberry ripple onto a cone and passing it over. A uniform blue apron was tied around his front, a name badge I couldn't quite read fastened on the left breast. If only I were just a little bit closer, maybe I'd be able to...

"Flo!" The abrupt version of my name yanked me from my thoughts.

"Huh?"

"It's our turn," Nora informed me from her spot at the counter, looking amusedly between me and the grinning cashier. Not only was he playing spectator to our conversation, he seemed to be enjoying it too.

"Oh." I could already feel my cheeks flaming under his gaze; I wondered if I'd be a melting hazard to the ice cream if I got too close. "Right."

Against my instincts I stepped closer, moving into the spot beside my sister. "Now let's get an expert's opinion," she was saying, leaning casually on the glass display as if the guy was one of her closest friends. "Tell me. Which one do I go for: mango, chocolate or caramel?"

My movement had brought me close enough to read the nametag pinned to the cashier's apron: Daniel. For some strange reason, it seemed to suit him – even if my assumption was based on approximately thirty seconds of knowing he existed. A few strands of wavy brunette hair fell over his forehead and he shook them away, shifting his eyes toward Nora. "Well," he said, in a mock-serious tone, "that's a tough decision. From an ice cream maker's point of view, there could be no right answer." Then, he lowered his voice, leaning in closer. "But personally, I'd recommend the chocolate. You can't go wrong with chocolate, you know."

"That's exactly what I said!" Nora exclaimed, clapping her hands together. Though her loud voice and outspoken manner had probably attracted the attention of the entire shop by now, she seemed unconcerned as always. "Go for it, then. And make it a double scoop, please, love."

"You got it," Daniel responded easily, the scoop already in hand. "And for you, miss?"

It took longer than it should've for me to realise he was looking at – and talking to – me, which, of course, was the cue for me to have a mini heart attack.

"Um," I said, cringing internally at my stuttering tone, "just vanilla's fine, thanks."

"Just vanilla?" Daniel shook his head solemnly. "You shouldn't underestimate the simplicity of vanilla, you know. Some might say it's the ultimate ice cream flavour."

I laughed, although its slight shakiness was hard to overlook. "Right."

I watched as he dug his scoop into the tub of pale yellow ice cream, transferring each dollop onto the cone in his other hand. Then he moved onto Nora's, embellishing the two creations with a Flake in the side of each. Honestly, I was surprised my sister hadn't started drooling beside me. I let my eyes follow closely the movement of his hands, deciding this was a significantly less awkward place to keep them, as opposed to his ridiculously well-formed face.

"I haven't seen you guys around before," he commented offhandedly, as he rang up our order on the till. "Are you here just for the day?"

"Oh, no," Nora cut in, "we're not tourists. We're from London, but Flo here's moving down to live with our gran. I'm moving in with my boyfriend, you see, before the little one arrives." She gestured downward to her stomach, as if it wasn't obvious she was ready to pop out a baby at any moment.

I looked over at her. "Nora, he really doesn't need to know our life story."

But, to my surprise, Daniel didn't look bored, or seeking a convenient escape from the conversation – instead, he was looking curiously between the pair of us, his expression conveying genuine interest. "Really?" he asked, his eyes zoning in on me. I became suddenly aware of how bare my face felt – the commotion of moving day hadn't left make-up one of my top priorities – and how I'd carelessly pulled my dark hair up into a topknot to hide its frizz. "That'll be great," he said. "There are hardly kids our age in town, so it's pretty boring sometimes. It's nice to have new faces. Ones that stick around, I mean."

"See!" Nora looked at me pointedly, handing Daniel a ten pound note. "You've got friends already. You'll be fine."

Praying my cheeks wouldn't flush, and smiling politely, I took the cone being held out to me. Though I couldn't deny its visual appeal, cool ice cream glistening beneath the shop lights, I forced myself to resist the compulsion to take a first lick. Experience had made me aware of my inelegance, and I was likely to end up with ice cream dribbled all down my chin if I made so much as an attempt. Instead, I kept it in my hand and remained quiet as Nora and Daniel said their goodbyes, like friends who'd known each other for five years instead of five minutes.

"He was nice," she commented, as we left the shop and started up the street again. Just off to her left sat the beach, waves creeping up the shingle on the shore, clusters of small children splashing in the water. This dull babble, combined with the squawking of seagulls overhead, seemed to make up the soundtrack of Walden-on-Sea. "See, this place isn't as bad as you think."

"I never said it was bad," I pointed out. It was then that I deemed us far away enough from the shop to take a delicate lick of my ice cream. My tongue got one taste of the creamy vanilla, and I was already a goner. "I'm just not crazy about the place, okay? He said himself there aren't many teenagers in town. It's not exactly London, is it?"

"That doesn't have to be a bad thing." Extracting the Flake from her sticky cone, she crammed it into her mouth in one go. "I'm telling you, by the end of the summer, you'll have changed your tune. You'll wonder why you ever thought twice about moving here."

I didn't want to dishearten her, but the thing was, she couldn't have been further from the truth. I could tell from the off I wasn't going to like it here; however much I tried to pretend otherwise, it was never going to be home. Maybe if Nora was coming with me, it'd be easier. But she wasn't. She was staying behind, leaving me to fend for myself in this unfamiliar, close-knit town.

It was as this thought crossed my mind that I became aware of a noise somewhere behind us. It was a kind of faint yet persistent calling, a voice getting carried away by the wind before it had a chance to reach us properly.

I turned around in time to get the shock.

Daniel was bounding towards us, wavy hair flying wildly in the sea breeze. The knot in his apron strings had become untied, leaving the sides flapping open. "Wait up!" he called. A few seconds later, skidding to an abrupt halt right in front of us, he heaved a deep sigh and flashed me a smile that made my heart melt like the ice cream in my hand. "Hey."

"Um... hey," I said awkwardly.

He held out his hand, to which at first I frowned. But then my gaze trailed downwards, landing on the small collection of coins lying in his palm. "You, uh, forgot your change."

"Oh." I blinked. "Thanks."

"That's okay," he told me earnestly. "I don't like to short-change my customers."

I didn't think putting us a couple of quid out of pocket merited sprinting halfway down the street, but my mouth remained shut, as it often did. It wasn't like I was complaining; here I was, having my second conversation with what had to be the cutest guy in Walden, and I had yet to embarrass myself. At the periphery of my vision I could see Nora grinning like an idiot, struggling to contain her glee.

"Oh, and by the way," he said, reaching into his apron pocket. He pulled out something I couldn't quite see, but when he pressed it into my palm alongside the coins, I realised it was a slightly crumpled slip of paper. "There's a party tomorrow night. A start of summer, beach party sort of thing. It should be pretty fun. You should come along."

At first, all I could bring myself to do was stare back at him. Was he really inviting me – me – to a party? I mean, sure, it was obvious there was a lack of teens in town, but I hadn't realised that automatically rendered me invite-worthy of cool beach parties. This wasn't what usually happened when I met people for the first time, much less unnervingly attractive guys.

"Um," was all I managed to force out, leaving the passing wind, ruffling both of our hair, to make up the rest of the conversation.

"She'd love to," Nora cut in suddenly. The look I shot her was caught somewhere between embarrassment an relief; I only hoped she'd be able to decipher it herself.

"Great," Daniel said, looking back at me. "It'll probably start around seven, down on the beach. My number's on that piece of paper if you need it." He glanced over his shoulder, where the yellow building sat, abandoned. A few customers were milling around out-side, seemingly bemused by the momentary lack of management. "I better get back. I'll see you around, Flo."

The smile he flashed made my breath catch in my throat, but before I could even begin to form a goodbye, he'd set off jogging up the street. My gaze subconsciously followed his retreating figure, it becoming increasingly smaller before disappearing completely through the door of the shop. Only when it had closed behind him did the unnatural pace of my heart become apparent, and I released the breath I hadn't realised I'd been holding.

It was also then that I felt a cold sensation on my hand, and I looked down to find that my ice cream cone had since been melting in the afternoon sun, leaving my hand covered in a sticky vanilla mess.

3

—— • ——

CHAPTER 3

"**Y**ou sleep okay?"

This was Gram's question as I stumbled into the kitchen the next morning, making a beeline for the coffee pot. She asked like the answer couldn't be found in my appearance: the way my hair was defying the laws of physics and sticking up in every direction; the multitude of creases running through my nightshirt; the dark shadows I knew lurked beneath my eyes. I put it down to the fact she was totally absorbed in her artwork, sweeping wide strokes of paint across the canvas on the easel set up in the corner of the room.

"Mm," I mumbled noncommittally.

To tell the truth, my night's sleep had been nothing short of awful, but I wasn't sure I wanted to spill the details to Gram. My mind hadn't been able to stop whizzing through the events of the day at the speed of light, forcing sleep further and further out of my reach. Packing up the last of my stuff from the flat, the two-hour train journey here, my unexpected party invitation. They'd all been replayed in my head at least a hundred times over the course of the night.

And that wasn't even counting how many times I'd gone over the worst part of it all: saying goodbye to Nora.

I'd braced myself for it, of course, but the real thing had hit home harder than expected. Really, it'd only been when she pulled me in for a hug, and I got a last whiff of the strong floral perfume she was never without, that the reality of the situation began to sink in. It was real, it was here, and it was happening. That was something no amount of preparation could ready me for.

And when she'd leaned in and whispered "You'll be okay, Flo," in my ear, I found myself, through the tears, doubting my sister for the first time.

It didn't matter that I wasn't moving to the other side of the world. The train journey between us was enough of a distance. Nora had been my rock for the last three years: the one thing that remained to always be counted on. While everything else in my life was morphing before my eyes, changing beyond recognition, she was always there. Until now. I couldn't tell how I'd handle it until she was really gone.

Three years ago, when I was fourteen and Nora four years my senior, marked the worst day of my life. Our parents had spent the evening at a dinner party across town, enjoying themselves, trusting that Nora and I were sensible enough to stay home alone. Naturally, we'd revelled in the freedom, loving the knowledge that even if just for the evening, we were totally independent.

We didn't realise how disturbingly accurate that statement would be until a few hours later. Asleep on the sofa, we were jolted awake by an urgent knocking at the door. The police.

There'd been an accident. An accident involving two cars, one of them my parents', as they made their way home. They were almost there; ten minutes longer and they'd have been pulling up on the driveway, unlocking the door, smiling to themselves when they came across Nora and I curled up together. They'd behaved themselves; they were sober. But the other driver wasn't.

They were taken to the hospital straightaway, but it made no difference. Their injuries were fatal.

And on that night, in a split second, Nora and I lost both our mother and father.

It was the starting point to the darkest period of my life: a blackened tunnel of hopelessness that seemed to have no light at its end. At just eighteen, my sister was forced to drop out of college and find a job. When she did, her hours were long, exhausting and unsociable, but the alternative was much worse. I didn't like to think about it, but I couldn't always stop myself, especially at late hours of the night when I found myself alone on whatever was serving as my bed that night. We camped on every one of Nora's friends' sofas, testing their hospitality to the edge of politeness, before we finally scraped enough money together for the rent on a flat of our own. It was by no account luxurious – cramped, slightly damp, and with a boiler that had a tendency to cut out just as you wanted to take a shower – but to us, it didn't matter. It was our home.

And things got better.

At least until the day, three years later, over a bowl of cornflakes balanced on her oversized stomach, that she announced everything was changing. We were moving out, not in favour of an upgrade, but a split between Lenny's cluttered apartment and a dinky cottage in Walden-on-Sea.

And I ended up here.

"What are you painting?" I asked, keen to move the topic of conversation away from what would only dampen my mood further. Flicking the switch on the kettle, my eyes forged a path towards Gram's easel, which was covered in what looked like random splotches of paint. While both of us shared a love for art, there was no denying we differed infinitely in style. I preferred sketches, minimalist and rough-edged; Gram, on the contrary, had a passion for all things bright, bold and abstract. Her walls were covered with personal artwork, most of which I struggled to work out what they were, let alone decipher their meaning.

"Oh, just a little something," she answered vaguely, her paintbrush continuing to assault the canvas with surprising force. "The idea came to me last night."

'The idea' didn't currently resemble anything, but I wasn't about to point this out. Instead, I nodded understandingly and returned to my coffee.

I felt considerably better once I'd taken the first sip, pulling up a chair and collapsing into it while Gram continued working quietly in the corner. The caffeine seemed to have an instant effect; maybe it was psychological, but within moments my brain was rendered significantly more alert, the prospect of my first full day in Walden – the one that was currently staring me in the face – no longer seeming completely terrible.

"No plans for today, then?" Gram glanced over her shoulder. Her glasses had slipped right the way down her nose, perching so far towards the end she was looking more over than through them. "Nora said you got invited to a party."

I sighed inwardly. Really, I should've known better than to assume my crazy sister would keep quiet about yesterday's happening before heading back to London. I didn't even know whether I was going to go to the party in the first place; I could make a safe bet on the whole thing being painfully awkward.

"Oh, that," I said, hoping I sounded casual. "I might not even go, anyway. I've got a lot of... unpacking and stuff left to do."

Now, Gram turned away from her painting, brush flying through the air with sufficient speed to send a splattering of green paint onto the wooden tabletop. "Oh, no, honey," she said, "you have to go! You'll meet the other kids in town. And it'll be fun!"

Oh, sure. Me inevitably making a fool out of myself in front of Daniel's friends would be so fun.

On top of this, it didn't seem the greatest day for a beach party. Gram's cottage sat in a small cul-de-sac uphill from the main streets, giving the house's front-facing rooms a sea view. Looking out, I noticed yesterday's pleasant weather had done a vanishing act, to be replaced by a dismal blanket of clouds that warned of impending showers, coupled with a strong wind that had already picked up. From here, at least, Walden's stony beach didn't look like the perfect party venue.

"I'll think about it," I told her, picking up my coffee and deciding to leave her alone with her painting.

I was going to think about it. It just didn't seem likely that when I did come to a final decision, it'd be to go to the party. Walden was a tiny town, and whilst its close-knit community of pensioners was sweet, the same didn't apply to teenagers. They'd probably all known each other since playgroup, friendships established before they could even string a sentence together. How on earth was I meant to waltz in and befriend them? Me, of all people?

I was awkward enough around people I did know, let alone a group of strangers. For me to throw myself into a situation like that voluntarily? Not likely.

It was an hour later that I got my first taste of the boredom that was sure to be common over the approaching summer. I'd dragged out getting ready for as long as humanly possible, even combing out the frizzy curls of my hair into something of a tamed style, which was just a few steps short of a miracle. But having accomplished that, I was stumped as for what to do next.

Weighing up my options, of which there were shockingly few, I grabbed my sketchpad and a jacket and headed out the door.

I thought maybe once I found a spot inspiration would strike. Maybe a pretty landscape or, at the very least, something rough and quick that I'd probably crumple up later. I just needed something to do: something other than the flurry of thoughts inside my head to focus on. But after I'd headed down past the neighbouring houses, each as compact and quirky as Gram's cottage, and settled on a grassy spot overlooking the beach, I realised I had nothing. My mind had gone completely blank.

My pencil was poised over the paper, ready to snap into action in seconds if an idea came to me. But nothing happened, and the empty white paper stared mockingly back.

It stayed that way for at least ten minutes. The wind whipped past me, trying to tug my hair from its ponytail, and I could taste the salt in the air. Eventually I gave up on creativity, resigning myself to a simple drawing of Nora instead. But I had no luck with that either; no matter how hard I tried, I couldn't seem to get the curve of her bump right, and my pencil refused to capture her ever-present smile, twisting it instead into an expression that was both forced and awkward.

My attempt lasted a mere few minutes. Then, frustration got the better of me and I ripped the sheet violently from the pad, tossing it away. The force of the breeze picked it up immediately and it floated downwards, cascading into the water below before disintegrating into tissue.

Tucking my sketchpad underneath my arm (though I wanted nothing more than to chuck that into the ocean too), I abandoned my spot on the grass and backtracked my previous path. My feet were acting of their own accord; I was heading somewhere, if not fully consciously. It was only when I found myself on the pastel-coloured seafront that housed Walden's main line of shops that I stopped in my tracks. I was about ten seconds from walking past – and maybe even into – the shop where Daniel worked.

Why had I even come this way? For someone who wasn't a fan of awkward social situations, I seemed to have a knack for creating them. Yesterday had served as sufficient proof that I turned into a dithering idiot around him, and without Nora to keep the conversation flowing, it would almost definitely grind to a painful halt.

But I couldn't deny the obvious. I did kind of want to see him. Just a little.

So, despite the – probably rational – part of my brain that shouted its vehement objection, I took a deep breath and continued walking.

I noticed the striped awning first, its blue clashing with the pale yellow hue of the building's exterior. Overhead was a sign I hadn't noticed yesterday; it simply read Walden Ice Cream in a mock-handwritten font. And sure enough, there he was. I could see him through the window, scooping ice cream onto cones for the customers forming a queue out of the door. Hair falling over his forehead, he was leaning over, adding a third scoop to a creation that already looked at risk of toppling over.

It happened then. He looked up, and our gazes met.

Oh, crap. Abort mission.

And then he smiled.

I had to blink a few times, wondering if I was imagining things. But then I realised he really was smiling, and at me too. Either that, or he was oddly happy to see the two elderly women sat on the bench behind me, engrossed in a conversation about what Margaret had heard at bingo.

So I smiled back, hoping my windswept hair didn't look too much of a mess, before hurrying past.

I wasn't really sure what to do next, so I crossed the road and headed for the steps that led down onto the stony beach. The pebbles dug uncomfortably into the sole of my pumps, and I had a feeling they wouldn't feel much comfier on my backside, so I hopped up onto the wall separating the boardwalk from the beach below.

Reopening the sketchpad and setting it down on my lap, I took out my pencil and set to work immediately. I was surprised to feel it glide easily across the paper, requiring a minimal amount of thought to pave its path. I tuned out of the noise of the waves hitting rocks and the loud chatter of the tourists surrounding me until the rough sketch of a figure, leaning down slightly to scoop a hearty helping of ice cream, began to take shape across the page.

It was as I sat there, recreating the previous moment in tangible form, pencil to paper, that I decided maybe going to the party wouldn't be the worst idea in the world.

There's a reason why England isn't renowned for its beach parties, and, walking down the winding path that led from Gram's to the seafront, I found myself being assaulted by that very reason.

The clouds had been threatening it all day, but right here, a short time past seven in the evening, they'd decided to let rip. We hadn't even been lucky enough to get away with a drizzly shower; the rain was battering the pavement with surprising severity, and what I was sure were gale-force winds persistently threw off my balance. I'd spent a good half an hour picking out my outfit, puzzling over what would fall within the dress code, but I needn't have bothered. I was already soaked to the bone.

I failed to see how much partying could be done in weather like this, but I was already more than halfway there; legging it back to Gram's would take longer than seeking shelter in the town centre.

Unsurprisingly, when I did make it down there, I was faced with the sight of an empty beach. The rain had warded off even the bravest of tourists, and there was no party in sight.

Ducking under the awning of the ice cream shop, I leaned back against the brick wall and sighed. My first day in Walden had been miles short of success, and I was seriously evaluating the logistics of hopping on the first train back to London. I was sure, with enough persuasion, Nora and Lenny could rearrange some furniture and find room for me in their flat. It'd be a squeeze for the three of us – let alone with a newborn baby added into the equation – but it had to be possible somehow. Putting on a brave face about moving here had seemed easier in theory; now, I wasn't sure how long I could keep it up.

Then, suddenly, my train of thought was interrupted by the sound of an approaching car. I kept my head down, hoping that all kidnappers favoured cities over sleepy seaside towns, waiting for it to pass. But the low rumble of the engine didn't seem to be getting any more distant; in fact, the car sounded as if it had stopped directly in front of me.

"The party's not out here, you know."

My head snapped upward, following the sound of the voice. A combination of embarrassment and relief washed over me as I recognised the grinning face that I'd seen through the shop window just hours before, now hanging out the edge of the car.

"Well, where is it then?"

"We're having it at Collette's place instead." He paused, taking in my drenched appearance with an air of silent amusement, the smile still tugging at the corners of his lips. I felt considerably less composed, water trickling down my face and dripping from the ends of my hair. "You want a lift, by any chance?"

"That'd be nice," I murmured sarcastically.

Bowing my head, I scurried quickly over to the passenger's side, wrenching the door open and collapsing, soaking wet, into the seat beside Daniel. He'd started the engine up before I even clipped my belt into place, and within moments we were heading up the street.

I didn't even have time to think about the many ways in which this evening could go horribly wrong.

4

CHAPTER 4

"Nice English weather, huh?"

Daniel smiled wryly as he flicked the windscreen wiper setting up a notch. The rain was hitting the glass with battering sound effects, and what of it had come down on me was now seeping unpleasantly through the fabric of my top.

"Very." I paused, the question frozen on the tip of my tongue. "So, um... who's Collette?"

He drummed his fingers on the steering wheel, keeping his eyes fixed on the road ahead. "A friend," he told me plainly, but I could've sworn there was a hint of hesitance in his tone. "She's nice. We all are. I promise."

A breathy laugh escaped me. "How modest."

"Well, I wouldn't want to scare you off," he said, shooting a grin in my direction that pushed my heart into overdrive. "It's not often we get anyone new around here. I mean, it's really just been the five of us since Scott moved here a couple of years ago. There are very few others our age – ones that stay longer than week, that is." The end of the beach emerged on the horizon as the car continued along the road; a few moments later, Daniel hit the indicator and took a left. We were soon moving through a residential part of town I'd yet to venture into. "Walden's not exactly a happening place for teens, believe it or not."

I quirked an eyebrow. "Did you just say 'happening'?"

He groaned. "See what I mean? That's what spending too much time with your mum does to you. This is exactly why I pounce on anybody our age who moves here."

"I feel like I should be scared."

To this, he laughed. "Nah, you're alright. You'll get used to the Walden bubble soon enough."

"You've lived here all your life?"

"Yup. My mum and dad, too. My whole family's been here ages."

"I see." My gaze trailed back to the windscreen. I watched as droplets of water hit the glass, as quickly as the wipers removed them. "Well, this place is different to London, I can tell you that."

"Oh, I can imagine."

We were already beginning to slow down, though we'd barely been driving two minutes. I gathered Collette's house was not a distant destination. Rolling up to the end of the road, we finally pulled up outside a large detached house that seemed to subtly dominate its neighbours. Maybe it was the large front door, or the iron fence that marked the perimeter of the garden, or the way the lawn was mowed in a perfect vertical line pattern. Needless to say, it was a far cry from the quirky cottages in Gram's neighbourhood.

"I think the other guys are here already," Daniel said, shutting off the engine and pulling the key from the ignition.

"Oh, okay." I was sure my quiet response was barely audible, but I couldn't help it. A clenching feeling had started up in my stomach, my palms already sweating. It's just a party, Flo, I told myself as I followed Daniel's lead and got out of the car. The rain was showing no signs of letting up, still beating down as ferociously as ever, leaving little time for admiration as we hurried up the front path and dived under the house's porch.

Daniel seemed to catch sight of my apprehensive expression, offering me a sympathetic smile. "You don't need to look so worried," he assured me, pressing hard on the doorbell. "They don't bite, I swear."

"I'm holding you to that."

I was joking, of course, but the moment the door swung open the doubt swept in like the tide. The girl who stood before us was strikingly pretty – so much so that she would've looked more in place on some kind of Walden reality show. Her chocolate brown hair was cropped into a short style, finishing above her collarbone, and the jeans that hung from her hips gave her a better figure than I could ever dream of. An array of gold bracelets on her left wrist jangled with every movement. "Look who finally showed," she said, her lips twitching upward into a smile at the sight of Daniel. Then, she noticed me. "And, um... who's this?"

"This is Flo," he responded smoothly, as I tried not to go dithery at his use of my name. "She just moved here, and I invited her along. Flo, Collette. Collette, Flo."

I smiled shyly, shrinking under the intensity of the brunette's gaze. "Nice to meet you."

"You too," she said slowly, but there was a blaze behind her eyes that I didn't like the look of. Though only having met her acquaintance for thirty seconds, I got the impression Collette was not a girl you wanted to get on the wrong side of. "Well, come in. The guys are in the lounge."

She moved aside to let us in, and I stepped across the threshold onto the cream carpet. Daniel kicked off his shoes so I did the same, hoping this would at least do something to stop Collette staring so intensely. Making a mental note to limit my interaction with her as much as possible, I followed Daniel through a door to the right and emerged beside him in the living room.

It was expensive; that much I gathered from the décor. Though not supersize, the house had a certain extravagance that seemed a running theme throughout the entire place. The lounge was painted a deep burgundy, its furniture decked out in matching shades of red and cream. A collection of sofas and armchairs were angled towards a large TV; onscreen, a music channel was playing.

"Look who it is!"

It took me longer than it should've to register there were people in the room, their presence suddenly strikingly obvious. One sat on the cream two-seater, one was perched on the edge of an armchair, while another was lounging on the plush rug in the centre of the room. Each had a can in their hand, and there were two unopened beer packets on the coffee table.

The guy who had spoken was the one on the sofa. His jet black hair contained way too much product, making it stick up in all directions in a way that completely defied the laws of gravity. "Alright, mate?" he said. Then, his eyes flickered towards me, about the same time as everybody else's in the room did the same. I could feel my cheeks warming under their scrutiny. "Who are you?"

"Jay!" The girl on the rug shot him a stern look. She probably would've looked normal, if it hadn't been for the fact that her hair was a violent shade of purple. "Don't be so rude!"

"I was just asking," he mumbled.

Daniel moved forward, snatching up a beer from the packet and gesturing towards me. "Guys, this is Flo," he announced for the second time. "She just moved to Walden yesterday."

I gave a little wave, which, I realised afterward, probably looked incredibly awkward. "Um... hi."

Daniel gestured toward the purple-haired girl sprawled on the rug. "This is Erin," he told me. "My sister. Twin sister. Unfortunately." Erin stuck out her tongue, scowling at him. As she did so, I caught sight of a glinting silver stud I guessed was an act of rebellion. "Then there's Jay," he pointed at the guy on the sofa, "and Scott." The guy sitting in the armchair was a brunet, with a gangly look about him. Even whilst sitting, it was easy to tell he towered over the rest of the group.

Daniel cracked open his can and sunk into the second armchair, Collette moving to perch on the arm of Scott's seat. Indifference was still painted across her pretty features, and I silently wondered how long it would be before any of us saw her crack a smile. There was definitely something off about her; she seemed to radiate tension, its quivering waves diffracting into every corner of the room.

When I returned to the present a beat later, I realised I was still stood awkwardly by the door, faced by the rest of the group's expectant stares. "You know," Erin started, "you can sit down."

"Yeah," Jay chipped in, patting the seat beside him, "come sit next to me."

His smile was flirtatious, and may have worked on some girls, but it just made me feel awkward. I briefly scanned the room for another space, but came up short; the empty spot next to him looked like my only option. So, praying I wouldn't trip and make a fool of myself, I made my way over and lowered myself tentatively onto the sofa.

They were all looking at me.

Daniel obviously hadn't been kidding when he said newbies were something of a rarity in Walden. I felt as if I belonged behind a polished glass screen in a museum, instead of perched on a cream sofa in somebody called Collette's house.

"So where did you come from?" Jay asked.

Erin, whose can was pressed to her lips, suddenly choked. She suffered a few spates of coughing before finally managing to compose herself, wiping her mouth with the back of her hand. "Weren't your parents supposed to have had that talk with you a while back, Jay?" she said, smirking.

He shook his head, while I wondered exactly how much gel was required to ensure total prevention of movement of his hair. "Don't worry. I'm completely clued up on the facts of life," he assured me with a wink. In my peripheral vision, I noticed Collette rolling her eyes. "But anyway. Where did you move from?"

They were all still looking at me, intrigued. I wished it hadn't become so difficult to form a coherent sentence. "London."

"That's so cool," Erin sighed wistfully. "God, I wish I lived in London. It'd be way more exciting than this stupid place. Well, actually, anywhere's more exciting than this place."

"Amen to that," I heard Collette mutter.

All of a sudden, noisy footsteps clattered from somewhere outside the living room door. Regular and fast-paced, they were undoubtedly the sound of someone making their hurried way down the stairs. A wave of silence fell across the room, leaving only the upbeat tempo of the pop song playing in the background to fill the empty space. But it was soon cut short by the door swinging open, thrust with so much force that it almost bounced off the wall behind it.

"Collette!" The high-pitched screech bounced off all four walls, its sound unpleasantly amplified.

I looked up to identify its owner; in doing so, I had to consciously stop myself from drawing a sharp breath. A girl stood in the door-frame, her tall stature emphasised by the sky-scraping heels that stood between her feet and the floor. Her features were unmistakably from the same gene pool as Collette's, but somehow hers were more strikingly defined and framed by honey-coloured curls instead of a cropped brunette style.

She was the type of girl who commanded immediately the attention of any room, and this one proved to be no exception.

"Alright, Beth?" Jay said.

She cast him a look that verged on tolerance before turning her attention toward what I assumed was her sister. "Collette, have you seen my keys?"

"I haven't touched your keys," she shot back instantly, tongue sharper than Erin's piercing.

"Well, I'm pretty sure I left them in my handbag, and now they're not there. You must have moved them. Didn't you take my car out the other day?"

Collette narrowed her eyes. "No."

"Oh, come on. It's pretty obvious you've moved them," Beth said impatiently, placing a hand on her hip. "Let's just hurry this up and cut to the chase. I'm late for this party as it is – they'll be wondering where I've got to."

"I told you. I haven't seen them."

"Jesus, Collette, are you trying to make my life harder than it already is?" she exclaimed, tone accelerating through a good few octaves. "You know how important these social events are. Not just for me, but for my career. What are people going to think of me when I can't even show up on time? I'll never get booked!"

"Hey." Daniel cut in, his voice an oasis of calm amongst the arguing pair. "Is it these you're looking for?" His hand had reached over, extracting a set of keys from the table beside him. The room's atmosphere shifted tangibly, but it was obvious that speaking was still very much out of the question.

Beth blinked. "Yeah," she said eventually. "That's them."

She stalked across the living room, her sharp stilettos digging into the carpet, before snatching the keys from Daniel and heading straight back out again.

"Have fun at your party!" Jay called, but Beth didn't spare him so much as a fleeting glance; with her, his attempts at flirting clearly fell flat.

"Well," said Erin loudly, once the front door had slammed shut, "isn't she just a ray of sunshine?"

"Don't even go there." Collette's warning was final: something not to be questioned. Her expression had intensified, passing through the stages of sulkiness into one of just anger. "She's only been home from uni a week and I'm already sick of her. We've still got another two months yet.

"I'm fed up of her thinking she's it all the time, just because she's doing a law degree and a tiny bit of modelling on the side. God, with the way she goes on you'd think she was the next Naomi Campbell or something. She's only done a couple of fucking catalogues."

An uneasy silence descended upon us; no one seemed to know quite what to say next. Collette was oblivious, taking an angry sip of her drink.

"So..." Scott said slowly.

"What now?" asked Erin.

"How about a game of Spin the Bottle?" Jay suggested.

The purple-haired girl just rolled her eyes. "We're not twelve."

"What? There's nothing wrong with Spin the Bottle."

"Oh, of course not," she countered sarcastically. "Because it's just a coincidence that every time you play it, you end up snogging every girl in the room."

"What can I say?" He shrugged. "I'm lucky." It was then that he turned to me, a mischievous grin forming across his impish face. "What do you say, Flo? Fancy a game? Maybe just me and you, if no one else wants to play..."

A collective groan resounded across the room. I could feel my cheeks darkening, although it was clear Jay would flirt with anything that moved. "Uh, I think I'm good," I told him.

To tell the truth, I was more than relieved by the others' opposition to the idea. I'd never freely admit it, but I'd never even played the game before. My experience was limited to Year Eight gossip I'd overheard in the school toilets: about who had ended up kissing who and had they really used tongue? It wasn't so much the game that made me nervous – more the fact that when the bottle landed on me (which, if Jay was involved, it undoubtedly would) it would become spectacularly obvious to everyone that I didn't have the faintest idea how to kiss.

It was shameful, I knew, at seventeen. But true.

"You might as well give up," Daniel said from across the room. "She's not interested."

"And your flirting technique seriously needs some work," Erin muttered.

An arm suddenly wrapped around my shoulder as Jay squeezed me into his side. Pressed against him, I got a strong whiff of hair gel and way too much Lynx. "Flo loves it," he announced, though my expression was very much contrary. Seconds later, I felt his grip loosen. "Hey, you know you're all wet, don't you?"

I wriggled away, wondering if it was my imagination or if the room really was shrinking in size. "Well, it was raining outside."

"And you were silly enough to go out in it." He shook his head, tutting. "Couldn't you have just got your parents to drop you off, or something?"

I froze; every muscle in my body seemed to simultaneously cease function. "What?"

"Your parents," he repeated, slower this time, as if I was hard of hearing. But of course I'd heard it perfectly, and the second time too; every drawn-out syllable was another stab in the gut. "What, they just leave you to walk places on your own in the pouring rain? That's kind of harsh."

I could feel the nausea rising inside of me, pooling in my stomach and throat, even though I hadn't touched any of the beer on the table. Jay's arm around my shoulder had turned unpleasant and restricting; I pushed it away, rising, somewhat unsteadily, to my feet. Five pairs of curious eyes were all trained on me, and I could feel my chances of a good first impression disintegrating with every movement, but I didn't care.

I just had to get out of there. If I didn't, I felt as if I might explode.

I could vaguely make out someone's voice from across the room, asking me where I was going. It sounded like Daniel's, but I couldn't be sure; only a fraction of my attention remained on them, the rest fixated on escaping by any possible means.

I think I mumbled something along the lines of Toilet, back in a sec. At least that's what I intended to do. The room was the size of a cupboard now, its walls squeezing together and trapping me hopelessly in the middle. There was no air – or maybe it just refused to enter my lungs.

I finally wrenched the door open and emerged in the hallway, my head reeling.

And, standing there amongst the painful emptiness, I wondered why it suddenly felt so hard to breathe.

5

CHAPTER 5

I didn't know where the bathroom was, but a stab in the dark led me to the door directly opposite; all I could do was hope it was the right one. Thankfully, as it swung open, I was greeted by a roomful of gleaming white tile and a significantly cooler temperature, both of which I didn't hesitate to stumble into.

What was wrong with me? Jesus, I'd never had a reaction like that before. I thought I'd dealt with the fact that my parents weren't around anymore long ago. Whilst I was still prone to onsets of sadness if they were mentioned, it was usually nothing more crippling than a twinge, or tears that I'd quickly wipe with the back of my hand.

But that?

I knew Jay hadn't meant anything by it. After all, how was he supposed to know that the girl beside him – the one who looked completely normal, with curly hair and freckles on her nose – had been ripped apart by grief only several years before? No one could tell. I didn't have a tattoo that read orphan on my forehead. I didn't come with a warning label that instructed the outside world to approach the topic with caution. I didn't have any visible scars.

So who could blame him, really? In fact, I was the one at fault.

I took a few minutes to compose myself, splashing cold water onto my face and furiously commanding my reflection in the pristine mirror to get a grip. But that was easier said than done. Honestly, I was considering making a break for it out the front door. It wasn't like I wanted to abandon the group of people who were my only escape from the prospect of a pathetically friendless summer. But what was I supposed to say to them?

I couldn't go back and explain the real reason behind my sudden exit. It'd ruin everything – and just fifteen minutes into the evening. I'd be stuck with a label that would stretch well beyond the end of summer. I could kiss goodbye to being just Flo, the new girl. The moment the truth came out, I was destined to become Flo, the new girl with the dead parents. The one who might freak out at any minute. And, as I knew from experience, that was an impossible stain to get off.

Back home in London, in the initial aftermath of the accident, the entire school found out within a matter of days. I still wasn't sure exactly how it spread so quickly, but I became a tragic case overnight, plagued by whispers and bated breath everywhere I set foot. People tiptoed around me, keeping themselves at arm's length like I was a bomb at risk of exploding at the slightest thing. And then there were the pity looks: those awful expressions, masking the faces of everybody I knew. I got them from everybody: my friends; classmates I'd never spoken to; teachers, especially. Suddenly I was never the girl picked last for teams in PE, never expected to go up to the whiteboard and explain one of the homework questions, never receiving detention for missing homework in the first place. I was permanently excused.

And I hated every second of it.

Here in Walden, I wasn't that girl. Daniel had looked at Nora and I with more than sympathy, and to the others, I was more than just a tragic past. I was the new girl, clinging with both hands to the potential to be anybody I wanted. For the first time in three years, I was without the label stuck over my forehead.

I couldn't tell them. I couldn't lose grip on those endless possibilities, of finally having people who knew me for me, not the tragic details of what had shaped my being.

And most of all, I couldn't handle Daniel taking pity on me.

I couldn't go back in there and face them. It was decided: the only thing for it was to make a break for it out of the door. I didn't even care about the rain. If I ran into any of them later, I'd have to conjure up an excuse about not feeling well.

Mercilessly, my plan was foiled the moment I stepped from the bathroom. I jumped slightly, suddenly noticing Erin standing in the hall, leaning against the doorframe and waiting for me. She looked up as the door clicked shut behind my frozen form.

"Hey," she said. "You okay?"

I cleared my throat, which, for some reason, felt like sandpaper. "Yeah. I'm fine."

"You look pretty pale." She was studying me through slightly narrowed eyes, but there was nothing judgemental about her gaze. "You sure you feel okay? I can get you a drink or something."

"Uh…" My own eyes flickered back to the living room. Its door was ever so slightly ajar, snatches of animated conversation escaping from the small gap. "A glass of water would be great, actually."

Erin pushed herself into an upright position, starting in the direction of a door at the other end of the hall. I followed after her. Seconds later, we emerged in a huge kitchen, all white tiles and granite worktops, each and every item stowed neatly in its allotted place. It was worlds away from Gram's pleasantly untidy workspace, where the mess seemed almost comforting.

Wandering over to the sink, Erin took a glass from a cupboard overhead and filled it from the tap. For a house that wasn't her own, she seemed to know her way around. Maybe she and Collette were close, though I couldn't imagine it.

"Here."

I blinked, realising she was holding the glass out to me. Tentatively bringing it to my lips, I took a shaky sip, well aware of Erin's eyes fixed on me.

"So," she said, as if deciding the moment of silence had stretched too wide, "you want to tell me what that was back there, or...?"

I swallowed. Really, I should've known it was coming. "Um..."

"I mean, you don't have to if you don't want to." Erin was leaning back against the counter, her hair seeming a shade brighter amongst the abundance of white tile. I found myself wondering what had possessed her to even go for such a colour in the first place. She was still looking at me, trying to analyse my expression, but all I wanted to do was squirm.

Desperate to detract from the question, but not really thinking, I blurted out, "What colour is your hair naturally?"

I couldn't read her look for the life of me. "Bright blue," she said, completely serious, before resuming her original topic with ease. "Look, I know we've only just met. But I thought you might want to talk about it, you know—"

"Did that thing in your tongue hurt?" I asked. I knew what I was doing was stupid, but I couldn't bring myself to stop. Stopping meant talking, and talking, I wasn't ready for.

"Like a bitch," she answered automatically. "Look, Flo—"

"I could never get something like that done," I babbled on. "I'd probably chicken out at the last minute, you know. I'd be way too scared for that sort of—"

"Flo." Her voice cut me off, and I froze. "Look, if you don't want to talk about it, then I'm not forcing you. Just say."

Biting my lip, my gaze trailed to the spotless tiles beneath my feet. Each one seemed too perfect – so perfectly in line, free from even the tiniest specks of dirt – to an extent that I found myself irritated. But it still wasn't enough to get me to look at Erin; she seemed too perceptive, like she could figure me out completely if she just looked for long enough. "It's kind of... personal."

Was it? Up until now, the details had pretty much been public knowledge. But this was Walden, and I didn't know where I stood.

"Oh. Right."

I felt bad for shutting her out, but how was I supposed to tell her? Let it slip, and there wasn't any way to take it back. Secrets were irreversible. Thirty minutes of knowing them – that was all – and I'd be labelled. Forever looked on with pity, listening to them censor their words for fear of saying the wrong thing. I'd had enough of that in the past three years. Was it really so wrong to disclose the truth for just a little while?

I didn't want to be Flo, the girl whose parents had died. The girl with only her sister left.

For a while, couldn't I just be Flo?

Erin had finally moved her gaze away, no longer scrutinising my face and what might lie beneath it. The awkwardness was quickly approaching, beginning to seep in faster than we could stop it. "I...

maybe we should go back." Bringing the glass to my lips, I drained the rest in one go. "They'll probably be wondering where we are."

"Oh. Yeah." She blinked, like she'd forgotten about the other four people in the next room.

I set the glass down quietly, starting towards the door. My damp socks squeaked on the polished floor as they skidded across it, the friction not quite enough to keep my feet steady. The sound of movement behind me confirmed that Erin was following my lead.

Or at least she was, until I'd reached the door. I had one foot over the threshold, the other still skimming the tile, when her voice cut in. Her tone was quiet, yet had an impact as sharp as a carving knife. "How did you lose them?"

I turned to ice, my body poised to take another step, but rendered physically incapable. Somehow, I regained enough composure to turn around, allowing my eyes to fall upon her solemn expression. "I..." I swallowed thickly. Could she really be referring to what I thought she was? I'd thought it impossible, but her gaze seemed to read nothing else. "What?"

"Your parents," she said evenly. "How did you lose them?"

She knew. She really knew. How could she know? How had she figured me out in such a short space of time?

She had. She knew. The words were buzzing around in my head, their movement wildly rabid, ricocheting off the sides and multiplying by the second. I wanted to lie, wanted so desperately to tell her that she'd got it wrong, but I knew there was no point. "It was a car accident," I forced out, barely louder than a whisper. "Three years ago."

"I'm sorry." I'd heard it hundreds of times before, each out of nothing more than politeness, but there was a kind of fiery sympathy behind her eyes that assured me it was genuine. There was something different about Erin. It was almost like she understood.

"How did you know?"

She sighed: a premonition. "We lost our dad," she said eventually. "Daniel and I. It was almost a year ago now."

I swallowed over the lump in my throat; this, I had not expected. I wanted so desperately to say something, assure her that I knew exactly how she felt, let her know somehow that I could empathise with whatever they'd struggled through. I wanted to do something to alleviate the vacant look of sadness that had glazed over her face. But the words had lodged themselves somewhere in my throat; I could almost feel their physical presence digging into my windpipe. All I could bring myself to whisper was, "I'm sorry."

A saying I knew from experience was meaningless. Weak. Empty. And I hated myself for saying it.

"It was cancer," she explained, uttering the word with disturbing ease. "So it wasn't like it was sudden, or anything. We knew he was sick for a while. Still... Daniel took it pretty hard."

His name sent a jolt of pain through me. I wondered if this was what other people felt when they heard about me, or whether my sense of grief had toyed with my emotions. Opening my mouth to speak, I racked my brain for something to say, but Erin had snapped out of it before anything could pass my lips. She shook her head vigorously, sending her purple waves flying.

"God, this is a depressing conversation, isn't it?"

I nodded as she took several steps towards the door. I wanted to ask her about Daniel, get her to elaborate on his recent past, but this was clearly a line not to be overstepped.

"Um, Erin?"

She was already halfway out by this point, pausing to look at me. "Yeah?"

"Could you not... you know, tell the others about this? Just yet." I swallowed. "I'm not ready."

I watched her features shift, expression morphing into something unrecognisable for a split second, but it had vanished before I could take a proper look. "Got it," she told me, with an almost melancholy smile. "My lips are sealed."

"Thanks."

"But Flo..." She paused, pondering her next thought, her voice gentle and tentative, forging a path through the silent air. "Just... don't underestimate the others, okay? They're more understanding than you think."

"I—"

"Just trust me, okay?" she cut in softly. "Trust me."

I thought of Collette, and how she didn't exactly seem the epitome of understanding, but something in Erin's tone held me back from saying anything else. The whole situation seemed vaguely surreal, as if this formed part of a hazy dream whose details would ebb away later. I couldn't even pinpoint the moment the uncomfortable clenching feeling in my chest had ceased.

"You okay to go back in there?"

I forced a smile, but I did feel infinitely more at ease. The lingering prospect of returning to Collette's living room no longer filled me with laden dread. "Yeah," I breathed, looking up to meet Erin's gaze. "Thanks."

"You don't need to thank me," she said. "What are friends for?"

Friends. An unknown reason sent an inner warmth spreading through me, igniting across every part of my body. It felt simultaneously peculiar and wonderful, a feeling so dated and unfamiliar I hadn't even known I'd experience again. Let alone in a stranger's shiny kitchen in the middle of Walden, after a conversation like that.

"Now, come on," she said, beckoning, "let's go back. Just, you know, mentally prepare yourself for Jay."

As the thought of the shameless flirt and his ridiculously gelled hair slipped back into my mind, I was surprised to realise that his bold advances and awful sense of personal space no longer brought on a fit of anxiety. Instead, I actually laughed out loud. And when we re-entered the living room, and I plonked myself back in my original spot in the midst of it all, it occurred to me that they weren't so intimidating after all. Even Collette looked considerably less frightening when she was giggling at something Scott had said.

In fact, if you took the time to look closely, maybe we were more similar than I thought.

Maybe.

6

CHAPTER 6

Downstairs, I could hear thumping.

It wasn't even soft, either; it was an extremely loud, incredibly distracting type of thumping that jogged my pencil each time it started up again. I was trying to sketch the view from my window – a relatively easy task, for lack of a better thing to do – but the way this was going, it looked like Walden was in the middle of a particularly violent earthquake. I just couldn't stop my pencil from jerking every few strokes. It sounded like Gram had taken a hammer and was hacking violently at the wall; this, perhaps, was the main reason I decided to rise from my desk and investigate.

I found her in the kitchen. She was bent over her washing machine, which she'd dragged out from the wall, whacking at it forcefully with her fist.

"Uh, Gram?" My voice was drowned out by another loud thump; I cleared my throat and tried again. "Gram!"

This time she stopped, spinning around to face me. Her glasses had slid right down to the end of her nose, so that she peered at me over the top of the frames. "Yes, dear?"

I frowned. "What are you doing?"

"Well," she said, "the washing machine's broken."

"Right," I responded slowly, wondering if I was missing something obvious here. "And, um… you're punching it why exactly?"

"I seem to remember I had the exact same problem a few years ago," she mused. Of course, when Gram said 'a few years ago', we were more likely to be looking at a timescale of around thirty years previously. "And Jim tried something like this, I'm sure. But it doesn't seem to be working this time."

I was pretty sure the washing machine's instruction manual would advise against physical assault as a method of repair, but I didn't voice my opinion. Instead, I suggested gingerly, "Well, maybe you should call someone out to take a look."

"Hmm… maybe." She was still frowning at it, as if by narrowing her eyes the problem would magically disappear. "The trouble is, I've got a huge pile of washing to do and it'll probably take a while for someone to come out." She paused. "Maybe I should just have another go at doing it myself…"

"No!" I interjected, a little too quickly. "I mean, the launderette's only down the road. I could go down there and do it for you."

Though spending an afternoon with the contents of Gram's wash basket didn't sound exceedingly appealing, I was more worried about her doing herself an injury tinkering with the thing. Not to mention flooding the kitchen if she managed to whack it hard enough. For such a little woman, she had a surprising amount of strength.

"Really? Well, that'd be a great help, Flo, but you don't have to."

"It's fine," I assured her. "I'll do it. You just go dig out the Yellow Pages and get a number for a plumber, okay?"

That was why, half an hour later, I found myself on the way down to the town centre with a zip-up bag of Gram's washing in one hand.

For once, the sun was actually shining over Walden, sending tourists flocking to the beach and making the pebbled shoreline busier than I'd ever seen it before. Free spots were disappearing at an alarming rate; everywhere I looked, there seemed to be another family piling in, setting up their windbreakers and tents whilst the kids made for the sea. I had to consciously block out the flashback that was threatening to set in – of seaside day trips when Nora and I were kids, filled with smiles and afternoon ice-creams and my parents holding hands. I was closer to them now than I'd ever been, yet the memories seemed a lifetime away.

As I reached the boardwalk, starting in the direction of the launderette, I couldn't help but let my eyes linger on the ice-cream shop. It sat a little further along the street, but even from here I could see the place was packed; the queue stretched right outside the door, and I could picture Daniel inside, scooping double and triple cones at top speed.

Five days had passed the party, but they'd been five days that had stretched on forever. Each time I ventured out of Gram's cottage I got my hopes up that I'd bump into one of them again, but I always seemed to be in the wrong place at the wrong time. I still had Daniel's number, scrawled on the crumpled piece of paper that now sat tucked safely inside my favourite book, but I hadn't worked up the nerve to contact him.

My conversation with Erin had left the evening looking up considerably. For once, I'd felt myself able to relax – and then of course there was the hilarity that ensued when Jay downed one too many beers and ended up dancing drunkenly to the Macarena on Collette's coffee table.

A bell tinkled overhead as I pushed through the door of the laundrette. The smell of washing powder was pungent in the air; I could feel my nose tingling instantly. Aside from an elderly lady engrossed in an edition of Knit Today on one of the plastic benches, the place was empty.

We exchanged a curt nod as I walked by, but when I approached the nearest machine and stood blankly in front of it for a second, I realised I didn't have the faintest clue about how to use it.

Deciding to go with the thing that seemed most sensible, I began pulling the pile of clothing from Gram's bag and stuffing it into the machine. I shoved the few pairs of her baggy white underwear in as quickly as possible, sincerely hoping that the old lady behind me was absorbed deeply enough in her knitting patterns to remain uninterested by my washing.

There was a powder dispenser over on the far wall, so that was my next port of call. Digging through the mounds of change Gram had equipped me with, I eventually came up with a couple of coins and slotted them in. So far, so good, I thought, as I took the cup. I only hoped that the lady would yell if she could see me doing something completely idiotic.

Like trying to put detergent in the dryer, or something.

In fact, it all seemed to be going pretty well. At least that's what I assumed several minutes later, once I'd actually managed to get the machine going. At any rate, I could see water splashing against the circular glass door, which had to be a good sign. Feeling pleased with myself, I sunk back onto one of the plastic seats and wondered if I was just a natural at doing laundry.

As it went, my good mood only lasted about ten minutes into the spin cycle. It was at that point that the boredom began to set in, and I realised it probably would've been wise to bring something to pass the time. Even if it did happen to be this week's issue of knitting patterns.

Contrary to popular belief, sitting alone in a silent launderette with only an elderly stranger for company wasn't the most exciting way I could've spent my afternoon.

Eventually I settled into people watching, which, considering the odd mix of tourists that could be found on any given day in Walden, had the potential to provide some entertainment. Still, that didn't mean I didn't get tired of seeing the same people walk up and down, striding past the launderette as if it were invisible to the naked eye. The most common passers included the single mother of identical triplets, who looked as if the weight of the world rested on her shoulders, a man who had possibly the worst sunglasses tan I'd ever seen, and a young couple that seemed to think it incredibly romantic (instead of just cheap) to share a single ice cream between them. Honestly.

I'd already transferred the clothes to the dryer, and was about to check how much time the cycle had remaining, when the sight of a familiar pair caused me to start. They were walking cheerily past the window: a tall brunet, ducking down slightly to hear what the other was saying, and the unmistakable violet ponytail of the girl beside him.

I went to duck out of sight, suddenly chickening out, but I wasn't quick enough.

Erin was the one to spot me; her peripheral vision must've been exceptional, because her feet dragged to a halt just moments after passing the window. Daniel, obviously less observant, continued walking for a few paces until he noticed the absence of his twin beside him, and looked back to see where she'd got to.

"Look!" I heard her say, her voice muffled through the glass. "It's Flo!"

Daniel, slightly bemused, took longer to grasp the situation. His gaze followed Erin's pointing finger dazedly, but a flicker of realisation appeared once his eyes had landed on me. "Oh!"

Maybe he was going to say something more, but he didn't get the chance; his sister had already taken hold of his wrist, yanking him toward the launderette door.

"Hi!" Erin called, thundering into the tiny place with as much force as a tornado. Her presence seemed to come in shockwaves, each one reverberating into every corner of the room. Daniel trailed behind her, much calmer by comparison.

"Hey," I said awkwardly, not quite sure how to go about our greetings. "Um, what are you guys doing here?"

"Lunch break," Daniel told me with a smile. "We were going to grab some chips. Didn't expect to see you in here, of all places."

"Well..." I scratched the back of my head sheepishly. "Our washing machine broke, and I offered to come down here, so..."

"Ah, right. So you're like, the good Samaritan of the family?"

My mind wandered back to Gram's unconventional repair method, and how my offer had only really been to prevent large-scale damage. "Something like that."

"Well, if you're almost done here, you could come with us," he suggested. "You know, if you want to."

"Oh. Sure."

The days since the party had been stretched wide with boredom, and I was in desperate need of some company from my own age group. Gram was sweet enough, but adjusting to her slightly odd lifestyle – often, I'd find her awake at one in the morning, dabbing her paintbrushes on canvas because, and I quote, 'inspiration had struck' – had been kind of taxing. At that moment, I was grateful for any kind of invitation.

The dryer's cycle came to an end then, beeping loudly to inform us. Weaving between the twins, I headed over and wrenched the door open.

"Need any help?" Erin's voice sounded beside me; she was leaning on the edge of the dryer, watching with amusement as I pulled the clothing out and stuffed it haphazardly back into the bag. An elastic band held her vibrant hair in an untidy ponytail, leaving a second silver stud in her cartilage on view. Remembering the brief exchange about the piercing in her tongue, I was left wondering exactly how many she had in total.

"I've got it, thanks."

I forced the last of the clean washing into the bag, yanking the zipper across. Daniel sauntered over, looking between the two of us. "You good to go?"

"Yep."

Then his eyes flickered downward, and I wondered what he found so fascinating about the greying tiles beneath our feet. "Um," he began, "I think you dropped something."

An immediate jolt of dread coursed through me; I was expecting the worst. It turned out I was right to. When my gaze followed his, landing on the patch of floor just in falling distance of the tumble dryer, my stomach performed a particularly unpleasant somersault.

Lying on the floor were a pair of polka-dot knickers.

Not Gram's. Mine.

A gasp of something between surprise and mortification left my lips, and I bent over instantly, snatching up the underwear and screwing it into a ball. I'd already zipped up the bag on my shoulder, so instead I went for the next best thing, stuffing them into the pocket of my shorts. My cheeks were on fire; I was sure their temperature would've been sufficient to fry an egg.

I dared to look upwards at Daniel and Erin, finding them staring silently back at me. It lasted, however, for a maximum of two seconds – after that, they simultaneously burst into hysteric fits of laughter.

"Okay, okay," I mumbled, as Erin clutched the side of the dryer for support, "it's really not that funny."

My cheeks, still flaming, showed no sign of cooling any time soon. Sure, it was funny for them, but they weren't the ones with their underwear on public display. Although, it occurred to me then, Erin probably wouldn't care in the slightest. Thirty seconds later, and it seemed like they were sobering up, but my hopes were soon snubbed; one look at each other, and both were set off again.

Glancing between them, I could feel my own lips curling into a smile. Their laughter was infectious, even if it was at the expense of my dignity. Even I had to admit my reaction was priceless.

"God, Flo," Erin said, when her laughter had subsided to a point that allowed her to speak, "you're hilarious, you know that?" She wiped a tear from her eye.

"Yeah, alright," I murmured, but the twitching corners of my mouth ruined my attempt at seriousness. "Come on, are we going to get some lunch, or what?"

The suggestion was met, as expected, by a collective noise of assent. Hitching the bag over my shoulder, and making a conscious effort to avoid eye contact with Daniel, the three of us headed out of the launderette into the afternoon sun.

Twenty minutes later, having ditched my belongings in the back of Daniel's shop, the three of us were sat on the beach, newspaper-wrapped chips in hand. I had to admit the food from the seaside chippy had a significant edge over the one back home, even if it did hold the disadvantage of lurking seagulls whilst you tried to eat.

"So how's your sister doing?" Daniel asked, glancing over. Though the sun was shining, the sea breeze was as strong as ever, ruffling his wavy hair. "No sign of the baby yet?"

"Your sister's having a baby?" Erin piped up.

"Uh huh." I nodded, spearing a chip with my wooden fork. "She's eight months gone. No sign of it yet, but you know, the panicked phone call could come at any minute."

"That's so cool," she mused. "You're going to be an aunt."

I paused as the thought passed over my head. It had done so on countless occasions before, but hearing it from Erin's mouth seemed to let the knowledge properly sink in. Of course, I'd known since Nora had first announced her pregnancy – and by 'announced', I meant running out of the bathroom, waving a positive pregnancy test and letting that speak for itself – but I hadn't really allowed myself to think too hard about it. I was only seventeen; I felt in no way ready to be an aunt. Weren't they usually gentle thirty-somethings, with blow-dried hair and fluffy jumpers? Awkward teenagers with frizzy curls and more of a preference for comfy hoodies? Not so much.

But still. Nora was on the brink of motherhood, and that was pretty hard to get your head around too.

"I know," I said. "It's weird when you put it like that."

"She thought of any names?" At least that's what I thought she said; it was difficult to tell when her mouth was full. Erin was clearly not one for elegance.

"I don't think so, but her boyfriend's completely bonkers. Honestly, I wouldn't be surprised if they ended up with a baby called Jesus."

Beside me, Daniel inhaled so sharply he ended up inducing a coughing fit, consequently attracting the attention of everybody in a twenty metre radius. Even the two toddlers in front of us, strapped into a double buggy and wailing for the entire time we'd been sat here, fell silent to stare at him curiously. I bit back a laugh as Erin and I slapped his back, trying to help him recover.

"Sorry," he said sheepishly, once he'd sobered up, "I was just imagining a kid called Jesus. I mean, come on, that's just asking to have the crap beaten out of you, isn't it?"

"Yeah. I mean, I had the mickey taken out of me enough just being called Flo," I said, "and that was before they found out what it's short for."

"Which is?"

"Florence," I muttered darkly. There seemed to be the ghost of a smirk playing at Erin's lips, but she refrained from commenting. "I'm telling you, you guys got off easy with normal names."

Daniel's retort was cut off by the shrill ringing from Erin's pocket, which only intensified in volume once she'd pulled it out. Making a face at the screen, she jabbed at a button and answered, "Hello?"

We watched with curiosity as her brow furrowed; whatever news the caller seemed to bear, she didn't exactly seem overjoyed. "You're joking," she said, which was soon followed by, "Really? There's nobody else?"

I shot a sideways look at Daniel, silently questioning, to which he mouthed back work. I nodded, albeit a little confusedly. I'd assumed Erin worked alongside him at the ice-cream shop; he'd mentioned before that his family owned it. And bearing in mind the way Daniel seemed to be swept off his feet all hours of the day, regardless of the weather, it didn't seem likely for him to turn down extra help.

"No, I can be there," Erin was now saying. "Yeah. In like, half an hour. That okay?" Setting down her portion of chips, she switched the mobile phone to her other ear in one swift movement. "Yeah, okay, I'll see you in a bit."

"Everything okay?" I asked, when she cut the call and slid it back into her pocket.

"Work emergency," she said, her response punctuated by an eye roll, "again. Two out of the three people meant to be in today have called in 'sick'. Apparently, I'm the only one available to cover."

"That sucks."

"Tell me about it. There goes my day off." She sighed. "Well, I guess I'll see you guys later. I better leg it up to the station before the quarter past train leaves. Let Mum know, okay, Daniel?"

"Yeah, got it."

She gathered to her feet, sparing the two of us a wave before setting off across the stones. Hands hooked inside the pockets of her denim shorts, her wavy ponytail bounced in rhythm with her pacing. She deserted us so quickly I didn't even have time to have an internal moment of panic at the prospect of being left alone with Daniel; without Erin to keep things running smoothly, I was about ten times more likely to embarrass myself.

I turned to look at him, but he'd beat me to it, staring back with an expression that made me feel uncomfortably like I was being studied. "Um," was all I could manage. I could practically feel my usual awkwardness creeping back in, no longer repelled by the barrier of Erin's bold personality. "I thought she worked at the shop with you?" I stammered eventually, for lack of a better conversation starter.

It took a moment for Daniel to snap out of his semi-dazed state. "Nah," he said eventually, shaking his head, "she's always refused to work more than a shift in that place. Only when she absolutely has to. I don't think she's ever really said why. I mean, it's not like we don't need the extra help over the summer – she could take a job there tomorrow if she wanted."

"And she doesn't?"

"Nope. Takes the train into town every weekend, even though it takes her twenty minutes. She works at this little clothing boutique in the shopping centre."

"Oh." I dragged my eyes away from Daniel's freckled face, letting them refocus on the vast stretch of ocean unfolding out as far as the horizon. The sun sat high in an almost cloudless sky, its light reflecting off the moving surface of the water, providing the remarkable illusion that somebody had poured a giant vat of glitter into the sea. "Maybe she just wants a break from this place," I said quietly. "You know, just for a little while."

"Maybe." His voice sounded suddenly distant, as if he'd been pulled down beneath his thoughts. I resisted the urge to look over again, to memorise his each and every feature and the way they seemed to fit together so perfectly. Instead, I chose a boat floating absently near the horizon, its white sail stark against the sky.

"Is it really that bad?" he asked a few moments later, turning to me. "This place, I mean. They all seem to talk about it being so awful, but... I don't know. It just feels the same to me. Familiar."

"Well, it's different to what I'm used to, that's for sure," I told him, "but it's not awful."

I was telling the truth. I mean, how could it be awful when people like him and Erin lived there? I'd known them barely a week, yet already there was something that weakened any doubt I might've had about trusting them. All the friends I'd had in the last few years I'd kept safely at arms' length, only fully opening myself up to Nora. I'd convinced myself that it was us against the world – that other people wouldn't understand. But somehow, in such a short space of time, I'd already told them more than I ever thought I would.

Maybe it was just the sea air.

"I guess," Daniel said.

We lapsed into silence again: a comfortable quietness, which lasted until he pulled out his phone, checking the time. "Ten minutes," he informed me wearily. "Then I've got to be heading back. It's going to be another crazy afternoon."

"How many other people work with you?"

The expression etched across his face was one I couldn't quite work out. "Right now," he confessed, "it's pretty much just me and Mum. Erin will help out if we're desperate, but that's not often. My cousin was meant to be coming down and helping over the summer, but he's hardly been pulling his weight. I take care of most of it. Even the business side of things."

"Really?" My surprise proved impossible to mask. "That's impressive."

"Yeah, well. I wanted to, you know, after–" He stopped abruptly, as if suddenly realising what he was saying. "I just wanted to. I'm good at that sort of thing."

"Right."

A few moments later had something occurring to him. I could sense it in the way his eyes – which, I noticed, were an unusual shade caught between green and brown – lit up. Like an actual light bulb, more than just a metaphorical one, had gone off somewhere inside his head. "Hey, I know this is a bit of a long shot, but," he conducted a brief gauge of my expression, "you wouldn't – maybe – be interested in a job at the shop? I mean, I'm not trying to force you or anything, but I've had an ad up for a while and haven't had much luck... and maybe, well, you know..."

"You're offering me a job?"

"Well, yeah." He scratched the back of his head. "If you fancy it."

Did I? I wasn't entirely sure. Of course, it would serve as something to occupy me over what was looking certain to be a very dull summer. Then there was the obvious advantage of spending more time with Daniel, if I got over the worry of my imminent personal humiliation around him. But...

Well, what was the 'but'? It was there, definitely; something very solid was stopping me from accepting straightaway. Yet when I tried to identify it exactly, it seemed to vanish, as if nothing had been there in the first place.

"Yeah," I said eventually, my face breaking out into a smile, "I do."

"Great! That's sorted, then. How does tomorrow sound?"

My heart fluttered as it caught sight of his award-winning smile, making it incredibly difficult to string together even the simplest of responses. "Yeah," I breathed, "tomorrow sounds great."

And then he was grinning again, saying something about how all I needed was an apron, and I'd be an official part of the crew. I found myself laughing in response, joking about how I couldn't wait. It was true, really, because despite my nerves, the prospect of spending entire days with Daniel seemed to make them shine in itself. My mind had been left reeling, whizzing over too many things to process, while my legs had turned to the consistency of jelly, but the bizarreness had an almost exhilarating quality. It felt as if I'd never be able to get enough of it, which was strange, especially considering this was somebody I barely knew. All of a sudden tomorrow seemed both seconds and light years away.

It was official. I was in over my head.

7

CHAPTER 7

"Triple scoop vanilla and chocolate, please, Flo."

Behind the ice cream counter, I glanced back over at Daniel. He was manning the till, currently stuffing a five pound note – which had come as payment from the slightly overweight customer he was serving – into the drawer. "Fudge stick?"

"Fudge stick," he affirmed, with a nod.

I swivelled my attention towards the pastel slabs of ice cream in front of me. They were all laid out behind the glass cabinet, corresponding labels displayed neatly underneath. Reaching for the scoop, I dug it deep into the tub on the far left – vanilla – then switched to chocolate, returning once again to vanilla. A week in, and I was definitely getting the hang of the job. It'd become considerably easier once Daniel and I had perfected our system, at least; while he took care of the till, I'd been officially presented with the title Director of Ice Cream Preparation.

Or so he jokingly put it.

Finishing off my masterpiece with a fudge stick garnish, I handed it over. "One triple scoop vanilla and chocolate," I announced, "with a fudge stick."

The customer thanked the pair of us, weaving round the existing queue and heading for the shop exit with his cone and change in hand. As the door clicked shut behind him, Daniel shot me an approving smile. "Nice job," he said, "and in quick timing, too. You know, it makes me wonder how I ever managed this on my own."

"What can I say?" I said sweetly, twirling the scoop in my hand. "I'm just an ice cream pro."

"Hey, now don't get too big-headed," he warned, as the next customers moved forward to the till spot. "You're still the newbie around here."

I stuck out my tongue. "A newbie who's at risk of beating you. You're just intimidated."

"Keep dreaming," he said, but he was chuckling. The customers – a pair of elderly women kitted out in floral cardigans – looked between us affectionately. Within moments he'd diverted his attention towards them, flashing a winning smile in their direction. "Hi there, what can we get you today?"

It wasn't as if I had thought working in the shop with Daniel would be terrible, but it had by all means surpassed my expectations. The days sped by much quicker than those cooped up at Gram's, and most of the time it didn't feel like work at all. This rung especially true when the clock began inching closer to the hour between twelve and one: when Daniel handed off the shift to his mum, and we headed off to grab lunch. A lot of the time it was only the sheer anticipation that steered me through the morning rush.

Most days we took to the beach, although several days ago the rain had prevented us from doing so. With our usual choice off the cards, we'd ended up dragging a couple of chairs out under the awning, settling down to watch the rain batter the street from our pleasantly sheltered spot. It was becoming increasingly bizarre to think that, technically, we'd only known each other for a fortnight; it seemed so much longer than that.

I couldn't deny it – at least not to myself. Maybe I did fancy Daniel the tiniest little bit, but could I help myself? It seemed impossible to avoid falling for his effortless charm and quirky habits. Of course, I knew it was pointless. It would never amount to anything, as much as I wished otherwise. It was simply implausible for someone so cool and calm and together to like someone so... well, not.

It was the nights that hit me the worst. Lying in bed, straining hard to hear the distant sound of the ocean, I'd be completely fine one moment, but the next would strike with a stifling sense of overwhelming. Like it'd only just sunk in that I was in a completely new place, surrounded by people who were, essentially, strangers, and miles away from the rock that had always made everything seem okay.

For the last three years, nights had always been the worst. Maybe it was the darkness, bringing with it a smothering wash of loneliness that did nothing but suffocate me. On the rare occasions that I did manage to drift off, the nightmares were another story. I was strange in the fact that these were not conventional nightmares; I didn't dream of the car crash or my parents' expressionless faces in the hospital beds. I didn't wake up screaming, sitting up in bed with a jolt. But the alternative was just as bad.

I dreamed of memories. Snapshots from an expanse of fourteen years, recreated by my unconscious mind. In my dreams I'd find myself a kid again, perched on my dad's shoulders for a better view of the fireworks. I was in the kitchen with my mum, her hands clasped over mine, as she showed me how to ice the batch of cupcakes we'd baked. I was there at the zoo, running along excitedly with Nora, looking back every now and again to see both my parents laughing, their hands entwined.

It wasn't always the past. Sometimes I found myself miraculously pulled into the future, plunged into moments that would never have the chance to exist. They were there, bidding me a teary goodbye as they dropped me off at university. Watching me graduate. Walking me down the aisle.

These were usually the times when it got too much: when I ended up clambering, watery-eyed, into Nora's bed. She was upset too, of course, but in daylight she forced herself to stay strong. She had to hold herself together for me, if nothing else. But the hours past eleven were another story; then, her pillow was usually as damp as mine.

She didn't try to fake strength. Instead, we clung to each other under the covers, and though the outside world remained as terrifying as ever, we had each other.

The grief had weakened since then, but it hadn't yet stopped from hitting me at random times, its blow so sudden I almost stumbled backwards.

And now, with Nora in London, and me stuck here, I didn't know how to handle it.

There was only one truth in the matter: I was messed up. I'd been permanently scarred by such a traumatic experience, the shattered remains only haphazardly pieced back together. And there was Daniel, so normal and happy and collected, despite what I'd found out about his dad.

Hurtling back into reality, I realised the guy in question was waving a hand in front of my face, trying to catch my attention. "Earth to Flo?"

I almost jumped. "Huh?"

"Single scoop mango," he repeated, peering at me curiously. "Hey, are you okay?"

Mentally, I slapped myself, trying to retune my consciousness fully into the present. "I'm fine," I assured him. "Just zoned out for a second. One scoop of mango coming right up."

I dug my scoop into the bright yellow tub, slapping a rounded portion onto a cone and handing it over. It didn't take long to get back into the swing of things; three orders later, and my mind had once again become so focused on ice cream that I could hardly remember what had distracted me in the first place. Just like that, the tension was slipping away again – at least it was, until the moment the door swung open, preceding a figure that strode right past the queue and towards us.

At first, I thought it was Erin – at least that was how I interpreted the sound of Daniel's bright "Hey!". However, once I let my gaze flicker upwards, noticing at once the significant absence of striking purple hair, I realised this wasn't the case.

"Oh. Hi, Collette," I said awkwardly, instantly feeling myself shrink under the scrutiny of her cat-like brown eyes. I could feel her looking over my apron, my nametag – which Daniel had scrawled across in permanent marker, embellishing my name with a smiley face – and every other detail, wordlessly totting up the criticisms in her head. Though she was dressed down, in a simple pair of shorts and a hooded jacket, this didn't stop her from immediately outshining me and everybody else in the room. By now, at least, I'd realised that this just came with the territory of being around Collette.

"Flo..." she said slowly. "I, uh, didn't know you worked here."

"Yeah." I tried hard to inject a shot of friendliness into my tone, but it turned out to be more difficult than I expected, especially whilst being looked up and down with blatant disapproval. "I just started."

"Right. That's... nice." Apparently deciding I was no longer interesting enough to hold her attention, she looked over at Daniel. "You need to come with me. You won't believe what happened."

He frowned, his brows knitting together. "What?"

"Look, you'll see when we get there," she said. "To be honest, I'm not even sure how to explain it. Just come with me. It's really important."

"Collette, I'm kind of working here..." He trailed off, awkwardly looking between us and the line of customers currently eavesdropping on the conversation. "Can't we sort this out later?"

"Come on. I just need to borrow you for ten minutes." She was growing impatient, I could tell. "Twenty minutes, tops. Flo can handle the shop on her own for that long, can't she?"

The internal jolt of horror was immediate; it took a conscious effort to prevent the alarmed look from appearing on my face. I had said I'd got the hang of serving, but that didn't mean – by any stretch of the imagination – that I was ready to be left alone. I'd only been here a week, for crying out loud. That was nowhere near the level of experience I deemed necessary to be in charge of the entire shop.

Daniel glanced over at me. "What do you say, Flo?"

I bit my lip. There were infinite possibilities of potential disasters in such a short amount of time, and my mind seemed unable to stop running through them all. I mean, there was fire, robbery, accidentally giving customers the contents of the till instead of the correct change – and they were just the first options that came to mind.

But how could I say no? The look of hope flickering in his hazel eyes – not to mention the impatience in Collette's – was already melting my defences. "Yeah," I lied. "I can handle it."

Those exact five words formed the reason why, ten minutes later, I found myself standing behind the counter of Walden's most popular ice cream shop, completely and utterly alone.

And feeling it.

"Sorry, what did you order again?" I asked, as I approached the glass cabinet and realised the customer's request had completely vacated my mind. It had probably been lost somewhere in the stress of using the till; I'd been concentrating too hard on counting the chance, desperate to avoid putting Daniel out of pocket with my bad mathematical skills. Evidently, my brain's capacity was limited to one thing at a time.

The customer, who happened to be the father of a set of incredibly boisterous twin boys, gave me a strange look. "Two chocolate chip cones," he repeated.

"Right," I said. "Sorry."

Quite frankly, I had no idea how Daniel managed it. Ten minutes and I was already in way over my head. I'd been thrown straight into the deep end, leaving me fighting to keep my head above water. But no matter how fast my limbs were sent flailing, trying to keep me afloat, I could barely keep up with the pace of customers coming and going. What had seemed simple enough with an extra pair of hands had suddenly become impossible.

And boy, did I feel stupid. I mean, what sort of an idiot couldn't even serve a few tourists some ice cream?

Single, double or triple scoop. A few different flavours. It was hardly rocket science.

"Uh, thanks," the guy said, as I handed over two very wobbly-looking cones. Both looked about ready to topple over; really, they should've been served with a warning label that read handle with care. Not that the rogue twins already terrorising the shop would pay any attention.

The queue was moving too quickly; as soon as I successfully served a customer, what seemed like another three would come in through the door. The constant stream was impossible to keep up with; the feeling likened to being on a treadmill, already running at full speed, but having someone constantly whacking up the setting until I could barely feel the ground beneath me. Needless to say, I was counting down the seconds until Daniel's reappearance.

Once the door banged shut behind the twins, I allowed myself a much-needed sigh of relief. The shop seemed to have expanded again at their departure; without them running rampage over every square inch, there was certainly more room to breathe. But there was little time for relaxation: I'd already begun taking the next customer's order, which included five separate cones, shoving their tenner into the till drawer.

Seriously, five? Couldn't they see I was struggling?

"Excuse me, could you speed it up a little?" someone from the back of the queue called, whilst I was halfway through dolloping a helping of strawberry onto the third cone. "I haven't got all day."

"Sorry," I mumbled, feeling my cheeks turn beet red. "I'm new."

Come on, Flo, I told myself furiously. You've got to get a move on. Daniel's counting on you. Determinedly quickening my pace, I powered on, though I could see my scooping skills deteriorating considerably.

"Actually, can we get Flakes on all of those, please?"

I had to stop myself from groaning aloud. Leaning over to grab the box where they were usually kept, my palm enclosed air when I realised the spot was empty. This time I sighed out loud, pivoting on my heel and heading towards the back of the room, where I'd seen Daniel fish out extra stock a few times. Sure enough, a familiar yellow box sat in the corner, the uppermost item on a tall stack.

I'd intended to step forward and retrieve it, but didn't quite get there.

Apparently, there had been a splatter of melted ice cream somewhere on the floor that had escaped my notice. I realised this only once my foot had landed right in it, my trainer losing its grip completely. Instantly, I was propelled forward, landing with a final thud right on my backside.

Not to mention going face-first into the ice cream cone in my hand.

Talk about graceful.

It might've been easier to live down had it only been the line of customers there to witness my embarrassing escapade. But, of course, my luck wouldn't allow that to happen. Milliseconds after my rear end had hit the tiles, the sound of a bell overhead indicated the opening of the shop door. Then, soon after, a familiar head appeared over the counter, peering down at me with the utmost confusion and what looked like restrained laughter written all over his face.

"Uh, Flo?"

Removing my nose from the ice cream, I dared to look upwards at Daniel. The throbbing in my lower back was already prominent, a bruise sure to follow, but I managed a sheepish smile. "Hi."

"You okay?" Daniel asked, when I emerged from the bathroom in the empty shop ten minutes later. His smile was strained, presumably by the effort of holding back laughter, but I supposed the image of me sprawled on the floor with a face full of ice cream was kind of funny. You know, if you didn't happen to be me. "Cleaned yourself up?"

I rolled my eyes, though I was more embarrassed than willing to admit. "Yes, thanks."

It seemed that Daniel felt bad about subjecting me to the stress of managing the entire shop alone. Though his first action had been to help me up from the floor, he soon decided to sweet-talk his mum into covering the afternoon shift so we could hang out instead. Whilst I'd been preoccupied scrubbing vanilla off my face, he'd finished serving up the last of the customers before switching the open placard on the door to its reverse side.

Now, he'd abandoned his apron, looking effortlessly together in washed jeans and a T-shirt. My appearance was much less composed; a few springy curls had fallen from their ponytail, a slight damp patch remained noticeable on the back of my trousers, and pretty much all of my make-up had been scrubbed off with the ice cream. I was by no means at my best, but there was nothing I could do.

"You know, I really feel bad for leaving you like that," he told me, after we'd slipped through the door and he locked it behind him.

"You've only been here a week, for crying out loud. It was completely unfair, and you can blame me as much as you like."

I shrugged. "Well, what Collette wanted was obviously really important, so…"

I didn't mean for the sarcasm to leak into my voice, but it did anyway. It was hard to stop myself; I had to admit the thought of Daniel and Collette spending time together alone struck a jealous chord. But this was Collette we were talking about. She had the looks of a supermodel, even if her sister had topped her by boasting an even better handful of genes. We were like chalk and cheese. And, as much as I didn't like to think about it, I couldn't see Daniel picking me if ever the choice was between us.

"It could've waited," he said. "I mean, she only wanted me to have a look at her car because the engine was playing up and she didn't want to be late for some hair appointment. Maybe I know a tiny bit about cars, but only because my dad was into them. It's not like I'm a mechanic or anything. I couldn't figure out what was wrong with it."

A brief delay ensued before the words could sink in properly. His dad. Had he meant to mention him? The only other time he'd been brought up was several days ago, when we'd had lunch with Erin, and even then it hadn't gone as far as saying anything aloud. Neither of them had uttered a word about it since.

But I was hardly in a place to blame them.

"Sorry."

"Honestly, it's fine," I assured him again. "Where are we headed, anyway?"

He stopped then, as if first realising his feet lacked any plan of navigation. "No idea," he said. "Where d'you fancy?"

I shrugged. "You pick. You're the expert on this place, anyway. Show me what's fun around here."

He looked around, skimming over our view of the seafront town as if searching for a source of inspiration. The beach lay ahead of us, clumps of tourists spread out across the stones, seagulls cawing overhead. To our left, the pier stood tall, the dark wood structure looking at least two hundred years old. Waves battered the rickety supports every few seconds, but the people milling around on it seemed far less apprehensive than I was.

"Have you been to the arcade?" Daniel asked, his eyes also drawn towards the pier. As they swivelled towards me, catching sight of my raised eyebrows, he pouted. "Hey, don't look like that. It's fun."

"You're just a big kid at heart, aren't you?" I said, to which he nodded eagerly. "Okay, okay. If you say it's fun, then we'll go."

"It is. You're just scared."

I frowned. "Scared of an amusement arcade?"

"Scared of getting thrashed on the 2p pushers," he corrected with a grin. "I'm telling you, live by a beach your whole life and you get good at them. I'm a pro. Prepare to be put to shame."

"Are you really making this into a competition?"

His smirk grew. "Yup."

"Actually, you know what? It's on."

"And," he added, "how about this for interesting stakes? Loser has to go swimming," he hooked his thumb behind him, though it was hardly necessary, "in the sea."

I stepped closer. "Bring it on."

Without warning, he grabbed my hand, the warmth of his fingers comfortably enveloping my palm. Then he tugged, pulling me in the direction of the pier. I quickened my pace as he broke into a run along the boardwalk, our trainers pounding on the wooden slats, and the two of us bounded towards the amusement arcade. We were laughing like idiots, and everybody was staring. But for what was probably the first time in my life, I couldn't have cared less.

8

CHAPTER 8

"**Y**ou've got to be joking."

I groaned as there came a noisy clattering from Daniel's machine for the twentieth time that afternoon. It had since become the warning sign that he was inching closer and closer to victory, leaving me lagging shamefully behind. In hindsight, agreeing to a competition against someone who'd lived in Walden their entire life had to be one of the worst decisions I'd made in a while. When he'd claimed that living by the sea had made him good at arcade games, he hadn't been kidding. It was hard to face, but the truth stood that unless I was blessed by some sort of miracle in the next five minutes, I was pretty much guaranteed a dip in the water.

"Seriously, how are you doing that?" I asked, as my own coin fell lazily through the machine, failing to even push anything off the top platform.

The rules, which he'd decided, were simple: we'd each been allocated a pound's worth of two pence coins, and the first one to knock one of the prizes off the end and down the bottom chute was the winner. Strictly no cheating.

Except there had to be some sort of foul play here, because there was surely no way Daniel could be having so much more success than me, just because he was, in his words, 'a pro'.

It just wasn't happening.

"Like I said, it's pure talent," he said, grinning as yet another pile of coins came cascading down his chute. Scooping the lot into his plastic tub - which was now teeming with copper - he waved it in front of my face. "Jealous?"

"Nope," I said stubbornly, pushing his hand away. "I'm doing fine."

"Really?" Looking down at my own tub, which held significantly less in comparison, he raised an eyebrow. "Doesn't really look like it. I hope you're in the mood for a swim, Flo."

Scowling, I turned my attention back to the machine. Daniel was right, of course. I was lagging miles behind, with no chance what-soever of catching up, but it didn't mean I was ready to give up. If the consequence was a dip in the sea, I wasn't about to go down without a fight.

"It's all in the wrist," he told me, pushing another coin through the slot.

I shot him a sideways smirk. "Oh, I bet it is."

It took a moment for him to realise exactly what he'd said; when he did, he began to laugh. "And here I was, thinking you were innocent," he said, shaking his head in mock disapproval. "Didn't realise you were almost as bad as Jay."

I was about to defend myself, but got robbed of the chance; I was instead cut off by the noise of yet another waterfall of coins clattering to the bottom of Daniel's machine. With a somewhat childish cry of excitement, he bent down to retrieve something that sat on top of them all.

Something that made my heart sink.

"Well, well, well," he drawled, "look what we have here."

It was a key ring: a cheap plastic heart, embellished with a toothy smile. Twirling it tauntingly around his finger, he looked over at me. "A prize," he said, as if it wasn't obvious. "I have a feeling this means I won."

I rolled my eyes.

"Aw, come on, Flo." He patted the top of my head, though the few inches between our heights were hardly of significance. "The water won't be that cold."

"You're horrible, you know that?"

"Hey, now would a horrible person give you their prize? Out of the goodness of their heart?" Smiling, he placed the key ring in the palm of his hand and held it out to me. "For you."

"How generous." I was being blatantly sarcastic, but reached out and took it from him anyway. The heart-shaped souvenir was only a bog-standard arcade prize - tacky, with the paint peeling off at the corners - but it didn't matter. It was the gesture that made my heartbeat quicken, combined with the sight of the adorable grin that had spread across Daniel's face once I clasped my fingers around the gift.

"Don't say I never give you anything," he said, affectionately flicking the end of my nose. "So, you ready to get out of this place?"

I let my gaze wash briefly over the room; a genius IQ was hardly necessary to work out that the arcade wasn't exactly the town's hottest attraction. I suspected this had something to do with the fact the building looked as if it'd been built sometime in the seventies and hadn't been upgraded since. A thick smoky odour lingered in the air, forcing itself uncomfortably down our throats, despite the clear No smoking signs dotted around the room. The carpet didn't look as if it'd seem a vacuum in the last couple of years, and the soundtrack - blaring sound effects, jangling coins and a cheesy Britney record - was sufficient to give anybody a headache.

But we'd had fun. I had to give Daniel that.

"Sure."

Abandoning our change pots - I couldn't help but remark internally that whoever found Daniel's would hit the jackpot - we weaved our way through the machines, heading for the back exit. Pushing through the doors, we emerged on the pier once more, immediately hit by a gust of cold sea air that proved more than welcome after breathing in stale cigarette smoke for half an hour.

"What are you doing?"

In my haste to get some fresh air, I hadn't noticed that Daniel had already sped ahead, now several paces in front of me as he approached the railing at the end of the pier. On it hung a sign displaying two clear rules: the first of which was No diving, followed by Do not climb this railing, both in bold red text.

He stopped in front of it, hoisting one leg up onto the lower bar. Then, realising I wasn't beside him, he glanced back over his shoulder. "Come on, what are you waiting for?"

"Can't you read?" I asked, gesturing toward the sign. "You're not supposed to climb that thing."

This fact, however, didn't seem to bother him in the slightest. Swinging the other leg over, followed then by the first, he took a seat on the uppermost bar. "Psh, whatever. I've been sitting on this thing forever, and I'm still alive. Come on."

I hesitated, eyeing up the stretch of railing Daniel was perched on. Though it looked far from the world's most stable piece of metal, he didn't seem to be in any great danger. In fact, I was mentally evaluating the chances of it totally collapsing when my thoughts were cut off by a voice.

"Chicken."

I quirked an eyebrow. "What did you say?"

Daniel grinned, a mischievous spark flashing momentarily across his eyes. "I called you a chicken," he repeated slowly. I could almost see him dangling the bait in front of me, waiting for a reaction. "Come on, Flo. Live a little."

"You know, if I die, that saying is going to become incredibly ironic," I warned, but something strange had ignited inside me - some kind of fiery sense of adventure I didn't know I had. My feet shuffled forward of their own accord, and before I knew it, I was standing beside Daniel at the base of the railing. Below us, the sea battered the pier's wooden stilts, but his charming smile seemed the only thing I was capable of focusing on.

I hoisted one leg over, leaving both my feet on different sides of the bar. "Now the second leg," he coaxed, but this was much easier said than done. I was straddling the gap between dry land and the depths of the water, not to mention hardly famous for my exceptional sense of balance.

Gritting my teeth and gripping the cold metal for dear life, I swung the second leg over and prayed not to wobble.

Heart pounding, stomach churning with an uncomfortable tor-rent of fear, it suddenly occurred to me that I'd managed it. I was teetering on the edge of the railing, my feet dangling below me, staring out across the English Channel. The feeling was bizarre: almost as if we were floating freely above it, if I concentrated hard enough on the horizon. Every so often, Daniel's arm would gently brush my own, the gentle contact offering a surprisingly significant amount of reassurance. I mean, all it'd take would be for me to lean forward just an inch too far...

"You're scared, aren't you?"

I looked over at Daniel. "Freaking terrified," I admitted. "Aren't you?"

He shrugged. "Not really. What's the worst that could happen?"

I couldn't help but look incredulous. Hadn't he grasped the fact we were balanced on the edge of an incredibly rickety pier, mere metres above the sea? I'd thought it pretty difficult to miss. "We fall and drown?"

"We won't drown," he assured me, laughing. "We're not that far away from the shore, and the water's still pretty shallow here. Trust me - I've swum out further than this before. You see that buoy out there?" I followed his pointing finger to the floating red dot amongst the waves, bobbing lightly up and down in the wind, marking the edge of the safety zone. "Even way past that, a couple of times."

"And you didn't freak any lifeguards out?"

"Oh, yeah. Plenty. I didn't care much, though. I was in a kind of rebellious phase, I guess. Convinced myself I didn't care what anybody else thought." He paused, reaching up to absently scratch the back of his neck. "It wasn't, uh... the best frame of mind I've ever been in."

Part of me wanted to lean over and cover his hand with mine, an inexplicable impulse, but the other was too scared to loosen my grip of the railing for more than a second. "Well, I'm glad you didn't go too crazy," I said instead. "Though I think sitting up here is pushing the boundaries a little."

"I wouldn't say crazy, as such. I prefer the term 'adventurous'. Don't you ever feel like trying it?"

"Trying what?"

"You know, doing something wild. Something no one would expect of you. Or even that you'd expect of yourself," he added, almost as an afterthought. As if he needed to prove his point, he released his hands from the bar, holding them in the air. "Like this. No hands."

I laughed at the sudden flash of impulsiveness, much like the decision to get up here in the first place. "Yeah, well, my sense of balance isn't as good as yours. For me, that wouldn't be crazy; it'd just be stupid."

He brought his hands back down, clasping the curved metal edge once more. Silence stretched between us, broken into even segments by the constant crashing of the waves below and the seagulls overhead. "Jump," he said eventually.

"What?"

"You could jump," he said again. "Like, right now. Just jump off this thing. That counts as wild."

I snorted. "Yeah. Right."

"I'm serious," he said, glancing over. "You could do it. I mean, you've already lost our little competition, so you have to go swimming anyway. You could get it over with right now."

"I agreed to swim," I pointed out, "not jump off a pier and fall to my death. Did you even take any notice of that sign? It says no diving."

"It also says you shouldn't climb on the railing, and look how much attention we're paying to that," he said, grinning mischievously. "Come on, Flo. For once in your life, don't you feel like being crazy?"

"Uh, I think I'm okay, thanks."

"What if I jump with you?"

I did a double-take, expecting him to be joking. His expression, however, remained impassive. "But you won."

"And yet here I am, agreeing to share your punishment," he said, laughing. "I think that counts as crazy too."

I shook my head disbelievingly. The entire situation was strange enough - so much so that I found myself wondering whether it was anything more than a dream my bored subconscious had conjured up. I hadn't ever considered that my summer in Walden might turn out like this, in any shape or form. And yet here I was, dangling off the edge of a pier, being dared to jump off by a guy I kind of fancied, in a town that I'd forgotten before three weeks ago. Surely that had to count as crazy enough.

"Okay," I said eventually, my grip on the bar tightening. "Okay. Fine. I'll do it."

Wriggling one-handedly out of my hoodie, I tossed it behind me for later retrieval. I kicked off my shoes, too, shoving them away from the edge with my foot. A salty breeze nipped at my exposed arms, an undeniable chill beneath the mild sunshine, and I tried not to dwell on how the cold was about to get a lot worse in a few seconds.

"I can't believe we're about to do this," I stammered, struck by a last-minute wave of panic as Daniel took my hand in his. "If I die, I'm suing your arse for all it's worth, okay?"

"Got it," he said. I didn't need to look at him to know that he was grinning. "You ready? Three... two... one."

It all happened so quickly, much too fast for my head to keep up. One moment we were teetering on what felt like the top of the world; the next, Daniel's gentle tug on my arm had sent us both freefalling through the air. The wind whipped through my hair, effectively backcombing the curls, and I knew somewhere amongst it all I'd started shrieking. The exhilaration was overpowering, much like my vice-like grip around Daniel's palm, and the only thing I could think of was how we were actually doing this, how utterly crazy it was, and the fact that I had finally let myself go. Literally.

The fall came to an end as quickly as it began, our figures crashing full-force into the water, sending salty spray flying in all directions. My head dipped under the surface, dragged downward by the impact, leaving just enough time to hold my breath. Somewhere in the landing my hand had lost Daniel's, and the stinging in my open eyes made it even harder to gain a sense of direction.

Flailing my limbs around wildly, hoping to propel myself upwards, my foot collided with something solid. I would've let out a yelp of surprise had I not been three feet underwater. Moments later, watery arms enclosed my waist, and I felt myself being pulled upward.

All of a sudden, my head was above the surface, and I was gulping down lungfuls of air like my life depended on it.

"I hope you're sorry for almost knocking me out," Daniel said, right in front of me. He was sopping wet, his brunette hair sticking like glue to the sides of his face. Only then did it occur to me that his hands were still on my waist, drawing us noticeably closer than usual. Had the temperature of the water not sucked every ounce of heat from my body, I probably would've blushed. "Your foot is vicious."

"Sorry," I apologised. "I was a little preoccupied trying not to drown, because some lunatic convinced me it'd be a good idea to jump off a pier."

He laughed, his hazel eyes crinkling with the motions, though somehow still seeming brighter than usual. "I knew you had it in you to be crazy."

I could feel myself struggling to keep myself above the water level, despite his steady hands at my side. All my effort was being ploughed into treading water, but I kept being caught by waves which dunked my head underwater. When a particularly strong current dragged me down further, with enough time for panic to set in, I felt arms wrap around me completely. He'd taken hold of me, prising my arms apart and linking them around his neck so I was, essentially, clinging to him.

Embarrassed, I tried to retract them. "I'll drag you down."

"Are you joking? You hardly weigh a thing," he said, treading water like it was second nature. "Don't worry, I can handle it. I took a lifeguarding course last summer."

"I can swim," I said. "The jump just... surprised me."

He was smiling. "You don't say."

The worst of the shock had passed by then, subsiding to make room for the sheer cold. I was wracked by shivers, my teeth chattering in accompaniment. In the periphery of my vision I could see clusters of people huddled by the railings, all seemingly eager to get a look at the teenagers crazy enough to jump straight over the edge.

It was in that moment that the absurdity of the situation hit me, and I was suddenly struck by the overwhelming urge to laugh. Throwing my head back, I broke into hysterics as we bobbed with the passing of another wave. It didn't take long for Daniel to join in too, and soon the pair of us were giggling like maniacs, the main attraction in Walden's newest freak show to an audience of tourist onlookers.

"I take it back," he said, when his laughter had retreated enough to allow him to speak. "You are crazy, Flo. You're the craziest person I've ever met."

I shot him a questioning look. "Is that a compliment?"

"Of course. But, you know, I think we better swim back. It's bloody freezing out here."

"Really? I hadn't noticed."

I forced myself to remove my arms from around his neck and put distance between us once more, though I'd been more comfortable than I should've in our previous position. Flipping over, I broke into a backstroke in the direction of the shore, and the sound of splashing soon afterward indicated Daniel was following suit.

I looked up at the cloudless sky above as we swum, trying to focus on the intermingling shades of blue, all blending together into an effortless blank canvas. But in the past few minutes this had suddenly grown incredibly difficult, for all I could see was Daniel's beaming face - the one that had been inches away from my own just moments ago - dancing in front of my eyes.

9

— ◆ —

CHAPTER 9

For the first time since I'd moved to Walden, it was hot.

Even here, with the sea breeze feeling at least slightly cool on my sticky skin, the air was humid and I could feel beads of sweat forming on my forehead and the back of my neck. Needless to say, the brief sunny spell over the south coast had sent tourists flocking to the beach in their hundreds, and right now, I was sandwiched between what seemed like the rowdiest groups in Walden. While the parents to my left were doing absolutely zilch to stop their kids shaking out their towels downwind, the couple on the opposite side were rolling around on the shingle in a way that was totally inappropriate for a family beach, and the group in front of me seem to have just given up on trying to quieten their screaming toddler.

It was, to put it plainly, chaos.

But I was here, out of sheer desperation that a spot on the beach would be even marginally cooler than Gram's place. Her cottage seemed to trap the heat and hold it hostage; every room could be likened to a greenhouse. Though such heat was rare, especially in this country, today was unbearable.

Once settled on the beach, I'd stripped down to my shorts and bikini top, though I could still feel the layer of uncomfortable perspiration settling over my skin. Cross-legged on a towel, I now had my head bent over my sketchpad, the grey strokes of my pencil slowly taking shape across the page. Every so often, I'd switch to a brighter colour, filling in the white gaps until the picture began to take form. I'd always found it sort of fascinating, how a movement as simple as the swipe of a pencil tip across paper could transform blankness into something so alive; this, I guessed, was the reason I always came back to draw more.

I was so absorbed in my creation that I managed to tune out most of the background noise, reducing the sound effects of the busy beach to a dull buzz around me. Hence why, when a set of footsteps and their owner approached me from behind, I failed to notice until they bent right over me, craning their neck for a good look at my sketchpad.

"What's that, then?"

I recognised the voice immediately; I snapped the book shut with a resounding slap: an automatic reaction. Maybe I was a little too jumpy, but the thought of prying eyes on my half-completed sketch was too much to handle. It was private: the snapshot of a moment I'd been afraid to forget ever since it happened. It had been much easier than I expected, actually, to illustrate the wild flailing limbs, the wind in our hair, the reassuring clasp of Daniel's hand around mine.

Foreign sets of eyes were unwelcome, particularly those of the girl hanging over me right now.

"C-Collette," I stuttered. My hands involuntarily tightened around the book in my hands; I wasn't convinced she wouldn't try to rip it from me herself.

She stood tall above me, her cropped brown hair brushed backward by the pair of sunglasses that sat atop her head. I could barely contain my envy at her tanned skin, leaving mine to pale in comparison, and the way her denim shorts hung effortlessly on her hips. Already I could feel myself shrinking, halving in size each second Collette's eyes stayed lingering on me.

"What was that you were drawing?" she asked.

"Nothing," I tried to say, though I didn't know who I was trying to fool.

"Didn't look like nothing to me. Don't I get a peek?"

"It's kind of... private."

"Oh. What a shame." I wondered if I was imagining the undertones of sarcasm to her voice. "Are you here by yourself?"

"Um." I ran my tongue over my lips; they seemed to have suddenly gone dry. "Yeah, just trying to cool down..."

"Oh, God. Me too. Mind if I join you?" I hesitated before nodding uncertainly, though she didn't appear to have been waiting for an answer anyway. She slipped her bag from her shoulder, not even pausing before dumping it onto the pebbles beside my own. "The weather here couldn't get any more bi-polar, could it? And then the moment you get the tiniest bit of sun, you get all this."

I looked around in the direction she was gesturing: the flocks of people closing in on all sides. With every passing minute, more seemed to pile in, filling in the gaps until we were packed together like bricks; I briefly wondered how long it'd take for the beach to reach full capacity, leaving us all cemented together, unable to move.

At that point, it seemed like it was getting close.

I still didn't really understand why so many people swarmed to Walden like bees to a honey pot. It wasn't like it was the only stretch of beach around, and there were far better bays and coves just a few miles in either direction. The entire south coast boasted a whole array of other options, most of them more sandy than the pebbles we found ourselves lounging on.

And yet still they continued arriving by the busload, clutching beach gear and craving ice cream, excited to spend the day in such a dinky little town.

It was alright for them, though. When the day drew to a close, they were free to pack up their belongings and head back home, to a place where more exciting things were sure to be happening. Their lives were full of concerns and happenings miles away from the quiet, hushed drama of the Walden seaside.

"You know your skin's looking really pink, don't you?"

Tumbling from my daydream and landing, with a thud, back in the present, I turned towards Collette's voice. "What?"

"You," she repeated. "You're going pink. You need more sun cream, or you'll burn to a crisp."

I lifted an arm for further inspection. It did look as if it had a slight reddish tinge, but I had just assumed that was my eyes trying to adjust to the bright daylight. The thing was, I hadn't really intended to end up sunbathing, as such. My trek down to the beach had originally been in search of relief from the heat; it just so happened that I'd ended up getting comfy with my sketchpad and the sound of the waves.

Sun cream had sort of slipped my mind.

When I didn't say anything, Collette shook her head. "You didn't put any on in the first place, did you? Honey, you're going to regret that."

There was something about the way she spoke, in a tone that seemed to edge into superiority, that irritated me slightly. But I knew she was right. I should've picked up a bottle on my way out, and though I wasn't feeling it yet, the consequences were sure to come.

"I... forgot."

We lapsed into a long silence – silence that wasn't really that at all, amongst the hectic babble of Walden beach. I could almost see the awkwardness unfolding between us, pressing its way into every gap. It was exactly what I'd feared from a conversation with Collette; this silent intimidation, the way I felt about six inches tall in her presence. I didn't know whether she intended to make me feel this way, or if it was just a natural demeanour that the rest of Walden had grown accustomed to. It wasn't that I disliked Collette. It was just exceedingly difficult to tell what she thought about me.

Eventually, though, she broke the silence by delving into the bag beside her. "Here," she said, as a white lidded bottle landed in my lap. "I've got some."

For a second, I couldn't do anything other than stare down at it, wondering if it was justifiable to believe that this could be some kind of sabotage in disguise. Something that would turn my skin blue, or painfully wax all the hair off my body? I wouldn't have put it past the icy version of Collette I'd met at the party. But when my eyes flickered hesitantly back to her, I noticed something about her expression that seemed more genuine. Like some of the coldness was finally melting away.

Maybe it had something to do with the heat.

"Thanks," I said.

"S'okay," she responded, shrugging. "Can't stand to sit there and watch you fry. I know how that one feels."

"Thanks," I said again, not really knowing what else I should say. I was sort of in awe of this new Collette, worried that one slip of the tongue could send her packing.

She smiled, a sort of knowing smirk: one that was neither offish, nor put me at ease with its warmth. "Well, you show me some of those drawings sometime, and we might be able to call it even."

My fingers clasped around the hard cover reflexively, gripping until I could feel the edges pressing uncomfortably into my skin. I didn't think she'd have the nerve to snatch it directly, but I didn't want to take any chances. Those sketches were my diary entries, moments of my life I'd tried to capture tangibly, trapping the memories into permanent form. On paper, they couldn't fade away. But other eyes would change things, twist the strokes into an interpretation that had the potential to taint the moment forever.

If you didn't want to lose something, you had to keep it close.

I forced myself to smile, though the thought of Collette snooping on the innermost workings of my head made my heart lurch. "We'll see," I said.

I hadn't meant to end up spending so much time with her.

When Collette had first materialised, I'd wanted nothing more than to vanish into thin air, reappearing somewhere I could resume my sketching alone. I had planned to make an excuse and flee the beach the moment an opportunity presented itself, but this intention seemed to have been lost somewhere in the conversation. When I thought about it, I couldn't really recall how it happened. All I knew was that the more we got talking, the more Collette's frosty front seemed to break down, and I was beginning to realise there might be something a whole lot more genuine beneath.

It was surprising, really, how easy it was to get along with her, when she wanted it to be. With every line of conversation, I could feel myself beginning to relax, finally regaining some of the height I'd lost earlier on. I could keep up, if I concentrated, chipping in at the right moments when she paused to share anecdotes about crazy things the five of them had done together. By the time she declared she was hungry, leaning in to tell me about this great restaurant she knew tucked away in the middle of town, I stood at my real measurements, only a couple of inches shorter than Collette herself.

And then, an hour later, I found myself seated opposite her in a booth in some shiny modern restaurant. It was quietly secluded from view on the street, in a corner of Walden I didn't even know existed. Shiny metal furniture felt cold against my backside, and huge glass windows swept the whole of the length of the back wall. A glass aquarium sat in the centre of the room, a whole assortment of rainbow-coloured fish darting wildly around inside. I hadn't even caught its fancy name before Collette ushered me through the door and somehow snagged us the best seat in the entire place.

At least that's what she called it. We ended up right next to the fish tank, which some people might've found pretty. To me, it was just off-putting, feeling like I was being given the evil eye as I scanned the menu and its array of seafood dishes.

I didn't know why I'd agreed to lunch with her, but I guessed it had something to do with Collette's newfound persona – and the fact that I was hungry too. She hadn't exactly become Miss Personality overnight, but freezing me out completely seemed to have at least turned to a thing of the past.

She was being nice to me, but I still couldn't relax. Not like I did when I was with Daniel, anyway.

Leaning back in her chair, Collette ran a lazy hand through her tousled hair. Over her bikini top she'd thrown on some sort of airy floral T-shirt, its dipped hem finishing far enough up her abdomen to show off a glinting diamond belly ring. She blended perfectly with the modern backdrop of the restaurant, whereas I felt awkward and lumpy in my baggy top and shorts. "Well, I know what I'm getting."

I peered over the top of the menu. "What?"

She smiled. "The smoked salmon salad here is to die for."

My eyes flickered back to the list, skimming over the lengthy names and descriptions. Half of the fancy dishes I could barely pronounce, let alone work out what they consisted of. With anybody else, I would've slapped down the card straight away, not even hesitating to order what could always be counted on: a simple burger and chips. But here, sat across from somebody who seemed to be willing to die for a pathetic leafy salad, I sensed this wasn't an option.

I ended up ordering the same as Collette, deciding I'd be subjected to less criticism that way, wordless or otherwise. When it arrived, I was faced with a salad that was masquerading as something posh, but in truth was nothing more than a few limp leaves and a dressing that was much too sharp for my taste. I forced it down anyway, to keep away Collette's impending cold shoulder, if nothing else.

"See, the good thing about this place," she told me, as she set her fork down neatly on her plate, "is that none of the day-trippers know about it. You can't stumble across it unless you're looking."

I merely smiled and nodded; I didn't like to admit that in fact I preferred the beach, with its rowdy families and constant hubbub, over the restaurant we were currently sat in. The customers here were all much too reserved, looking over at the smallest disturbance with intense disapproval. At least by the sea I didn't feel so out of place, like I could be turfed out at any moment for simply not belonging.

"Of course, now you know about it," she continued, "but don't go spreading it around." She smirked. "I think I can trust you, though."

I laughed, wondering if I was reading too much into it, or whether her words really did mask some kind of deeper meaning. Maybe this was the reason my voice came out more nervously than I intended. "Yeah."

I didn't get a chance to elaborate; the loud buzz from my pocket cut me off. My phone had pinged to life with the arrival of a text message.

"Who is it?" Collette asked, as I fished it out and started scrolling to locate the newest message. Biting my lip was the only way to stop a ridiculously girlish grin spreading across my face when I saw its sender: Daniel.

Got any crazy plans for tonight, he'd written, or do you fancy meeting up? Punctuated with a smiley and a couple of kisses, it made my heart flutter unnecessarily.

"Come on, who is it?" she repeated, leaning closer.

"Oh, just Daniel," I said, without thinking.

Within an instant, Collette's newfound warmth had disappeared, vanishing into thin air as if it'd never existed in the first place. Now, she was staring at me from across the table with an expression I neither could nor wanted to decipher. "Well," she said eventually, her words turning the atmosphere to ice, "who else would it be?"

I wanted to kick myself. All afternoon I'd been careful, double-checking my words before I was careless enough to let them slip. One moment of lost concentration, a slither of attention spared on Daniel, and I'd messed up completely. My mouth had gone dry; I wasn't sure I could've said anything even if I wanted to.

If I wasn't so intimidated by Collette, I might've asked her what exactly was the deal between them. I'd still yet to work it out, but I wasn't fully convinced she wouldn't bite my head off if I so much as mentioned Daniel's name again.

"I–"

"I mean," she continued, "you work together now, right? You're spending practically every day with each other."

"Well, just–"

"It's only natural that you fancy him, really."

My head snapped upward; I couldn't stop my jaw from dropping. "What?"

"Oh, sweetie, you don't need to deny it," she said, her condescending term already shrinking my posture, letting the sense of inferiority come seeping in. "It's okay if you like him. I mean, free country and everything, right? But there's something you should know about him. Daniel... well, he's sensitive. He's had a really rough time over the past year, and quite honestly, I'm not sure he's ready for a relationship right now. Let alone with someone he just met."

"I don't–"

"Look, I'll tell you something. We used to go out, a while back. We were together for six months. Now I'm not saying that he doesn't like you, but what's best for him right now is a sense of familiarity, you know? Someone he's got history with. Not someone he barely knows." She was looking pointedly at me, a look of silent warning expertly concealed by her well-practised smile. The exact words might not have been out in the open, but the message couldn't have been clearer: Back off.

The anxiety was simmering inside me, a rising feeling of déjà vu from the night of the party already threatening to consume my entire being. I could feel a hot flush creeping up my neck, and the restaurant suddenly likened to a sauna, despite the air con being on full blast. "I don't—" I stammered, unable to get the right words out. "I mean, I just remembered I need to..."

I was already snatching up the bag from under my seat, fumbling inside the pocket of my shorts for the money to cover my part of the bill. "There's this thing," I explained vaguely, feeling the searing effect of Collette's stare through my whole self. "I have to go."

"Right now?"

"Yeah." I swallowed hard. "I forgot, but I have this thing to go to... with my gran. I sort of promised."

I'd already started to move away from the table, desperate to put distance between Collette and I, though aware that my swift exit was attracting the attention of nearby customers.

"Oh." I didn't look round; I could only hear her voice behind me. "That's a shame."

"Sorry." I wasn't quite sure what I was apologising for, but I didn't wait for a goodbye as I weaved through the labyrinth of tables in the direction of the main door. Pushing past a group of twenty-some-things in rainbow-coloured flip-flops and almost tripping over my feet in the process, I earned several strange looks. But I was focused on one thing and one thing only: getting the hell out of there. It was only when I'd made it outside, standing on the street amongst the humid summer air, that I allowed myself to stop and breathe.

And, right there, any hopes I had about getting on good terms with Collette crumbled into dust.

10

— ◆ —

CHAPTER 10

"You're telling me that was twenty minutes? It can't have been."

"It was," I assured Erin. Sat in front of the sink, she had her head tipped backwards so her hair dangled into the basin. "I checked."

Clearly, she wasn't convinced. "Well, maybe we should leave it on a little bit longer. You know, just to be safe. I want it to be bright."

"Erin, you leave this stuff on your hair for another minute, and it's going to fry. We're taking it off right now."

We were both sat in her bathroom, as we had been for the last half hour, trying to work magic with the packet of dye she'd picked up from the pharmacy. In my opinion, her hair looked fine, but she was having none of it; she'd insisted her roots were returning with a vengeance, and decided a second packet of chemical colour was her sole defence against them. Hence why, on a Saturday evening, somewhere amongst agreeing to stay the night at her place, I'd been appointed chief coordinator of the hair-dying mission.

I'd never done it before, but my lack of experience didn't seem to be a concern of Erin's. All she cared about, it seemed, was ensuring her hair stayed as bright as the sun from root to tip.

It didn't help my concentration that the bathroom was as humid and sticky as any other room in the house; though it'd been three days since my encounter with Collette, the freak heat wave the country had been experiencing was showing no sign of letting up any time soon. I was growing tired of the clammy heat, of nights spent tossing and turning under fans that seemed to do little more than push hot air around the room. And then there was the constant bustle of the town: you couldn't go anywhere without running into a herd of day-trippers clogging up the pavements and shops.

It was even worse than rain. But then again, this was English weather we were talking about, and I knew the sun could turn to a thunderstorm in a heartbeat.

"Okay, fine." Finally, she'd resigned herself to following my instruction. "Go ahead and rinse, then."

I did as she said, unhooking the showerhead from its spot above the bath and stretching it over to the sink. Upon turning the dial, water began running through her hair immediately, the excess dye turning it a vivid colour as it pooled in the bottom. Any normal person probably would've been alarmed by the sight of such a bright hue, seeing as it had just been plastered permanently onto their head, but not Erin. In fact, she seemed more concerned by the risk of it not being bright enough – as if she needed any more help standing out from the crowd.

What had surprised me, though, was the fact that Erin had returned with a packet the exact shade of the one already on her head. I'd expected something different, although equally as daring – sea green or bubblegum pink, maybe – instead of the colour that had lately become her signature look.

"I like it," she said, shrugging, when I'd asked her. "It just feels right, you know? I don't feel like I'm ready for a change just yet. Maybe next time."

Now, she looked up at me. "It's coming off alright, I take it?"

"Yeah, I think so." I continued running my gloved hands through her hair, a little worried by how the previously white sink seemed to have taken on a distinctly lilac tinge. Though Erin had assured me she'd done this hundreds of times – and on this, I didn't doubt her – I still wasn't convinced it wouldn't leave a permanent stain. "Just this last little bit, and then I think you're good to go."

"Thank god for that," she said. "My neck is killing me."

The way she was sat did look uncomfortable, but it was the easiest way for me to help. And so Erin was sat there, her T-shirt abandoned and slung over the towel rack – "You don't want to get this stuff on your clothes," she'd told me. "It stains like a bitch." – in just her bra and jeans, her head tipped back into the bowl of the sink. I stood beside her, taking charge of the actual hair colouring, and hoping to god I didn't screw anything up because Erin might actually have killed me.

But for a first attempt, I thought it had actually gone pretty well.

The water trickling from the ends of her hair had turned almost clear again, which I took as a sure sign we were nearly done. I was seconds away from shutting off the water when the door across the room swung open without warning, revealing a tall figure which proceeded to barge right in.

"Oh crap, sorry," Daniel exclaimed, stopping in his tracks when he caught sight of the two of us. "I didn't realise you were in here."

He looked adorable, as always, the face of surprise painted across his features. I was sure I looked like a complete freak, staring dumbly back at him, but I couldn't help myself. When I finally did come to my senses, I quickly ducked my head, diverting my attention to the showerhead that was dripping water down the side of the sink.

"Oi, you perv, get out," Erin said, when she caught sight of her brother in the doorway. Had she not been bent backward over the sink, her hair dripping fresh dye, I would've counted on her to shove him out herself. "It's just me in here without a top on, you know. Sorry to disappoint, but Flo's fully clothed."

I willed myself not to blush beetroot, but nevertheless I could feel my cheeks flaming.

"Sorry, but some people need to pee around here," he said, although I could've sworn I saw him steal a sideways glance in my direction. Caught in the middle of their sibling rivalry, I stood awkwardly, unsure of what else to do. "Believe me, I don't want to see my sister in her underwear."

"Right back at you, pervert."

Shrugging off his sister's insult, he seemed to catch sight of the opened dye packet balancing on the edge of the tub. "Oh god. Purple again?"

"What's wrong with purple?"

"Nothing. I just thought you might've finally ditched the crazy colours and gone for something normal this time," he commented, eyeing my handiwork. Though his words were sharp, they were softened by his tone; I could tell he was only joking. "Guess not."

"Get out of here. Go pee downstairs."

"I'm on it," he said, hooking his thumb behind him and shooting us a smile. "Have fun."

"Out!"

Marking the end of our conversation, the door swung shut behind him. The two of us were left standing in a bathroom that seemed oddly empty without him, despite the fact it had only been us in the first place.

Weird.

"I can't believe you like him," Erin said, shaking her head as she cast me a disbelieving look. "You know that's kind of disgusting, right? That's my brother."

"I don't—" I could feel my face heating up as I struggled to get the right words out. "I mean, who said that I—"

"Oh, sure," Erin drawled, smirking. "Of course you don't fancy him. Where on earth did I get that idea from? Hmm, maybe the fact that you practically go weak at the knees whenever he's around?"

"What? I don't—"

"You know, me and the other guys have practically been taking bets on how long it's going to take you two to get it on."

My face, I knew, was the picture of incredulity. "You have?"

"Well," she said, with a dismissive wave of her hand, "not exactly, but we might as well have been." Seeming to notice the look I was giving her, she shook her head. "Look, it's fine. You don't have to deny it. Sure, I think it's gross, but each to their own, right? I mean, he's not your brother."

Instead of responding, I just stood there, wishing my cheeks would at least make some attempt to cool down.

"It's a good thing anyway, you two," she continued. "I mean, you're heaps better for him than Collette. Not that I have anything against her, it's just... she was always a bit clingy."

"Oh." My voice seemed to have shrunk.

I was torn. One half of me longed to change the subject as fast as possible, but the other was itching to find out more about what exactly had gone on between Walden's most infamous couple. They'd gone out for half a year, but that was the full extent of my knowledge. I'd realised my feelings weren't exactly secret from Erin, and eventually I swallowed over any niggling doubt. "Um, what exactly happened between those two, anyway?"

Erin, who up until that moment had been looking up at me, averted her gaze conveniently elsewhere. A small delay followed, as if she found herself searching for the right explanation.

"Well, for as long as they've known each other, everyone sort of expected them to get together," she said eventually.

All I could manage was a small "Oh."

"They did, eventually. But... I don't know. Daniel never seemed quite as into it as she was. She was always a bit possessive over him, even before they started going out.

"They broke up when... well, you know. When things started to get bad with our dad. Daniel said he just couldn't handle a relationship while he was going through something like that. Let alone one with Collette. Of course, she wasn't happy, but what could she do? It was just sort of an unspoken agreement that they'd get back together once Daniel was in a better place."

I didn't know what to say, let alone make of it. An uncomfortable pang of jealously coursed through me at the thought of them together, but I had to take comfort in the fact he no longer seemed interested. Right?

Heat was prickling at the back of my neck, underneath where I'd scraped my hair up into a half-hearted ponytail. All of a sudden the bathroom felt excessively warm, its air sticky and stagnant.

"Of course, we didn't plan on you showing up here." Now, she looked back at me, smirking. "No wonder Collette's not happy."

I sunk down onto the closed loo seat, sighing. "Well, she does seem to hate me."

"Nah, she doesn't hate you," Erin said reassuringly. She pushed herself into a standing position, draping a bath towel around her shoulders to catch the dampness of her hair. "She's just a bit jealous that you've been getting on so well with Daniel."

"So she hates me."

"Look, Flo." Erin turned around, exhaling deeply. "I know Collette's not the friendliest person in the world, but she's not all bad. The thing is, she and Daniel ended over a year ago now. It's not like you've just waltzed in and stole her boyfriend. A bit of time, she'll get used to it. And it'll all turn out fine. I swear. I've grown up with these guys, remember?"

"Okay." I did feel better; Erin seemed to have a knack for talking things up until they didn't seem quite so hopeless. "Thanks."

"What're you thanking me for, stupid?" she asked, grinning. "I didn't do anything. In fact, all I ask is that when you do finally hook up with my brother, you both keep quiet. My bedroom happens to be right next to his."

Needless to say, I took great pleasure in chucking the hair-dyed glove at her face.

I hadn't realised Erin was such a restless sleeper.

While I wasn't the soundest even at the best of times, this girl was in a whole different league. Had I known, I would never have allowed myself to fall asleep on her double bed, twisted awkwardly in the blankets next to her. At least that way, I would never have had to experience the pain of being rudely awoken by none other than a brutal kick to the face.

Somehow, we'd ended up in a top-to-toe position: hence why her foot happened to be so close to my head in the first place. Still, that didn't make it any easier to sleep with her sporadic jerky movements, the last of which involved a painful collision between my skull and her heel. Evidently, she was deep in a dream that required a lot of violent kicking.

I was used to night-time disruptions, especially living with Gram, but even I couldn't sleep through that.

"Erin!"

My hissed exclamation didn't cause her to so much as stir. Arms hugging the pillow, hair fanned out across the mattress, she continued snoozing without a care in the world.

Unravelling myself from the twisted blankets, I sat up. Erin's bedroom was dark; the only source of light was the faint blue glow of her alarm clock, its blinking digits reading 2:04. An electric fan hummed in the corner, blasting cool air onto our feet, but the rest of the room remained horribly muggy. The most I could make out of my surroundings was rough silhouettes; Erin's newly-coloured hair was really the only thing I could see clearly, even after my eyes had adjusted to the lack of light.

The lack of fresh air was already getting to me, so I pulled back the covers and hopped off the edge of the bed. I knew where the bathroom was, having spent so much time in there earlier this afternoon, and I only hoped it had a window I could throw wide open to let some cool air in. At the very least, I could splash cold water on my face and pray for a change of weather.

The door handle rattled as I tugged on it, moving from one silent room to the next. It was almost eerie, how quiet it was; no matter how still I stood, or how much I strained to hear sounds that were basically nonexistent, the silence was there, weighing everything down like a heavy blanket. Trying my best to shake off the feeling, I emerged on the dark landing and started towards the bathroom door.

However, it was not empty. Cracks of light were escaping from the gap between the door and the frame, indicating that it was already occupied.

I stepped tentatively forward, hoping that whoever was in there would finish up quickly so I could cool myself down and get back to Erin's room as quickly as possible. The quiet didn't seem so daunting there, at least. But just as this thought crossed my mind, and I stopped about three steps away from the door, the lock clicked and the door suddenly swung open.

It was Daniel who stood there.

I inhaled sharply as my eyes locked onto his, but this time it was not merely the shock of bumping into the guy I sort of fancied, in the dead of night no less, that caused this. The lack of light didn't stop me noticing the way his hair was sticking up in all directions, like he'd been running his hand through it, and how his eyes were rimmed with red.

"Flo?" His voice was raw, as if the word was physically scratching at his throat.

"Daniel..."

I didn't have the faintest idea what I was going to say, but his name escaped me anyway. For a moment the both of us stood rooted to the spot, unable to do anything but stare dumbstruck at each other.

Then, swallowing, I worked up the nerve to say, "Are you... are you okay?"

It was pretty obvious he wasn't, but I felt like I needed to ask anyway. He'd emerged from the bathroom in the middle of the night, with sore eyes and a husky throat; it was a situation I knew like the back of my hand. I couldn't count the times I'd gone through it: the helplessness, the inability to do anything but sob, knowing it'll never get better.

Suddenly I was back there again: tears streaming down my face, screaming into pillows in an overwhelming mix of frustration, anger and pulsating grief. Knowing nothing on this earth could ever bring them back, questioning how I was meant to survive the rest of my life without them. Terrified, because what if I forgot the taste of my mum's pancakes on a Saturday morning? Or what it felt like to have Dad hug me and call me his angel? It's those things you cling to, a thread with the spindly strength of a cobweb, that keep you just feebly connected to what you've lost.

But memories start to fade eventually, and when they do, they're gone forever. For real this time.

Nights were always the worst, dominated by the darkness that did nothing but smother me, and silence that left my thoughts free to perform their torture. I felt it. I'd been through it. Yet I seemed unable to do anything but ask the most pointless question there was.

"I..." He was just staring back at me, almost as if he didn't quite believe I was standing there. Like I was some kind of mirage formed from a half-conscious dream. There was a definitive vacancy glazing his eyes; even though he was a couple of feet in front of me, he was miles away. "I just... I'm fine. I swear."

"You're not fine," I whispered. "What's wrong?"

"It's just…" He sounded tired, but a long way off being able to fall asleep. The familiar feeling was imprinted in my mind: being so utterly exhausted and wanting nothing more than to drift off to a place where your thoughts can't reach you. But your head won't allow it, instead going over and over the thing you're trying desperately to forget. "It's just been a really rough night. I don't… can we not talk about it?"

"I never said we had to," I said softly.

"Okay."

I know it's about your dad, I wanted to say. I know how it feels.

But I didn't. He just looked so hopeless and upset, standing there in his pyjamas in the quiet hallway, the end of his nose rubbed raw, I knew I had to do something – anything – to make him feel better. So instead I moved closer and pulled him into me, wrapping my arms around his back. I squeezed him as tightly and reassuringly as I could manage, trying to remove every last centimetre of distance between us. He smelled of washing powder, combined with the faintest hint of toothpaste, but I tried not to think too hard about that, instead praying to god that I was doing something here. I had to be.

"Flo," I heard him mumble quietly into my shoulder. His arms had moved around me now, keeping me pressed to his chest like he was scared to let go. I knew I was the strong one here, but there was something undeniably comforting about being enveloped in his grip – something that made me want to melt into his arms and stay there forever. I was shielded from the outside world, even if it was just for a moment.

"We don't have to talk about it," I reminded him. "It's fine."

I'm not even sure what happened from that point. When I try to recall it, I can't even remember how we went from being locked in each other's arms in the empty hallway, to his room, and then his bed. Nothing happened; we just lay there, arms wrapped around each other in the place of words we didn't have the courage to speak out loud.

In the light of day, there would've been questions, awkwardness, faked strength. But the sky was dark, and things were different.

We both drifted off eventually, his arms around my waist and my back pressed to his chest. I could hear his steady breathing, even his faint heartbeat if I listened hard enough; it was these unchanging rhythms that lulled me to sleep.

In a few hours, the darkness would dissipate, to be replaced by the first signs of sunlight nudging their way through the gaps in the blinds. Somewhere between that things would start to change; there'd come a point when night would crossover into the normality of daylight, though you might not be able to feel it yourself.

Maybe that was why I woke before the clock showed six, untangled myself from Daniel's arms without causing him to stir, and padded back to Erin's room before she could even wake up and realise I'd been gone.

11

———— ◆ ————

CHAPTER 11

It was sometime past midnight, about fifteen minutes after I'd drifted off to sleep, when Gram's landline trilled into life, echoing through the quiet cottage.

I woke to the sound of an opening door from somewhere across the landing; this was shortly followed by slipper-clad footsteps padding down the stairs. Seconds later, the phone stopped.

My room was too distant from the hallway to hear much more than Gram's muffled speech, but the way she was struggling to limit the volume of her voice confirmed whatever news she was receiving was exciting. It continued for several minutes before I decided I'd had enough of straining to make out muted words, threw the duvet back and padded downstairs after her.

The further I ventured downstairs, the clearer the one-sided conversation became. My feet landed on the last step just as I heard Gram say, "But how long? How long do you think it'll be?"

"Gram?" I whispered, tentatively stepping towards her. The phone was pressed tightly to her ear, brows furrowed in a concentrated frown as she listened intently to person on the other line. "Is everything okay?"

She looked up at the sound of my voice, noticing only for the first time that I stood there. "Flo," she said, louder now. "Sorry. I didn't mean to wake you up."

"What's going on?"

"Nora." The mention of her name had my heart leaping. "She's gone into labour."

"Wait – now?" I did the mental calculation, but it worked out. A few days early, maybe, but essentially right. I'd been in Walden over three weeks; when I'd left Nora, she'd just passed the eight month milestone. Had time really passed that quickly? She'd looked ready to pop for a while, but I figured the last few weeks of her pregnancy would drag.

"Yeah. She's in the hospital."

I froze. My head was instantly laden with snapshot-like images of Nora lying in a hospital bed, crippled by agony, screaming at the top of her lungs. Lenny would be there, of course, but aside from him and a couple of doctors, she'd be alone. How could I be here, one hundred and fifty miles away and so blissfully unaware, when somewhere in London my sister was about to go through the scariest and most painful experience of her life?

"I'm going." The decision was easy; there was no other answer. "I have to be with her."

"Flo..." Gram protested. In the dim light of the hallway, standing there in her faded dressing gown and pillow-flattened curls, she looked so startlingly different. By day, she was eccentric and unpredictable: Flo and Nora's crazy grandmother. Now, she looked more normal than I'd ever known. Like a regular grandma, who knitted jumpers and played bingo and carried a never-ending supply of toffees in her handbag. Not the one who'd paint random murals on any free walls she could find in the house. "It's late. You can't go now."

"I have to."

"It'll take you two hours to get up there, and it's the middle of the night. It's dangerous to be out in London at that time."

Of course, I knew that better than anyone; I'd lived there all my life. It was more than dodgy to be wandering the streets at two a.m., but what choice did I have? I couldn't just go back to bed and leave Nora on her own. She might've had Lenny, but I was willing to bet he didn't know the first thing about childbirth. It wouldn't have surprised me if he thought the baby was going to come out of Nora's bellybutton.

"Why don't you go back to sleep? You can get up early and catch the train out then. That way you can still go see her."

"The baby might've been born by then," I said. "Gram, I can't just leave her on her own. I have to go."

"It's not safe."

"I don't care."

"Well, I do!" Gram's voice suddenly escalated several notches in volume, a fiery glare igniting behind her eyes. "I'm responsible for you, Flo, and I'm not letting you go marching off to London alone at this time of night. Nora's an adult, and she's got Lenny with her. She can cope."

"But what if she can't?" I was verging on desperation now. "What if she can't, Gram? What if she needs me, and I'm not there?"

"She's two hours away, she'll understand if—"

"You don't understand!" I cried. I wanted to take Gram by the shoulders and shake her, make her see somehow how desperately I needed do this. "We promised each other we'd never leave. She kept her side of the deal. She's always been there when I needed her. What kind of sister would I be if I just left her now? Please, Gram. I have to go."

We lapsed into silence; the only sound left in the hallway was that of our steady breathing alternating with each other. I stared pleadingly back at her through a glaze of potential tears. Didn't she know what it had been like for us? Didn't she realise that Nora had been the only thing there when my world had fallen apart at the seams? I knew tonight wouldn't make up for it completely; I'd always remain indebted to her. But being there, even if I was just another hand to hold, couldn't have been more important.

Gram was staring back at me, her chest rising and falling with each deep breath. I couldn't read the expression written all over her face. She'd turned into one of her own abstract works of art, the true meaning concealed from any onlooker. In her hand, the receiver was dangling by its cord, and I briefly wondered whether Lenny was still on the other line. I only hoped he was too busy comforting Nora to play witness to the first argument I'd ever had with Gram.

When she finally spoke, it was only one word. "Okay."

I blinked. "Okay?"

"I understand. You can go, but not on your own. I'm coming with you."

"Really?"

"Yes," she said quietly. "I can see how important this is to you. If you want to go see Nora, then so be it. We can take the car instead."

It took a few seconds for the words to sink in, but when they did, I could think of nothing else to do but rush forward and throw my arms around Gram. There was a slight delay in her response, but a few seconds later I felt her arms enclose me, squeezing me tighter. "Thank you," I breathed, my voice muffled by the fabric of her dressing gown.

"You're welcome, Flo," she answered. Then, I felt her grip loosen. "Now come on. Grab anything you need as quickly as you can. We need to make a move and hope Nora's little one's not too eager to get out."

It took two hours to reach the hospital Nora had been admitted to, even with Gram pushing the speed limit most of the way there. The time on my mobile read quarter past two as we tore across the scarcely lit car park and arrived, breathless and sweaty, at reception.

The receptionist stationed at the front desk looked startled, to say the least, by our arrival. I suppose she had a right to be, really; seeing a seventeen-year-old and a pensioner, both in pyjamas and slippers, burst through the revolving doors into an otherwise empty room wasn't exactly the most normal of occurrences. But, to be honest, she should've abandoned all normal expectations the moment Nora was admitted to the maternity ward.

"We're here... to see... Nora... Kennedy," I stammered breathlessly, steadying myself on the front desk.

The woman, who seemed yet to recover from her initial shock, paused. Her pristine appearance – tightly pressed uniform, fluffy blond hair, pearly lipstick – indicated she was neither used to nor fond of surprises, and Gram and I appeared to be the biggest shock she'd had all shift. Regaining her composure, she began tapping away at the computer, squared nails hitting the keyboard with perfect rhythm.

"Ah, yes," she said. "She's upstairs in maternity. Are you immediate family?"

"Yes," I told her. The most immediate she has left, I added mentally. "I'm her sister."

I could've sworn I saw the receptionist purse her lips. "Very well," she said slowly. "You can head on up, I suppose."

That was enough of a cue. I wasted no time in dashing past the front desk, heading in the direction of a sign that read stairs. The sterile stench of the hospital was already threatening to trigger a wave of terrible memories, memories that originated three years previously, but I forced them away. Right now, I had to focus on one thing, and one thing only: finding Nora.

The maternity ward was on the third floor. Being much too agitated to wait for the lift, my legs were aching severely in protest by the time I'd dashed up the last flight of stairs. But I was too close to stop now. I pushed through the doors to be faced with a bustling ward, where countless monitors beeped in synchronization, nurses hurried to and from every corner of the room, and babies screamed somewhere off the corridor.

It seemed bizarre that this was the place where new life began; it just seemed too normal and too busy for that.

"I'm here to see Nora," I panted for a second time, to one of the midwives absently sorting through a hefty stack of paperwork.

"Ooh, are you her sister?" she asked, her face brightening. I could tell immediately she was a hundred times friendlier than her downstairs counterpart; for starters, her smile didn't look like it was causing severe muscle strain. "She's been asking about you for hours now. We've been telling her you live a way away, so it's not like you can just pop down the road to visit. But you're here now! One sec, I'll take you through."

She slid the pile of paper into a plastic folder, tossing it aside. Then she rose from her seat, beckoning for Gram and I to follow.

"How is she?" I asked. My shoes squeaked on the burnished floor while the midwife, whose nametag read Sally, strode ahead with great purpose.

"Oh, she's absolutely fine," she assured me. "Everything's running smoothly so far. She's doing brilliantly. I'd say we can expect the baby in the next couple of hours. Maybe even sooner."

We rounded the corner, coming to a stop in front of the first door on the left. Sally knocked loudly, not even bothering to wait for an answer. Opening the door right up, she stepped straight inside and motioned for us to do the same.

I don't really know what I was expecting, but it was far from the sight that stood before me. My previous experience of childbirth was limited to years-old tales of how Nora was the biggest newborn the nurses had ever seen, and how she'd put our mum through so much pain she almost didn't have a second. I had visions of her lying on blood-soaked sheets, screaming fit to burst as nurses flitted around, trying to calm her down.

Thankfully, the reality was much less horrifying.

Nora was propped up by pillows on a bed in the centre of the room. Swathed in a baggy hospital gown, she was lying with her knees apart and a blanket draped over her lower half. Her blond hair was pulled into a straggly ponytail, her skin pastier than usual, the painful twist of concentration across her face sent a jolt of alarm through me. However, once Sally stepped aside to reveal Gram and I in the doorway, her features relaxed and a smile full of relief appeared over her frown.

"Flo!"

"Nora!"

I made a beeline for her immediately; arms wrapped around me the moment I got close enough. We were soon enclosed in each other's grip, my nose buried in her shoulder, breathing in the floral scent that remained noticeable over the sterility of her gown. We'd only been apart for a few weeks, but suddenly it felt so much longer – and as if we'd been separated by several thousand miles, instead of a two hour train journey.

"You're here," I heard her say. "And Gram too."

"Of course," I mumbled, willing away the tears of relief pricking at my eyes. "Why wouldn't I be?"

"And I wasn't going to let her come alone," Gram chipped in. "She insisted she had to see you."

I could've sworn I felt her smile into my hair. "Thank you," she breathed. "It means so much that you're here."

When her grip loosened, I moved backward, taking a second look at her small form. Though her stomach was anything but, and my five foot eight only topped her by an inch or so, she seemed so tiny beneath her gown. Maybe it was the lack of make-up, or the absence of hair framing her face, that made her look younger, but I was sure anybody who didn't know us could've easily mistaken me for the older sibling.

I noticed a chair propped up against the wall, which I dragged forward and positioned right by Nora's side. It was so close my knees were pressing into the bed frame, but the thought of putting any more distance than necessary between us now felt utterly unbearable.

Only then, glancing round the room, did something occur to me. "Hey, where's Lenny?"

"I think he went to get a drink or something," she said, screwing up her face as she rubbed her stomach. "He got a bit squeamish, anyway. He's been looking pale for the last couple of hours. Bless him."

"Oh. Right." I hadn't expected it; I'd always assumed Lenny would delve right into the experience of childbirth. It seemed suitably hippie to go wild on the whole miracle of life thing, but apparently he was full of surprises. "Are you okay, though? Is it really that bad?"

"Yes. It's the worst bloody pain I've ever felt in my life," she groaned, throwing her head back against the pillow. "The midwife keeps insisting everything's going brilliantly, but it doesn't feel like it."

"It's childbirth, love," Sally interjected from across the room. "Trust me, having the baby is not going to be as much fun as making it."

My head whipped around so quickly I got a crick in my neck; I couldn't help but stare open-mouthed at the midwife, who was busying herself inspecting the clipboard at the end of Nora's bed. When she caught sight of me gawking, she grinned. "What? I'm just telling it like it is."

Whatever response I might've come out with died in my throat when a load groan erupted behind me. Nora was clutching the sides of the bed, gripping the sheets so hard they wrinkled beneath her fingers, eyes squeezed tightly shut. Panic coursed through me like a shot; I looked from her to Sally, to Gram, and back to Nora again in despair.

"Another contraction?" Sally inquired.

My sister nodded slowly, the entire movement seeming to require extortionate effort. The pain then intensified; in the space of a second, her hand had left the mattress and found mine instead. She was squeezing it so hard I was sure the bones were being pulverised, but the sensation barely registered. I remained focused solely on Nora, my eyes never leaving her, letting my hand get crushed as we waited for the worst to pass.

When her eyes finally fluttered open, she was panting, and beads of sweat trickled down her forehead. "I. Want. To. Push," she forced out.

"You can't yet, honey," Sally said, her tone too cheery for the situation. "It's not quite time."

I felt the front of my top being gripped; Nora had hold of it in her fist, dragging me closer to her. "Flo," she said through gritted teeth, "tell her. I want to push. Now."

"I, uh…" I looked between them.

Nora screamed, her fingers curling, causing her nails to dig deep into my palm. "She wants to push," I told Sally, in a voice that sounded surprisingly unlike my own, "and I don't think she's going to take no for an answer."

The midwife rushed forward at that point, yanking back the blanket that was covering Nora's legs. "You feel like you want to?"

"Just a bit," Nora shot back, sarcastic as ever.

"Well, if you're ready to. Just a heads up: this bit's going to hurt."

She groaned again, pressing down harder on my palm. As I winced, the door swung open. It quickly revealed an eye-wateringly colourful T-shirt, worn by its owner as much as his wary expression. In fact, Lenny looked as if he happened to be venturing into a sleeping lion's den, where one wrong foot could have disastrous consequences.

"Everything okay?" he asked gingerly.

"Lenny!" Nora yelled. "Get over here right now."

Evidently too scared to disobey his girlfriend, he stumbled forward, almost tripping over his feet in his hasty effort to reach Nora. Her fingers immediately enclosed his palm, pressing hard, and I knew at once from his wincing expression that his hand was suffering the same treatment as mine. But it wasn't like we were in a place to complain. Nora was the one about to push a baby out of her, after all.

"You ready?" Sally asked, from her position at the foot of the bed. Somewhere amongst the commotion she'd donned a pair of gloves, and was now forcing Nora's knees apart. "You're ten centimetres dilated, so we should be good to go."

All she got in response was an ear-splitting scream.

The next hour was, to put it simply, a complete blur. It passed in a hazy mess of blood, wailing and the pulverizing of the bones in my hand, and was punctuated by Sally's breezy updates from the other end. Time whizzed past in an agonizing rush: a chaotic hubbub full of yelling, deep breathing – from everyone involved – and huge gulps of gas and air. It was difficult enough to watch; I could only imagine what it was like for my sister, who already had hours of agony under her belt.

Lenny, for one, seemed to be growing progressively paler with each second. At one point, I was convinced he'd be making a dash to the adjoining bathroom any second, because the slight greenish tinge his face had taken on was nothing if not ominous. But he stuck it out, keeping the nausea at bay, and doing so paid off.

Because at forty minutes past three, he and Nora officially became the proud parents of their first daughter.

Sometime later, Nora and the baby had been cleaned up, and with the umbilical cord cut – courtesy of Lenny, who really did look about to puke after that – I found myself back in the seat beside the bed. The newborn had been swaddled in a pink blanket, pale face peeking out from the fabric, held tightly against my sister's chest. Needless to say, they both looked considerably more peaceful than they had done an hour beforehand.

"So," I said softly, daring to break the comfortable silence that had fallen across the room. It had become almost like a blanket: one as warm as that tucked around the tiny baby. I almost didn't want to shift it, to disturb the frozen snapshot we found ourselves trapped in, but there was an important question on my tongue. "Have you come up with any names yet?"

Nora looked down at the bundle in her arms; it already had tufts of dark fuzzy hair, a button nose that was squished slightly against her mother's skin. Glancing up to lock eyes with Lenny, she shifted slightly in the bed. "We were thinking of Summer," she whispered, "but we weren't sure."

"Summer," I repeated slowly.

Gazing down at the baby – my niece – in her arms, an unfamiliar sensation washed over me. It was heavy, dense, though its weight on my shoulders felt comforting rather than restricting. I thought back to the past few weeks, how everything had changed beyond recognition in such a short space of time. I backtracked to the nerves I'd had about moving to Walden, the people I'd met, the crazy happenings that had become part of daily life.

And Daniel.

"Summer," I said again. "It's perfect."

12

CHAPTER 12

"So," Nora began, as I settled into the opposite seat with my hands around a hot cappuccino. "How's it been? You have to tell me everything."

It seemed strange that, tucked away in a busy Starbucks during the first time alone we'd had since Summer's birth, Nora was asking me this. She was, after all, the one who'd just had a baby; the past seven days had seen her being hurled headfirst into the deep end of motherhood. I was sure that ranked a little more exciting than what I had to talk about – which was, of course, my summer so far in England's sleepiest seaside town.

And yet we were both here, tucked into a two-seater by the window, while Nora smiled expectantly at me over her coffee.

Conforming to the rest of London's routine at this time of day, the place was bustling. Clattering mugs and room-wide chatter made up a larger part of the shop's soundtrack than the radio blasting over the speakers, and almost every table was occupied; we'd had to dash the moment another couple vacated their spot. It was hectic, but it felt normal. Everyone here was just a face in the crowd I'd likely never see again.

It stood a stark contrast to the lethargy of Walden-on-Sea.

Summer was now a week old, and Nora almost recovered from the ordeal, though I was yet to make my return to Walden. Gram had driven back several days ago, offering to take me with her, but I'd declined. I wasn't quite sure why, but I found myself wanting to stay in London just that little bit longer.

It was still my home, and yet I couldn't deny something felt slightly off. It was as if three weeks in a cottage on the south coast had already altered my perception; I'd become used to waking up to the sound of the ocean rather than traffic rattling the window frames. One morning I even found myself wondering if Walden was in for some kind of freak tsunami, before realising that I was in fact one hundred and fifty miles away, in a flat in the country's busiest city.

The camp bed in Lenny's living room wasn't exactly the most comfortable living arrangement, but I couldn't bring myself to leave just yet. I may have been as sleep-deprived as they were, now accustomed to the sound of Summer's crying at all hours of the night, but I didn't like the thought of separating from Nora again so soon. For now, at least, I felt as though I had the sense of stability back in my life – even if it was preoccupied with a newborn baby and I was living out of an overnight bag.

"Well," I said slowly, as Nora leaned back in her chair. I could tell she was preparing herself for a long story, detailing the adventures that had filled the time we'd been apart. "There's not really much to tell."

It seemed true, at least on the surface. It was only when I began to think about what really had happened over the last few weeks that I began to doubt myself. Walden-on-Sea could undoubtedly bag prizes for being the dullest town in Britain, but that was only the case if the judge hadn't met Daniel, Erin and their friends.

"Oh, come on," she said, stirring her coffee. "You've been away for almost a month. There has to be something to tell me. What's Gram's place like?"

The cottage's image was surprisingly easy to conjure up in my mind; I could instantly picture the whitewashed walls, the vibrant paint of each room, the thatched roof I was always convinced was going to collapse at the first sight of rain but never did. "It's nice," I said truthfully, "and my room overlooks the sea."

"Really?" Nora's eyebrows raised. "God, I'm so jealous. I mean, Lenny's place is okay, but a sixth storey view of the main road doesn't really compare to something like that."

"Lenny's place isn't that bad."

Bringing the cup to my lips, I took a drink of the steaming liquid, jolting as it scalded my tongue. I'd been unprepared for the heat against my mouth, but soon realised the damage was done; there was nothing for it now but to go in for another sip.

"So, have you made any new friends?" Nora wasted no time in diving straight into the next question, her expression eager. "There must be some kids your age, right?"

I went in for a longer sip this time, deliberately delaying my answer. Nora was the equivalent of an embarrassing mother, and I wondered if spilling the details about my sort of – maybe – new crush was wise. After all, she wasn't exactly known for keeping her nose out of things.

"Yeah," I said eventually. "I've met a few people. I went to that party – you know, the one I got invited to on the day we got there?"

"You did?" Her face practically lit up. "That's great, Flo! How was it?"

"It was…" I was hit by a sudden flashback, of what could only be described as my freak-out at the mention of the word parents. I remembered hiding in the bathroom, the crippling nerves, the scrutiny of Collette's gaze as she looked me up and down. It was almost strong enough to bring back a second round of the panic, but it merged into something else just in time.

The conversation in the kitchen with Erin, the intangible bond that linked us together. How I'd returned to the party and done something I hadn't, at that point, thought possible: I'd enjoyed myself, without being in London and without my sister. "It was fun, actually."

Her grin widened, though I wasn't quite sure how. "Oh, Flo. I'm so happy for you." Inching forward, she placed her elbows on the table. "So, tell me… any fit Walden guys?"

I'd expected the question at some point, attributing my straight face to the mental preparation I'd had time for beforehand. Tactfully averting my gaze downward, focusing on the specks of chocolate floating atop the coffee foam, I shook my head. "Not really."

I had never been the world's most talented liar. Since I was a kid, I'd been no good at it. One Christmas, I remember stumbling across Mum's hiding place for all our presents and not being able to resist sneaking a peek at every single one. It would've been fine if the guilt hadn't racked me from then onward, eventually leading me to blurt out the truth and burst into tears on my mother's lap several hours later. I just couldn't lie.

Maybe I could've gotten away with it. If I just kept my head down, letting my hair's loose curls shield my face from view, I might've been able to get off scot-free.

As it turned out, my phone chose that exact moment to come to life. With a buzz that vibrated the entire table, its screen illuminated, flashing the six-letter word that gave it all away.

"Text from Daniel?" Nora asked, struggling to hold back a smirk. Though I snatched the mobile up as quickly as I could, my reactions had been just that little bit too slow. She'd seen the name, and by now I was blushing full-force.

Whichever way I looked at it, there was absolutely no wriggling out of this one. Because while Nora had her slightly ditzy moments, she was by all means persistent.

"It's nothing."

"Oh, really?" Her smirk intensified. "It doesn't seem like nothing. He's obviously got something to say."

I gripped the phone more tightly, half-afraid she would rip it out of my hands and read the message herself, but the hot coffee on the table seemed to deter her.

Lowering my phone safely into my lap, well out of Nora's reach, I ducked my head to check the message. It flashed up immediately onscreen, my eyes scanning over it eagerly. We'd exchanged a lengthy text conversation spanning the week I'd been in London, although there had been no mention of what had happened the night I'd stayed over. It was much too heavy to discuss over text messages, but even in person, it wouldn't feel right to bring up in daylight. Some things were banished to the safety of darkness, where the slate would be wiped before sunrise. I wondered if we'd ever get round to mentioning it, even after I arrived back in Walden.

His messages, however, rarely failed to make me smile – especially when they consisted of tales about Erin being roped in to cover my shifts at the shop. Just imagining her scowling face behind the counter as she scooped ice cream into cones made me have to bite back a smile.

You coming home soon? it read. We miss you.

A round of butterflies instantly erupted in my stomach. I almost forgot that Nora was sat across the table from me, watching my girlish expression with amusement painted across her own.

Only then did I notice the most significant part of the text: the way Daniel had referred to Walden as 'home'. Of course, it was to him; he'd lived there his entire life. But to me? The world almost didn't sound strange enough.

"What's he saying, then?" Nora asked, obviously fed up of watching me smile idiotically at my phone. "Text message love letter?"

I rolled my eyes. "You're so immature."

She stuck her tongue out, effectively proving my point. "Come on, Flo. You said there was nothing to tell. You were lying. You and Daniel have got something going on, haven't you? You little sneak!"

"No," I said firmly. "He's just a friend, that's all. He just wanted to know when I was planning to head back."

"Are you sure?"

"Yes," I told her, knowing better than to elaborate. One slip-up could be disastrous; Nora had a knack for twisting my words into something one hundred times more embarrassing. Years' experience had taught me it was better to keep quiet. "What? Stop looking at me like that."

Though I tried to sound irritated, we'd both noticed the way my cheeks were warming considerably – and I couldn't put it down to the heat of the coffee I'd been drinking. Nora, averting her gaze to the table on which she was drumming her fingers, merely smiled.

"Nothing," she said, though it was clearly the opposite. Then, she added, "Looks like Flo's got a little crush."

"I do not!" I protested, but the squeakiness of my voice begged to differ.

"So you've been hanging out with him?"

"I..." Whatever negative response I might've had died in my throat. Nothing could come from lying, so I took a deep breath and prepared for Nora's potential squealing. "A little. And he, uh... he kind of gave me a job."

"In the ice cream shop?"

"Uh huh."

She clapped her hands together, leaning back in her seat with a huge grin on her face. I couldn't really see what was so amazing about this revelation, but Nora obviously could. "Oh, Flo," she gushed. "You know, I was so worried about you settling into that place. I thought we might have to reconsider if you found it too difficult... but this is wonderful. It's all worked out. I'm so happy for you."

My cheeks reddened. "It's not that big of a deal."

She reached over the table and clasped my hand, the conversation suddenly serious. I blinked back at her, focusing so hard on her face that the people walking past the window were reduced to indistinguishable blurs. "You're really okay?" she asked. "Because I swear, if you're not happy, we can figure something out. All you have to do is say the word."

"Nora," I said, "I'm fine. Honestly."

It was hard, adjusting to a whole set of new surroundings, but I had to stick it out. Even if I hated life in Walden-on-Sea, I couldn't ask my sister to uproot her whole life – the one she'd only just started living – for my benefit. The thing was, despite the extent of the surprise that came with the fact, I didn't hate it. Though taking some getting used to, I was getting there.

Nora had her own life now, and I had mine.

And though the thought pretty much scared me shitless, there was nothing I could do but accept it.

"Okay." She seemed satisfied with my answer, or at least that's what I took the loosening of her grip on my hand to mean. "I'm so glad."

Keen to steer the conversation toward a lighter topic, I cleared my throat. "So, uh... how's motherhood treating you?"

She sighed, blowing her fringe from her face. "Oh, just brilliant. I mean, it's a complete doddle. And I get eight hours of sleep every night." She rolled her eyes. "No. It's freaking hard, Flo. It's only been a week and I'm exhausted. Seventeen years and fifty-one weeks to go, huh? Not that I'm counting."

I shot her a sympathetic look. "That bad?"

"Well..." She paused for thought. "Not completely. I mean, I love her to bits. I couldn't imagine being without her now. It's just... I don't know. I always thought I'd be a bit more clued up – that once I actually had the baby some kind of maternal instinct would kick in. But right now, I'm basically just winging it. It wasn't until the midwife visited that I realised I'd been putting her nappy on backwards for the first three days."

Laughter bubbled up inside me, escaping before I could stop it. I pressed a hand to my mouth to suppress the giggle. "Oh, God."

"Hey, don't laugh." She pouted exaggeratedly. "I'm a first-time mum. No one gave me an instruction manual."

"You'd have thought all those baby books you spent a fortune on would've done the trick."

"So did I. And then there's all the worrying. Worrying about whether she's having enough milk. Worrying about whether she's gaining weight quick enough. Worrying if her cot's the right temperature. You know, I even worry about whether I'm worrying enough."

Now, I could sense it was my turn to be sentimental. "You're doing fine," I told her honestly. "You and Lenny are going to make great parents."

She blinked back at me, widened eyes making her face look younger than ever. "You really think so?"

"Of course."

A small, genuine smile graced her features. "Thanks, Flo."

Over the table, she stared at me, her eyes scanning over me with more intent than they had all afternoon. It was as if she found herself determined to see past the walls of my exterior – and for that, Nora had always possessed a talent like nobody else's. "You know what? I'm not worried about you at all. You're going to be absolutely fine in Walden."

Though I had doubts in my sister's ability to fasten a nappy, I had a feeling she might have been right about that one.

13

CHAPTER 13

I couldn't sleep.

It was sometime past one o'clock, several hours after I'd arrived back in Walden, showing up on Gram's doorstep with a suitcase as I had already done once before. The place had seemed eerily empty when I first stepped inside, but I guessed that was what seven days in Lenny's cramped flat – accompanied by two hippie parents and a newborn with surprising lung capacity – did to you. Considering my current level of exhaustion, I should've been asleep in seconds.

It wasn't just Summer's sporadic screaming that had worn me out. There had also been Nora herself to contend with. I mean, I loved her more than anything, but our time spent apart had definitely weakened my immunity to her craziness. Living with Gram and her occasional odd habits was nothing compared to my older sister.

Not to mention I'd eaten more organic lentils in the last seven days than I could stomach.

But still, here I was: curled up on top of the duvet, tossing and turning in the heat of my bedroom. The alarm clock appeared to be mocking me as I watched the minutes turn into hours, with no sign whatsoever of sleep descending upon me anytime soon.

The whole town was still, the only sound being that of the faint lapping of waves on the shore from my open window. Even the seagulls had quietened, the absence of their loud cawing leaving perhaps the biggest gap of them all. I was shattered, both physically and mentally, but my mind wouldn't stop racing, hurtling through my thoughts faster than I could keep up. Every movement only pushed sleep further from reach.

Eventually, I concluded that lying there was pointless, swinging my feet over the side of the bed. Once up, I pulled on a jacket over my pyjamas, slipped grey pumps on my feet and set off for the landing. My sketchbook and phone easily slipped inside a small bag, but I had no idea where I intended to go. All I knew was that I need to clear my head; at least having my sketchbook would provide something productive to fill in the hours I spent not sleeping.

Sneaking out of the house wasn't likely to be a challenge; Gram was usually the world's heaviest sleepier. Padding down the stairs, crossing the hallway and slipping out the front door – remembering, at the last minute, to take a key – made for an easier task than I could've hoped for.

A chilly breeze rustled through the flimsy fabric of my clothing as I stepped outside, and I pulled my jacket tighter around me. Though the day had been pleasantly warm – a waste of nice weather, considering I'd spent most of it packing and crammed into a stuffy train – the lack of sun brought with it a distinct temperature drop, and the wind had definitely picked up.

The noise of the ocean was even louder in the town's silence; undoubtedly, everyone was sleeping at this hour. I was sure I'd be able to hear the collective sound of snoring pensioners if only I listened hard enough.

My feet felt strangely heavy on the pavement as I headed down to the town centre. In the distance sat the familiar street of shops, their windows darkened, broken up by the artificial light of the twenty-four hour minimarket. It stood the bright spot in a line of darkness, and a split second decision steered me towards it.

The cashier seemed to suffer the shock of his life when I passed through the door. Clearly, late-night customers in Walden were a rarity. Exchanging a brief nod with him as I walked by, I headed straight for the junk food aisle.

Sleep didn't seem to be on the cards tonight, so I was determined to find the most unhealthy, sugary I could think of. In fact, I was so deep in deliberation about whether I was more in the mood for a chocolate cupcake or a double pack of iced doughnuts that the opening door and footsteps from another customer completely escaped my notice.

Until they poked their head around the aisle.

"Flo?"

I was so surprised to hear another voice that I almost dropped the packet of doughnuts. Head darting in their direction, I came face-to-face with someone I recognised instantly. "Daniel?"

"What are you doing here?" we both cried simultaneously.

"Hey, that was good," he said, laughing. "We should be a double act or something."

I found myself grinning, rendered suddenly speechless by the sight of his adorable smile. Unlike me, he was dressed in clothes more sensible for the occasion – jeans, and a hoodie that looked much thicker than my own.

But as my eyes scanned over him, it occurred to me that this was the first time we'd been alone together since the night I stayed over.

For a fraction of a moment I was transported back, his red-rimmed eyes and visible sadness brought to the forefront of my mind. I almost wondered if he'd bring it up, or at least do something to acknowledge it had been more than just my imagination, but the burnished glare of the supermarket lights reminded me this was not the place. "Yeah," was all I managed to force out.

"I didn't know you were back," he said, leaning on the shelf full of packaged cupcakes. "How was London? Did everything go okay with Nora?"

Composing myself, I met his gaze. "Yeah, everything went fine. She had a little girl. Summer."

"Aw, that's great. Cute name, too."

"Yeah," I breathed.

"And you stayed up there a while, didn't you? I was beginning to wonder if you'd fallen back in love with London and abandoned Walden forever."

I laughed. "Not quite. I only stayed a week – I got back this evening, actually."

"Right." I noticed his eyes drifting downwards, stopping only when they landed on the packet clutched in my hands. An amused smile tugged at the corners of his lips. "Midnight snack?"

I could feel my cheeks darkening. "I couldn't sleep."

"Me neither. Again," he added, quickly averting his gaze to the shelves beside us, an abundance of all things sugary piled up on every one. Though he'd dared to scrape the surface of the taboo, he chickened out of anything further, retreating as quickly as he could for fear of the reaction. "I kind of came here for the exact same reason."

Feeling my embarrassment drain away, I held up the packet. "Well, can I interest you in any doughnuts?" I offered. "I've got two."

"Sounds great," he said. "They're on me."

We headed up to the till, where the cashier rung up our food and Daniel handed over a few coins. I couldn't help but think we must've been the most excitement he'd had all shift; he even looked slightly disappointed to watch us go, returning to his game of Angry Birds on his mobile with a look verging on wistfulness.

"So, where to?"

The door of the shop clicked shut, leaving us standing quietly in the empty street. It was odd to see it in such a state – cloaked in darkness, with a distinct absence of its usual bustle. The gap stretched astoundingly wide without clumps of rowdy tourists, caw-ing seagulls and the yelling of the coastguard from somewhere on the beach. Walden would've been unrecognisable had I not gotten to know it so well.

"Where were you headed, anyway?"

I thought back to the sketchbook tucked into my bag, my intention to find a quiet spot for sketching like I'd done on my second day in Walden. "I don't know," I said truthfully. "I was just going to go with the flow."

He cracked up then, his sudden bark of laughter echoing around the silent street. "Go with the Flo," he repeated, when all I offered in return was a strange look. "Oh, come on. Don't tell me you didn't do that on purpose."

I rolled my eyes, though I was smiling too. "You're way too easily amused."

"And proud."

He stuck out his tongue, eyes twinkling. Somehow they seemed brighter in the darkness, their hazel colour more striking against the tint of the moonlight. The realisation led me to wonder what my own face looked like. Sleep-deprived and lacking make-up, I assumed I looked a state, but Daniel's intent look took me by surprise. It was almost as if he was trying to memorise each little detail – even the mass of freckles dotted across my nose and cheeks.

"Where were you going, anyway?" I chipped in. "I don't believe for a second you were going to have your little midnight feast at home."

"'Course not. I was going to go to the beach."

"Really?" I couldn't help but raise an eyebrow. "Isn't that kind of mainstream for someone who's lived here forever?"

He laughed, shaking his head. "Well, sort of. But it's different at night. Come on, I'll show you."

Without warning, he took my hand, but my heart barely had time to flutter in excitement before I was yanked forwards. He was already heading for the stone steps leading down onto the beach, and I trailed after him. But as our shoes hit the shingle below, he turned right and began striding purposefully to the beach's edge, where the chalky cliffs stood tall. I hadn't paid them much attention before; they pretty much marked the end of Walden. At the top sat a small holiday park, whose outermost caravans teetered alarmingly close to the edge, but I hadn't yet had a reason to venture over there.

"Where are we going?"

A mildly amused look was sent in my direction, over his shoulder. "I didn't mean this beach," he said, like it was obvious. "Come on. Trust me on this one."

Strangely, I didn't need much more persuasion. It was like I already did trust him, on anything and everything he said. It was sort of scary, how much of myself I was willing to give to someone I'd known for so little time. A matter of weeks was all it'd been, but with Daniel it felt more: so much so that I could barely remember the pre-summer days without him. It was terrifying and exhilarating, all at the same time.

And so I trekked on after him across the stony beach.

"Almost there." We were now approaching the edge; metres ahead began the towering cliffs, beyond which there was no more of Walden. He stopped here, and our intertwined hands dropped between us. "Close your eyes."

I frowned. "What?"

He came up behind me, placing a hand over my eyes and effectively blackening my vision. I might've tried to wriggle away, had my mind not been so caught up in how warm his skin felt against mine. "What are you doing?"

"Showing you something."

"I think you'd find that a little bit easier if I could actually see."

"You'll see in a minute," he assured me. "Now hold the doughnuts."

With a sigh of resignation, I took the packet and let him press into my back, gently ushering me forward. I could feel my breathing getting shallower as I took several wobbly steps forward, too aware of the thousands of jagged rocks just waiting to trip me up. And yet I couldn't deny that the feel of Daniel's arms encircling me, the warmth of his body against mine, was a slight comfort.

It must've been about five minutes before we finally came to a halt – a journey which would've taken much less time had I not been robbed of my sight. "Here we are," Daniel announced softly, his voice surprisingly close to my ear. Then, I felt the pressure lift from over my eyes.

I knew my life couldn't get any more cliché than it was in that moment, but it didn't stop me from sucking in a sharp breath when my eyes fluttered open. We had navigated around the edge of the rock face and were now standing on the edge of a secluded cove, completely separated from the main part of the beach. Chalky cliffs curved around the perimeter, stretching tall against a background of stars. Waves shattered onto the shore in a mess of white froth, and it seemed to be the only place in Walden with any sand at all. Of course, it was more coarse grains mixed with pebbles than tropical paradise, but beautiful nevertheless.

"What is this place?" I asked, dragging my gaze away from the view long enough to look at Daniel. There was a tiny smile across his face, almost content, as if he was pleased to be the one to let me in on the secret.

"The other part of the beach." He started down the slope, trainers skidding on the grassy patch that led down onto the sand below. "I don't think anyone else really knows about it apart from the five of us. And now you, of course."

"It's amazing," I breathed.

"We sometimes have barbecues and stuff down here, or we'll just hang out if the beach is too busy. It's definitely quieter."

"No kidding."

I trailed down the verge after him. With the wind blowing full force, even in the secluded bay, I found myself suddenly very aware I was wearing nothing thicker than linen pyjama bottoms and a jacket. The chill was creeping in, advancing with every gust of cool air.

Daniel soon found a spot on the sand, sinking down onto it. I went to join him.

"So you come here a lot?" It felt strange to break the silence that had begun to settle, like tiny snowflakes accumulating, piling up into a thick layer. The only interruption was the steady sound of unsettled water just metres ahead of us. I watched as each wave fell onto the sand, creeping its way up the beach before retreating just as quickly. "On your own, I mean?"

"Sometimes." He picked up a handful of sand, letting it run through his fingers. "Just when I need to think."

The words were on my tongue; I could almost taste them. No matter how far I tried to steer my thoughts away, they always came wandering back to that night. The glassy eyes, the look of hopelessness, the way he'd clung to me like I was the only thing he had to hold onto. I was haunted by the lingering feeling of his hug, of how it had felt to fall asleep listening to his steady heartbeat.

Should I? Shouldn't I?

"What you needed to think about," my voice came out hardly louder than a whisper, "was it the same as that other night? The one before I went to London?"

For a painfully long moment, he didn't say anything. My eyes scanned his face, trying to gauge any sort of reaction, but it remained impassive. I knew I'd said the wrong thing. Why on earth had I dared to bring it up? He'd told me at the time he didn't want to talk about it; what could possibly be to gain from forcing him into it now?

Just as I was about to apologise, he spoke.

"Are you sure you want to get into this?" he asked. "I mean, it doesn't exactly make for the happiest conversation in the world."

"Hey, that doesn't matter. If you want to talk about it, then I'm here to listen. Promise."

He smiled then – a small, tentative smile that tipped my heartbeat past overdrive. I could feel it pounding beneath my jacket. "Well, I guess you've probably heard it from somebody else by now, but..." He took a deep breath. "Erin and I lost our dad last year."

"I heard," I murmured softly.

The ghostly image of the moon was reflected on the water; this was what Daniel seemed to be focusing on to keep his gaze away from me. "It hit me pretty hard," he admitted. "I mean, he was always the one I was closest to. I could talk to him about anything, you know? We thought the world of each other. Mum's okay, but we've never got on particularly well, even when Dad was still here."

I nodded, knowing better than to interrupt.

"It wasn't like it was sudden or anything. He'd been ill for about a year, and even though we didn't say it out loud... well, we all knew what the end result was going to be. Still, just because you know it's going to happen... it doesn't make it any easier."

"Of course not," I whispered. "It's your dad, Daniel. It'd never be easy."

"I thought I was doing okay. I've taken over the shop, just like he wanted. That place was his dream. He'd always talked about having his own business, and when he finally got the chance, he was over the moon. Except he only got to enjoy it for a couple of months before he got ill. It crushed him, not being able to work anymore. More than anything else, I think." He drew a long, deep breath. "It's been hard, running it almost on my own. But it's what he would've wanted. I have to carry on. For him."

He reached down and picked up a pebble from the space between us, turning it over in his hands. Then, drawing back his arm to give the throw some leverage, he sent it plummeting into the sea. First skidding expertly along an incoming wave, it soon plunged out of sight into the water below.

"I thought I was doing okay. I thought I was getting used to the fact that he was gone – I was beginning to deal with it, at least. But suddenly it's been a year and it's almost the anniversary and... I don't know. It feels like I'm just coming to realise that maybe I'm not okay."

It could've been a trick of the light, but the glassiness appeared to have returned to his eyes, making them shine with unshed tears. Without thinking, I leaned over and took his hand, giving it a reassuring squeeze: the way Nora had done to me countless times before. He looked over in mild surprise, but didn't pull back.

"You don't have to be okay," I told him. "I mean, it's been a year. Losing your dad, that's... that's hardly any time at all."

"Erin handled it so well," he said. "She's so... together, you know what I mean? I feel like a wreck in comparison. Sometimes it'll just hit me... like it's only just sunk in that he's gone. And it scares me. That's what happened the other night." He paused, shaking his head. "God, I'm sorry about that."

"You don't need to apologise. You're not a wreck, Daniel. I mean, do you even realise how big this is? It's not something you can get over in a week. But you'll get through it, no matter how hard it seems. I promise."

I squeezed his hand again. He managed a small smile, but it didn't reach his eyes. "I just wish it could've been somebody else," he admitted in a low voice, like he was telling some sort of shameful secret. "I know it's selfish and horrible and awful but... what did my dad do to deserve to die like that?"

"I know," I murmured. It sounded strange to hear the words out of someone else's mouth; for three years now, similar ones had remained hidden deep inside my head. Some I hadn't even confessed to Nora. I'd lost count of the times I'd lain awake, wishing it could've been someone else's parents who had to be taken like that. I'd wished it upon strangers I passed in the street, our neighbours, even my friends. Anything – anything – to have my mum and dad back. "Trust me. I really do know."

He looked up, blinking at me through watery eyes. "You do?"

I closed my eyes, inhaling deeply. The waves seemed to suddenly double in volume, until I realised most of the crashing was coming from inside my head. Torn between two sides, I could already feel the internal soldiers raising their weapons. One half seemed desperate to let the words tumble from my lips, but the other dreaded the idea, yanking my thoughts away from its consideration with surprising violence.

You've kept it a secret for this long, it reminded me furiously. You tell, and what happens then? They all know. You become the sad girl with the tragic back story, and there's no recovering from that one.

I knew that. I knew I was taking a risk, that once the words were out in the open, I couldn't take them back. I'd no longer be the same person to Daniel – but was that such a bad thing? Didn't he have the right to know? If sat on his secret beach at a crazy hour of the night wasn't the right moment to do it, would there ever be one?

So I took a deep breath. And I took the plunge.

14

— • —

CHAPTER 14

Really, I don't know what I expected.

Some kind of spontaneous fanfare? A physical weight being lifted from my shoulders? A sprinkling of confetti? Either way, nothing like that happened. In fact, without the meaning behind them, without the emphasis placed on keeping them locked inside, they were just words. Nothing more than just a combination of letters, strung together as a means of communication from the mind to the outside world.

Just words. They couldn't hurt you physically, but they were extremely good at tricking your mind into thinking differently.

"It was my mum and dad," I whispered. My voice was barely audible, let alone against the background of the ocean, but it didn't seem like Daniel was having any trouble hearing. "Three years ago."

Three years and fifty-one days. I didn't mean to count, mentally tallying up another twenty-four hours I'd got through without them, but I couldn't help it. It just happened.

"Oh, Flo."

Daniel's face had transformed. Usually, this was the cue for pity to set in; I was almost afraid to see it etched across his features. Yet when I lifted my head, daring to meet his gaze, I came face-to-face with the sight of something very different. Understanding. Empathy.

"What happened?" he asked, before cringing at his outright question. "Sorry. We don't have to talk about it if you don't want to."

Silently, I shook my head. "A car accident," I forced out, my throat suddenly raw. "The other driver was drunk. I was only fourteen."

His expression could only be described as horror-struck; it must've had something to do with the fact I'd kept it quiet for the last month. Maybe he'd assumed he was the only one with a secret. "Oh, Flo, I know it doesn't make it any better, but I'm so sorry…"

I shook my head again. "It's not your fault."

"I know, but–"

"Daniel."

His name trailed off into heavy silence; he stared back at me, eyes searching my face. I resisted the urge to squirm under the scrutiny. "I'm fine," I tried to say, but my voice cracked before it had even hit the last note. The dam was breaking, the memories flooding back, and suddenly all I could see through a glaze of blurred tears was the moment Nora had opened the door to see the police officer.

One moment I was composed, expertly concealing my greatest weakness. The next, my mask was crumbling, tears rolling delicately down my cheeks.

"Sorry," I mumbled, swallowing hard. "I shouldn't be making this about me."

I was ashamed by my selfishness. It was obvious Daniel was having a hard time dealing with his grief, and what he needed was support. Having to comfort me, bawling over something I should've already got to grips with, wasn't going to help. It was stupid, I knew, to choose now of all moments to miss desperately the security of being enveloped in my mum's arms, or the deep, hearty sound of Dad's laugh that had always made everything seem okay, but that didn't stop it from happening.

"Shh, you idiot. Come here."

He edged closer, and before I knew it, I'd been scooped into his arms. They were oddly warm against the harsh, salty breeze whipping through our hair, squeezing me tight as if returning the favour from the other night. Only then did I realise what I'd previously thought impossible: this, right here, was perhaps as comforting as being curled up with Nora in the darkness of her bedroom. The grief was still there, of course, rushing in like the tide and constantly threatening to pull me under. But with Daniel I felt safe, reassured by a buoyancy aid, settled in the knowledge that the hopelessness couldn't consume me completely.

Without thinking, I rested my head against his chest. My arms, acting of their own accord, wrapped around his torso. We were pressed right up against each other, the gap between us dwindled into nonexistence, a single shadow made up of two silhouettes.

"Why didn't you tell me?" he asked. I could feel soft pressure on the top of my head; he was stroking my hair.

"It's not the sort of thing you can slip into casual conversation," I murmured into his chest.

"Tell me about it." He laughed shakily. "No secrets now though, right? We both know each other's depressing back stories."

"Sorry," I apologised again. For the most part, the tears had subsided; my eyes were still damp, but I'd never known the feeling of despair to dissipate so quickly. Even with Nora's arms to fall into, it had been worse than this. "This wasn't exactly the pep talk you were looking for."

"Stop apologising. It doesn't matter."

"But–"

Before I could continue, a finger was pressed to my lips, effectively cutting me off. I tried to ignore the jolt of electricity induced by the contact, but my pounding heart did enough to remind me. "No buts. It's been a rough night for the both of us, okay?"

Sighing in defeat, there was nothing left to do but agree. I still felt guilty – Daniel had obviously been seeking comfort, and all I'd offered was the burden of my own problems – but there was no denying the weighty sense of relief that had settled over us. We might've been getting somewhere after all.

Daniel knew. And, surprisingly, that was okay.

His finger trailed away from my lips; reaching up, he wiped the last few tears from my cheek with his thumb. Our faces were in closer proximity than they ever had been, his eyes sweeping intently over my features. In fact, there was such a blaze of intensity behind the speckled hazel that I was sure something was going to happen any moment now...

"You know, I think now would be a good time for those dough-nuts."

I was struck by a brief pang of disappointment, but broke into laughter at his serious expression. "Because doughnuts solve everything, right?"

"Of course they do."

His face stayed as straight as line while he reached for the packet, tearing it open and waving it beneath my nose. "First pick?"

I rolled my eyes but wasn't one to refuse such an offer.

And somehow, sitting on a beach in the bitter cold at two in the morning made these doughnuts – cheap, sticky and probably full of chemical fats linked to early death – taste like the best thing in the entire world. As unlikely as it sounded, Daniel's theory that they solved all problems was looking increasingly believable.

"The best doughnuts you can get for miles," he concluded triumphantly. Having polished his off in record timing, he'd now resorted to licking the rest of the icing off his fingers – all while I was still a measly halfway through. "Damn, we should've picked up another pack while we were there."

I laughed, the action now much easier than it would've been ten minutes ago. "That'd just be greedy."

"After the night we've had, I think we deserve it."

"I suppose that's true."

He turned to look at me, once again with that searching expression that felt as if all my innermost thoughts had been placed under a beaming spotlight. It was oddly similar, I realised then, to the one Erin often wore when she was trying to figure something out. Their differences may have been dominant on first notice, but if you looked close enough, Daniel and Erin had some peculiar similarities that could only be present between twins.

Unnerved by the look's intensity, I swallowed my last mouthful and blinked back. The atmosphere seemed suddenly charged, as if the air between us had been zapped with a shot of electricity.

"You know, if you ever feel like you need to talk to someone, or if you're just having a rough day, you can always talk to me," he said earnestly. "Any time of day. I'm your guy." His smile was iridescent, as bright as the moonlight bathing the cove. "And I'm not one to turn down midnight doughnuts. They really do make everything better."

A smile of my own edged its way onto my lips. "Actually, I'm beginning to believe you on that one."

"I told you, didn't I? Seriously, though, I can't stand to see you upset."

A particularly strong gust of wind whipped past us, its chill forging a path through the fabric of my jacket and inducing shivers throughout my body. This, of course, didn't escape Daniel's notice. "And I can't stand to see you cold either," he added, shrugging off his own jacket and draping it over my shoulders.

I tried to protest. "No, really, you'll be cold–"

"I'm fine," he countered, even though removing this outer layer had left him in a T-shirt that looked much too thin. "Used to the sea air and all that, remember?"

"Right," I said. "Well, thanks."

"That's okay."

Perhaps it was my imagination, but he seemed to have inched closer, the gentle smell of washing powder on his clothes even noticeable over the salty scent of the air. A strand of my hair blew forward from its ponytail, but before I could tuck it behind my ear, Daniel had reached up and was doing it for me. His face was now so close I found myself holding my breath, my mind subconsciously joining freckles on his nose.

"I know we haven't known each other that long, but..." His gaze swept over my face, as if searching for permission to voice his next thought. "I don't know what it is about you, Flo. I can't help it. I'm crazy about you."

I inhaled sharply. This couldn't be happening. It all seemed too surreal; surely it had to be some part of a restless dream, conjured up whilst stumbling through the realms of light sleep. Things like this just didn't happen to me. Any moment now I would wake up sweating, not to mention crushed with disappointment, in my bedroom, coming to realise that my suspicions had been justified. Wouldn't I?

But suddenly Daniel was edging closer than he had been before, and it occurred to me that this was all very real. It hit me all at once, hurtling at full speed, a realisation and onset of elation all rolled into one. In a dream I'd never pick up on the slight tentativeness in his movements, the feel of the sand beneath me, or that one tuft of his hair sticking up in an opposite direction to the rest.

No, this was most definitely real.

And as soon as I'd come to the conclusion, my lips were faced with the unmistakable – yet totally unfamiliar – sensation of another pair being pressed against them.

I was kissing Daniel. On a secluded beach in the middle of the night, where, for a little while, nothing existed but that one moment. We were enclosed in a single snapshot, an instant not intruded on by anybody else. Even if only for a few seconds, we were just us. And that was all we had to be.

The kiss was soft; I could barely feel the pressure of his lips as they brushed over mine. My head was much too fuzzy to think straight, but that didn't stop me from wondering if my lack of experience was showing through too boldly. It wasn't like I actually knew what I was doing. In essence, I was floundering, hoping that my apprehensive movements were at least slightly in sync with his.

Still, I was sort of in the middle of my first kiss with the guy I'd liked for weeks. Even if I did stop freaking out long enough to concentrate, it wasn't exactly my most refined moment.

But that was okay. It didn't have to be.

We ended up staying on the beach longer than anticipated. I didn't have a watch, but I could see the darkness gradually dissipating from the sky, stretching wide to make room for the sunrise due later. We must've spent over an hour there, just talking, until my eyelids started to grow heavy and I realised I could easily drift off on Daniel's shoulder if I didn't stop myself.

It was surprising, how easy it was to talk to him. I'd been afraid my confession would make things stilted or awkward between us, but Daniel's personal experience had led him to be more understanding than anyone. Conversation flowed freely between us, moving through the silliest topics with little friction, punctuated by crazy anecdotes and persistent laughter.

I was more than disappointed when we came to realise that we really had to be heading back, or else risk facing the wrath of some incredibly pissed off Mums or Grams. The night had taken a rapid turn from restlessness to total elation, as if I was soaring above the clouds themselves. For once in my life, I was actually thankful for the nightly plague of thoughts that kept sleep at bay. Without them, tonight would never have happened.

Backtracking our original path, we trailed up the edge of the cove and ducked past the rocky outcrop that isolated us from the rest of the beach. Our hands stayed intertwined as we stumbled over the uneven surface, the warmth of his jacket still hugging me from the waist upward. I'd tried to give it back to him at least three times, claiming it wasn't fair of me to leave him cold, but he refused to take it. Even when we'd wandered all through Walden, creeping through the house-edged streets and up to the hilltop cul-de-sac where Gram's cottage sat, he still wouldn't let me shrug it from my shoulders.

"It's your jacket," I told him.

"Keep it."

I looked over at Gram's front door; it couldn't have been more than a few metres away. "Daniel, I'm not exactly going to contract hypothermia in the time it takes me to walk up the front path."

"I don't want to take the chance."

I rolled my eyes, despite being secretly overjoyed that he was giving me his hoodie. It was much too big for me, hanging awkwardly from my torso, but the thick fleecy material was warmer than it looked, and the scent of Daniel seemed to cling to every fibre. Maybe if I closed my eyes and hugged it tightly enough, I could kid myself he was there with me.

"Well, thanks. And thanks for walking me back."

"That's okay." Though for the most part he was keeping eye contact, every so often his gaze seemed to drop to my lips, as if he couldn't help himself. "You know, though, it was kind of an excuse."

"An excuse for what?"

He stepped closer. "To do this again."

And then he'd ducked down to kiss me, his hand trailing the edge of my jaw as his lips brushed gently with mine. My heart was pounding so loudly I was sure he must've been able to hear it, and an electrified shiver coursed through me despite the hoodie.

"You do realise that was incredibly cheesy, right?" I said, once distance wove its way between us again.

The returning grin was sheepish, and he reached up to scratch the back of his neck. "Yeah, I know," he admitted, "but it worked, didn't it?"

"I suppose so."

Looking over my shoulder, I studied the cottage. The curtains were pulled across the windows, the entire place deadly still. It was almost like I was looking at a photograph: a snapshot frozen in time, lacking the faintest hint of movement. But I couldn't let myself be fooled: Gram was inside, and she had a tendency to wake up at strange hours of the morning if she was in one of her creative mindsets. "I need to go in now."

His gaze flickered to the house and back again. "I know."

"Thanks, though," I breathed, squeezing his hand, "for tonight. For everything."

"Shh," he said quietly. "I already told you: you don't need to thank me. We're just two sad cases who've got to stick together. Anyway, I don't know how I would've got through tonight without you."

I smiled, reluctantly untangling my fingers from his. "See you tomorrow?"

"Today," he corrected.

"Right. See you later."

I started up the front path, all too aware that he was watching me go. Glancing briefly back, I noticed he stood in his original position, having made absolutely no attempt to head back home. The corners of my lips tugged upward again as I reached the front door, unlocked it as silently as I could manage and slipped inside.

Even when I'd tiptoed up the staircase – careful to avoid every spot I'd discovered had a tendency to creak – and returned to my bed, still encased in the warmth of Daniel's jacket, I found myself unable to wipe the smile from my face.

It just wouldn't budge.

15

CHAPTER 15

Several hours later, I was roused from my slumber by the trilling of my phone on the bedside table. Letting out a low groan, I rolled over under the covers and snatched it up, but refused to raise my head above the comfy mass of duvet. "Hello?"

"Flo?" Erin's loud voice didn't exactly make for the smoothest transition from sleep to consciousness. "Wait, you're not still in bed, are you?"

"No..." I mumbled sheepishly, my voice muffled by the sheets.

"You lazy arse. God, you're just as bad as Daniel. It's half eleven and there's been no sign of him this morning either."

Blinking hazily, I lifted my head to catch sight of the glowing digits of my alarm clock; true to Erin's word, a large 11:32 stared back at me. I didn't usually sleep in this late, but then again, it wasn't like I'd spent much of last night doing any sleeping. A hearty chunk had been spent breaking about fifty different rules with Daniel, before returning to my room at just past four in the morning. Quite frankly, I hadn't known I had it in me.

"Yeah, whatever," I dismissed, blinking away my sleepiness. I pulled myself into a sitting position, keeping the phone pressed to my ear. "Did you want something?"

"Actually, yeah. I was calling to tell you about this party happening at Collette's place later. Fancy thing. Her parents are throwing it to show off to their friends, I think. Or maybe it's got something to do with getting contacts for Beth's modelling... I don't know. I wasn't really listening."

"Right..." I said slowly. "So?"

"You're invited," she told me. "All five of us are. Apparently Collette's got her hands full with helping her parents set things up, so she's lumbered me with the job of making sure you all drag yourselves along."

An uncomfortable sinking had become prevalent in my stomach, and I shifted my position. "What? We're going?"

"Yeah. She wants us to come. It won't be the most exciting thing in the world, but it's free food, right? With you guys there it'll be bearable, at least."

"I don't know if that's such a good idea."

"Oh, come on, Flo," she pleaded. "Look, I know you and Collette aren't the best of friends, but it's not like you two are going to be locked up in a room together or anything. She'll be too busy having to prance around in front of her parents' cronies to bother with you. We'll just hang out together."

"I still don't—"

"Please?"

Sighing in resignation, I sunk back against the head of the bed, feeling the cool metal press into my back. An evening at Collette's wasn't exactly appealing, but the other guys were going to be there. If what Erin said was true, we could just have a laugh together. And I couldn't exactly cop out, leaving them to suffer their friend's upper-class acquaintances alone. I wasn't that selfish.

"Okay," I said reluctantly. "What time?"

When I found myself stood on Collette's porch that evening, the front door swung open before I'd even had the chance to take my finger off the bell. The woman behind it had obviously been expecting somebody; her eyes swept over me with hopeful expectation, but her face fell when recognition – or lack of it – kicked in. She was a tall lady, uncomfortably slight in an expensive-looking cocktail dress, and possessed deep brown eyes that looked vaguely familiar. It was then that I realised I was standing face-to-face with what had to be Collette's mother.

"Oh," she said. Clearly, I was not the guest she'd been hoping for. "And you must be...?"

"Flo," I told her, understanding now where Collette and Beth had inherited their intimidating manner. A mere few seconds under the scrutiny of this woman's gaze gave me the urge to squirm. "I'm Collette's... friend."

"Right!" Through her falsely bright tone, I could tell she didn't have the faintest idea who I was. "Well, come on in. The party's in the garden; go right through."

She ushered me inside, but made no attempt to point me in the right direction, clearly too agitated in the anticipation of another more important guest. I made my way through the hallway, guided by the sound of lively chatter from the back of the house, smoothing the skirt of my dress as I went.

The patio doors at the back of the lounge gave way to a huge garden, one of a size you'd expect to find a home furniture brochure, not belonging to someone you knew. It was almost a wonder how they had room for such a monstrosity in a place as tiny as Walden. Still, Collette's family were obviously not short of money, and this fact showed in everything from the marquee on the lawn, to the floral decorations lining the patio, and the intricate paving around the pond.

The only thing that was missing was a fountain.

It was pretty intimidating, really, especially as the scene came complete with suited waiting staff milling around, juggling canapé platters in their hands. Needless to say, when my gaze landed on three familiar faces gathered on the lawn, I made an immediate beeline for them.

"You came!" Erin breezed as I approached. "Thought I was going to have to come over to your place and drag you out of bed myself."

With her hair tamed into neat waves, the stud in her cartilage noticeably absent and a heart-shaped necklace resting below her collarbone, she looked more normal than I'd ever seen her before. Scott also looked distinctly more well-groomed, with Jay the exception, still yet to ditch the bucket-load of gel in his hair.

"Excuse you. I got up right after you called, actually."

"You sure? You wouldn't be if you were anything like Daniel. He didn't grace us with his presence until about three o'clock."

Alongside Collette, he was the only person missing, his absence inducing a mild pang of disappointment I'd never admit to. I was kind of nervous about seeing him again, especially considering the way the thought of last night still made me break out in tingles, but the excitement had the edge. Briefly scanning the garden, my gaze caught upon a couple of brunets about his height, but there was no sign of him.

"Daniel as well?" Scott raised an eyebrow. "What, did you two sneak out together or something?"

He was joking, but the harsh pink hue that rose to my cheeks instantly gave me away. I ducked my head, but knew I couldn't escape; they'd all picked up on it.

"You did as well!" Erin screeched, disbelieving. "You dirty little stop-out!"

"Shh! You don't need to be so loud!"

Predictably, Jay was smirking. "You and Daniel sneaking around at night? You bad girl, Flo," he drawled. "You're not as innocent as you seem."

"Nothing happened!"

"Lies," Scott chipped in. "Come on, spill. What'd you get up to?"

"But keep it PG-rated," Jay added, "there are kids around here."

"Nothing!" I insisted through gritted teeth. "Neither of us could sleep, and we just happened to bump into each other…"

"Tut tut." Scott shook his head in mock disapproval, before shooting an amused look at Jay. "We'll have to quiz Daniel about this later."

"Oh, God, definitely. I'm not leaving him alone until he tells everything."

I groaned in frustration. "Stop it. It wasn't like that."

Erin looked over at me. "So what was it like?"

I was tempted to send daggers in her direction, but the truth stood that they were all bound to find out sooner or later. Maybe it was easier to get it over with, like ripping off a plaster. Though I wasn't overly keen on reciting a full recollection just yet – and here, of all places – I knew it was better than the ridiculous stories Erin and Jay were likely to make up.

It wasn't that I was embarrassed about what had happened. In a way, it just seemed… private. Like a secret that was meant to be kept between the two of us. It was pathetic, I knew, but there was a tiny part of me that was afraid if I shared it with other people, the memory would lose its charm.

"We just talked, okay?" I said, picking at a nonexistent thread on the waist of my dress. "And maybe he sort of kissed me just once… or twice."

Erin clapped her hands together loudly, attracting the attention of a few of Collette's acquaintances in close enough proximity. "I knew it!" she practically yelped. "I knew there was something going on between you two."

"God, didn't everyone?" Jay rolled his eyes. "I mean, you can practically feel the sexual tension every time they're in the same room."

This time, I decided a look wasn't sufficient to convey my feelings towards him. Instead I reached over, whacking him across the arm with all the force I could muster. It wasn't a lot, but it did make me feel better; I'd wrinkled his pressed shirt, if nothing else. "You're a pervert, you know that? I'm going to regret telling you anything."

"Don't pretend you don't love it." He winked. "You know, one day you'll fall for my charm."

"Not me, but I'm sure one day some poor girl will." I paused, making an exaggerated display of looking pleadingly up to the sky. "God help her."

"Hey, I don't like this Flo." Jay was pouting now, looking over at Erin for support. All she offered him, however, was a smirk, arms folded over her chest. "The innocent one was nicer."

"Just because she didn't shoot you down when you tried to flirt with her," she said.

"It's only because she's getting it on with Daniel."

"Excuse me," I interjected. "I'm not getting it on with him."

"Yet."

I groaned. "Why am I friends with you guys? Seriously, you're all annoying as hell."

"Because Walden is a pathetically small town and we're your only option?" Scott offered.

"Yeah," I replied. "You hit the nail right on the head with that one, actually."

"And then there's the attraction of Daniel, of course," he continued. "Except the rest of us just come as part of the package deal. If you're screwing him, then you're screwing us too. Wait, hold on, that came out wrong—"

We all turned to stare at Scott momentarily; Jay was the first to splutter with laughter, shortly followed by the rest of us. I shook my head at the four of them, realising I'd completely forgotten that we were at some posh party with Collette's parents. Though upper-class guests still milled around us, I'd completely tuned out from the buzz of their chatter. "Well, you know, I could say the same thing about you two," I said innocently, gesturing between Jay and the bright-haired girl next to him.

As expected, their laughter dried up immediately. "What?"

"You two," I repeated. "Come on, don't act like you don't know what I'm talking about. You can almost feel the – what did you call it again, Jay? – sexual tension."

He was stuttering now, tripping over his words in his haste to get them out into the open. The role reversal was strange; he usually made me feel uncomfortable with his shameless flirting. Maybe they couldn't see it, but I remained convinced there was something more between them, even if hidden beneath sarcastic banter and sideways smiles they thought nobody else noticed.

Or maybe there wasn't – but it was worth it, just to see Jay's cheeks tinged pink as he shook his head vehemently.

"You have got to be joking."

Erin, to say the least, did not look amused. Her brows were creased, and I was pretty sure it was me intended to be on the receiving end of her glares. If looks could kill, my gravestone would've been sat right in the middle of Collette's garden. Yet even through the intensity of her stare, I couldn't overlook the faint pink tint that was dusted across her cheeks, making her look distinctly girlish.

Clearly, I'd touched upon a nerve for both of them. And I was enjoying every second of it.

"Me and Erin?" Jay was trying to scoff, but instead just ended up coughing awkwardly. "Yeah. Right."

Her response, as I should've expected, was a little more creative. "Are you joking? I have more sexual tension with my brother than I have with him."

Holding my hands up in mock surrender, I smirked. "Okay, okay," I said, "you made your point."

However, now they'd put themselves on my radar. I'd had a previous suspicion, but the reaction had only strengthened my theory. Erin did pay the most attention to Jay's jokes, even if her responses were usually dripping with sarcasm, unconcerned by their sheer cheesiness. I watched as Jay shot her a sneaky sideways glance, double-checking her reaction.

I was so onto them.

"So," I said, trying to sound casual, "where is Daniel?"

"Missing him already?" Jay cooed. I could see him making exaggerated kissing faces at me in my peripheral vision but did my best to ignore him.

"Beats me," Erin said, shrugging. "He got dragged off by Collette the moment he walked through the door, so he could be anywhere."

"Oh." Though I tried to keep my expression impassive, I couldn't hold back the chord of jealousy that struck me at the mention of her name. What had happened between us last night should've been enough proof that Daniel liked me, but I couldn't erase the niggling doubt in the back of my mind. Collette obviously wanted him back, and she didn't seem like the type of girl to give up easily. She'd probably be more than happy to make a move on him, and who was to say that Daniel wouldn't resist?

"Actually," Scott said slowly, his eyes fixed on a point over my shoulder, "I think we just found him."

I turned around, following his line of vision until my gaze fell upon the guy I was looking for. My heart leapt when I saw him; he looked as adorable as ever, his wavy hair trying to break free of its tamed style, one corner of his mouth curled upwards in a half-smile. The image of that same face, the inches between us closing rapidly, bringing us close enough to count each other's freckles, flashed across my mind. It took all I had not to blush.

He was standing in the doorway with his hands dug into his trouser pockets, giving the garden the once-over as he scanned the lawn for familiar faces. It didn't take long for him to locate us, and when his eyes locked with my own, his smile widened into something so incandescent I wanted to melt on the spot.

I was expecting him to come over – mostly because he sort of moved his foot, like he was about to take a step towards us. However, he didn't get the chance; in a matter of seconds, someone had appeared by his side, hooked her arm through his and brought her lips alarmingly close to his ear.

Collette whispered something that was impossible to make out before tugging gently at his arm. Though he looked like he wanted to say more, he nodded and followed her mutely in the opposite direction, seeming to forget all about coming over here.

16

CHAPTER 16

"**H**ave any of you seen my parents?"

Reluctantly, I dragged my attention away from the foursome they'd been fixated on for the past hour, refocusing it on the tall blonde who'd just strode over. In fact, for the first time since we'd met, the sight of Beth standing before me was actually a minor improvement its preceding scenery. Then again, it was what had been torturing me all evening: seeing Daniel, paired with the girl who seemed to have been permanently stitched to his side.

It was enough to make my stomach twist into an unpleasantly intricate knot.

I had no idea why he and Collette had turned into conjoined twins overnight, but it wasn't as if I'd got the chance to ask him. The moment she'd hooked her arm through his, he'd barely spared in a glance in our direction, let alone made an attempt to come over and say hi. I guessed it had something to do with the fact he was sort of preoccupied, listening intently to the end of the conversation Collette was holding up as the pair stood opposite her parents.

My heart lurched uncomfortably each time, but I just couldn't stop my eyes from wandering back over there every few seconds. These were classic symptoms of jealousy, I knew, but didn't I have a right to feel that way? I thought last night had meant something to Daniel - something bigger than unnecessary physical contact and false, simpering laughter. Maybe I was wrong.

Swallowing my distaste, I forced myself to tune into Collette's older sister. Wearing stilettos I was sure could function as stilts, Beth towered over most of us; her height was only matched by a gangly Scott. Tagging behind, and looking like he was under the influence of some kind of hypnotic charm, was a slightly greasy-looking guy with long, dark hair and a half-buttoned shirt. A fleeting thought had me wondering if he was just a hardcore admirer of Beth's, but her lack of concern with his proximity suggested it was something more than that.

Jay's awe was badly concealed; he'd taken to staring almost open-mouthed at her, and I didn't fully trust him not to start drooling. "Hi," he breathed, smiling giddily.

Beth threw him a look of what could only be described as utter disgust, before averting her precious attention to the group as a whole. "So, are any of you actually going to answer my question?"

Since Jay didn't appear to be in a position to speak coherently, let alone provide her with a rational answer, Erin stepped in. However, with her arms folded defensively over her chest, a frown creasing her brow, she didn't exactly look happy to oblige. "They're over there," she said, nodding across the garden. "Just past the marquee."

"Right. Come on, Angelo."

Without bothering to offer so much as a thanks in return, she pivoted on her sharp heel and stalked off in the opposite direction, 'Angelo' at her heels like a lost puppy. Whoever he was, she clearly had him wrapped around her little finger, willing to obey any command that slipped from her pouty lips. Then again, this seemed the case for almost every male on the planet when it came to Collette's sister.

Sure, she was attractive, but did that really overshadow the fact she had the worst attitude I'd ever had the displeasure to deal with? Stuck up, conceited and completely self-absorbed, I couldn't help but feel a brief pang of sympathy for Collette; she had to suffer being related to her, after all. I tried to imagine how I would've coped over the last three years with someone like Beth instead of Nora, but the concept was unthinkable.

I couldn't imagine getting through it with anyone but my own sister.

The momentary compassion soon vanished once my eyes trailed back to their original position. Collette was still hanging from Daniel like a limpet, her free hand pushing back a strand of hair that had fallen in front of his face. Just watching made me feel nauseous with jealousy, not to mention stinging irritation, but I wasn't going to give either the satisfaction of seeing me flee. I'd let it happen too many times before, and I was determined to stay strong. This time, I wasn't going to let my emotions get the better of me.

Instead, I did my best to stifle them, hoping my facial expression didn't betray me. I didn't want the others to know how close I was to bursting into tears.

They'd noticed what was going on, though. That much I could work out from their shifty expressions and reluctance to meet my gaze. Even Erin, usually as bold and outspoken as the colour of her hair, had been reduced to an odd quietness. It was her silence that added perhaps the most tangible awkwardness of all.

By now, Beth had located her mum and dad, her air suddenly transforming from one of utter moodiness to false smiles and laughter as she caught her mother in a hug. Collette's eyes narrowed for a split second, annoyance temporarily exhibited, before her slightly strained smile reappeared.

Then, without warning, her gaze darted in our direction. Flickering evenly across the three others, it hesitated only when she got to me. I held my breath, preparing myself, though for what I wasn't sure. Just before my lungs began to ache in protest, she animatedly beckoned us over.

"Is she...?"

"Yeah," Erin concluded.

"Brilliant," Jay muttered. "Looks like it's meet the parents time."

I'd briefly encountered Collette's mother at the door, so at least she vaguely recognised my face once the round of greetings started up. She was a remarkably skinny woman, her collarbones protruding above the neckline of her dress, her slight frame seeming hardly substantial to hold her up. She had an antique aura of beauty about her: one that suggested she was as beautiful as her daughters in her younger years. Her husband, on the other hand, stood tall and broad, even more intimidating in his tightly pressed suit. His loud, booming voice made it seem as if he was stuck permanently at the head of a business meeting, and just being put under the spotlight of his scrutinizing gaze made me want to shrink to half my size.

"I don't believe we've met," he said. "You are?"

"That's Flo," Collette interrupted, as if I was incapable of answering for myself. "She's new to Walden. She moved here a few weeks ago."

"Isn't that wonderful." He stuck out a hand, his shake too firm and commanding to allow any room for comfort. "I hope you're enjoying yourself. It's even more wonderful, of course, to have such a success in the family to call for this sort of celebration."

He looked over at his eldest daughter, who giggled coyly. "Dad."

"But it is," her mother interjected. "An opportunity like this at your age! I would've killed to get a contract abroad when I was in your position, you know. And in Italy! You know, Beth's worked so hard for this. She deserves every bit of success she gets."

"Italy?" Erin echoed.

"Yeah." Beth smirked. "See, Angelo managed to get me a casting with this super cool agency in Italy, and they loved my portfolio. Signed me straight away." She looked over at the guy beside her, silently commanding his input.

"She is very beautiful," he told us, the words difficult to make out underneath a thick Italian accent. He said it as if the living proof didn't stand right before us, looking on smugly as if he were a dog she'd trained herself. "Everybody loves her."

"Oh, stop," she simpered. "God, you guys really know how to embarrass me, don't you?"

It might well have been my imagination, but Collette's grip on Daniel's arm seemed to tighten. The fire behind her eyes burned visibly as she glared with absolute loathing at her sister. "Actually," she interrupted, her sharp voice effectively cutting off Beth's next statement, "I kind of have something I want to announce. Well, we do." A pointed look at Daniel left him nodding in agreement.

"Oh?" I could see her parents' attention visibly swivel back to her.

"Well, we've kind of been keeping it a secret," she continued, "but I think now's the time to announce it. Daniel and I... well, we're back together."

From the corner of my eye I saw Erin open her mouth, about to say something along the lines of "What?!", but something stopped her. She closed her mouth abruptly, watching as Collette's parents' faces were lit up by smiles. About the same time, my heart suddenly turned to lead, falling to the pit of my stomach with what I was sure must've been an audible thump.

I tried desperately to meet Daniel's gaze, to question him wordlessly about what was unfolding before us. All I got from him, however, was a tiny shake of the head. I assumed it was supposed to mean something, but what, I didn't have a clue.

"Oh!" Collette's mother's smile lifted her prominent cheekbones as she looked between what was apparently the happy couple. "You are? How lovely!"

It was the first time I'd seen her genuinely pleased with her youngest daughter, and the same went for her father, who nodded curtly at Daniel with a contented smile. Impressively, the news seemed to have twisted the spotlight of her parents' affection from somewhere other than Beth for over ten seconds.

Said girl, however, seemed far from happy with the new arrangement. With her parents gushing over Collette and her apparent new boyfriend, Beth grew visibly bored within seconds. She nudged Angelo, silently communicating something through her heavily outlined eyes, and made her next action snatching the nearest piece of silverware from a passing waiter's tray to clink against her glass.

"Excuse me, everyone," she simpered, her voice projected to the guests milling around on the lawn. "If I could have your attention for just a minute."

The chatter quickly dulled to a low murmur, just as Beth flashed a toothy grin towards her onlookers. "Now, you know how much I hate to steal you away from the wonderful party my parents have thrown, so I'll keep this short. Oh, and speaking of that, I'm sure you'll join me in thanking my mum and dad for organising this whole thing and, of course, for being exceptional hosts." She raised her glass, smiling sweetly, a 'perfect daughter' mask expertly concealing the evil underneath. "Love you guys."

Widespread agreement ripped through the crowd, and Beth glanced back at us, though her eyes lingered on Collette slightly longer than they needed to. "So, anyway," she continued, "back to the point. Some of you might know my boyfriend, Angelo." She paused, placing a hand to her heart and looking off into the distance in a sickeningly exaggerated manner. "Fate brought us together about six months ago when it paired us for a swimwear photo shoot. It was love at first sight. Since then, the last few months have been... well, the best of my life. In a way, I feel like we were meant to meet each other. He's the most amazing person, so supportive, and I honestly couldn't imagine being without him."

Collette stuck a finger in her mouth, making silent vomiting motions, but sobered up pretty quickly the moment her parents' eyes flickered in her direction.

"And, well, there's a reason why I'm telling you this." Beth looked over at Angelo with an expression that only made Collette's actions more understandable. "We have something to announce."

Under her breath, Erin muttered something that sounded suspiciously like "Oh, shit."

"We're engaged."

Collette's mother gasped in surprise, while a couple of others dotted across the lawn followed suit. Smiling smugly, Beth took Angelo by the shirt and pulled his lips to hers for a sloppy, drawn-out kiss. A smattering of polite applause started in one corner, sweeping the rest of the party until Beth was grinning coyly and basking in the spotlight, her arms snaked around her fiancé's waist.

Swallowing, I dared to let my gaze drift back to Collette, whose dark irises were burning so intensely I was kind of scared to make eye contact. Her hand had tightened around Daniel's arm, squeezing the muscle until I was sure it must've been painful. And then, just like that, she seemed to snap. Yanking back her arm, she marched towards her sister until they stood a foot away, pure loathing scrawled all over her face.

"Are you fucking joking?" she screeched, the pitch and volume of her voice causing a hush to fall over everybody within a ten-metre radius.

Beth raised her arched eyebrows, placing one hand on her hip in a stance that seemed to ooze confidence. "Excuse me?"

"Don't you dare act like you don't know what I'm talking about," Collette hissed.

Beth smirked. "Actually, honey, I haven't got a clue."

"You do this every time. You can't stand the attention not being on you for one second, can you? I have one bit of news, and you can't even let me have that? You have to go and announce that you're fucking engaged?!" Collette was fuming. Her face was rapidly turning an unnatural shade of red, fists clenched, visible fury consuming her entire being.

"Oh, for Christ's sake." Beth rolled her eyes. "You're really going to make a scene? Grow up, Collette. No one cares about your petty little boyfriend dramas."

"Fuck off!"

Before I could even realise what was going on, it happened. Collette reached up and landed a stinging slap on Beth's face, the noise resonating throughout the entire party. Time seemed to freeze for a moment, leaving us all rendered motionless, every other sound drying up to leave a painfully loud silence that was swathed in tension.

It only lasted for a moment. Beth's shock was the only thing that stopped her from reacting immediately, and when it wore off, all hell broke loose.

She launched right at her, slamming into her younger sister with so much force they were both knocked off their feet and fell, scrambling, to the grass. In a matter of seconds they'd become a single mass of flailing limbs, clawing nails and angry screaming. Beth looked dangerously close to landing a punch on Collette's face; the next moment, her fist was blocked, and Collette had regained control by rolling over and pinning her to the ground.

The initial shock was beginning to wear off, the realisation of what was occurring before my eyes finally sinking in. A couple of people rushed forward to prise the brawling girls apart; a flash of violet hair confirmed Erin was among them. Stumbling forward to assist, I approached the fight just as she and Jay each grabbed one of Beth's arms, yanking her away from her opponent.

Thoughts were racing across my mind too fast to comprehend, but I noticed Collette looked as if she was about to go in for a second - more vicious - attack, and I had to stop her. Making a desperate grab in her direction, I felt my palm encircle her upper arm and pulled towards me, preventing her from any forward motion.

"Let me go!" she screamed, fiercely battling against my hold. "Let me go right now! I swear, I'll fucking kill her!"

"Stop it!" I yelled, my voice reaching a volume loud enough to rival her own. "Come on."

Maintaining a tight grip on both arms, I steered her away from the scene, across the patio and in the direction of the house that loomed over the garden. Though she was still struggling, her resistance weakened as we moved further away from the action, evidently accepting the fact that the fight was over. Once I'd successfully ushered her through the back door and into the empty kitchen, she wriggled out of my clutch without making any attempt to escape.

"Look, let's go upstairs," I suggested quietly. "You can calm down and get yourself cleaned up, okay?"

I expected her to put up a fight, but instead she silently obliged, letting me lead her up the carpeted steps and towards the upstairs landing without so much as a word. Head hung low, her messy brown hair shielded her face from view as shaky steps led her towards the bedroom.

I didn't even notice - at least not until we'd slipped inside the room and she collapsed, defeated, onto the bed - that her shoulders were shaking, the first stray tears rolling down her cheeks.

An involuntary shot of panic sent my heart lurching, unnerved by the prospect of seeing Collette in such a state. A part of me wanted to flee, leaving her to deal with the personal aftermath in private, but there was something about the way her face was crumbling, the sobs increasing exponentially, that stopped me. This was a type of crying that radiated hopelessness, of breaking down and shattering into a thousand pieces. So, as much as my head opposed the idea, I stepped closer.

"Hey," I said softly, sinking onto the bed. Slowly, I stretched an arm around her, beginning to rub her back in slow, circular motions, hoping it was at least slightly soothing. I didn't know whether to take the fact she didn't push me away as a good or bad sign. "What's the matter?"

"Everything," she said, her voice broken by sobs. "God, just everything."

"Is this about Beth?" I asked. "Because if it is-"

"It's always about Beth, isn't it?" she interjected, burying her head in her hands, sniffling. "That's just the thing. It always has been. That's why I end up doing things like... that. God, I'm so stupid."

"What happened down there wasn't all you, Collette."

"I just... snapped. I don't know what came over me, but all I knew was I couldn't take it anymore and..." She trailed off, taking a deep breath that just ended with a fresh round of tears. "My parents are just going to hate me even more now for ruining their precious party."

"Don't say that. Your parents don't hate you."

"No, you're right. They don't hate me. But it'd be nice if they sometimes acknowledged the fact that I exist."

"Oh," I said quietly, my hand freezing on her back. "Is that what this is about?"

"That's what it's always about." As she slowly lifted her head from her hands, I got a look at her face - hopeless, smudged with make-up and crumpled like a piece of paper - staring back at me. I'd never seen Collette like this before: weak and vulnerable to an extent that she no longer intimidated me. Underneath her tough exterior, there was a horde of insecurities she never let anybody see. "Beth's always been the favourite. Her A-levels, getting into uni, all this modelling she's doing... it's all they see. It's all they care about."

"That's not true," I whispered. "It can't be true."

"Except it is." She looked over at me, her chocolate eyes glassy. "The only thing I have that gets my mum and dad to even look in my direction is Daniel. They love him. When we were going out, everything was fine. But once he broke up with me..." The tears started welling again, and she looked up to the ceiling, as if willing them to stay back. "It was almost like I was a failure. It all went downhill from there."

I didn't know what to say. The tension had set in now, and I shifted uncomfortably on the bed, feeling the awkwardness become almost tangible. I felt suddenly so awful, even if I had no real reason to. Collette had been waiting desperately for a year for the time Daniel would come back to her, and instead I'd waltzed in and interrupted everything. Now look where she'd ended up.

"I knew he'd moved on, really. Even before you showed up here. You're just so goddamn perfect for each other, you know? If only you could see how happy you've made him. I've never been able to do that."

"I..." My throat felt suddenly tight; the words couldn't get through.

"I know about what happened last night," she told me, blinking through teary eyes. "With you two. And yet I still went ahead and got him to do that in front of my parents, knowing you'd be there... God, I'm such an awful person."

"You're not awful," I assured her, shuffling closer. "You just did what any normal person would've done."

"I loved him, you know?" She took a deep, sniffling breath and blinked rapidly to keep the new tears at bay. "It just... I didn't know it would hurt so much to see him begin to love you the same way."

"Shh," I said soothingly, pulling her into a one-armed hug. "Look, just because things didn't work out with Daniel doesn't mean it won't with anybody else. I mean, have you seen yourself? You get guys dropping at your feet wherever you go. And Jesus, do you know how many girls would kill to look like you? Me included."

"What does that matter?" she mumbled. "I'm a bitch."

"No, you're not," I said firmly. "Don't say that. You're just a person who's hurting a lot right now. And you did what you thought would make you feel better. You're wonderful and beautiful and any sane guy would kill to have you. In fact... I can think of one who's downstairs right now."

Her head snapped upwards; her curiosity was evident even through a glaze of tears. "What?"

"Oh, yeah," I said, nodding. "Can't you see Scott's completely head over heels for you?"

She seemed to sit up a little straighter, reaching up to dab at her eyes with the sleeve of her dress. "What are you talking about?"

"Everyone can see it, you know. Most of the time he can barely keep his eyes off you. And all those times he tries to make you laugh? He's got it bad."

"Scott doesn't fancy me," she said, though her voice was wavering, and I could tell she was toying with the idea. "Of course he doesn't. Why would he?"

"Just take a look, okay?" I told her, smiling. "You'll see what I mean."

It took a while, but the smile that eventually graced her own features was worth the wait. Though her eyeliner had smudged into semi-circles beneath her eyes, and her nose was an unflattering shade of pink, the joy of her smile radiated through. "Thank you," she breathed. "Seriously... I didn't deserve all that, but you stuck around here anyway. Thank you."

"It's fine, honestly. What are friends for?"

She looked at me then, studying my face closely as if trying to work out some kind of deeper meaning that lay beneath my features. "Daniel's lucky to have found you," she said. Her voice was suddenly so level and sincere that it startled me. "We all are."

And as I pulled her into a hug - this time, one infinitely less awkward - I could feel the unspoken bond clicking into place, a loose end being tied up, and I knew that Collette and I were finally at peace.

17

CHAPTER 17

There was something on Daniel's mind.

It was obvious in the way he worked: how he kept stumbling over actions as basic as handing over the right change; the hesitance and stiltedness of the conversation that usually flowed so freely; how I'd caught him, more than once, zoning out completely from what was going on. There was something bothering him, I could tell. And it was something big enough to hold back his usual, charming self, leaving this bundle of jitteriness in its place.

It didn't seem right to question him properly while the shop was busy with customers; such a hectic environment was not the place. Even so, I couldn't stop myself from glancing over and checking he was okay at more-than-regular intervals. He always nodded, ducking his head and quickly going back to whatever he was doing, but I could see through this transparency. It was later, when the shop had closed for the day and we were in the midst of clearing up, that the opportunity finally presented itself for me to probe deeper.

"So," I started, leaning on the mop in my hand and blowing away the strand of hair that had fallen from my topknot. "How long's it going to be before you actually tell me what's bothering you?"

From his spot by the door, he looked up; in doing so, the collection of keys he was holding slipped through his hand and dropped to the floor. "What?"

I watched as he bent over to pick them up, his fingers fumbling to get a grip on the metal. When he straightened up, the eye contact established between us was reluctant at best. "You've been acting strange all day," I said softly. "There's something on your mind, isn't there? We can talk about it, if you want."

Sighing, he ran a hand through his ruffled hair. "I…" The keys were slipped into his pocket, and he made his way towards the counter to grab the second mop. "I have no idea how you do that," he settled for eventually, picking his words carefully and expertly dodging the question.

"You almost gave someone a twenty pound note when they only paid a fiver," I pointed out, "and you're just… distracted. It honestly wasn't that hard to figure it out."

I moved to the opposite end of the shop, dunking my mop in the bucket and beginning to wipe. My strokes were sideways, slowly advancing in Daniel's direction, so we'd eventually meet in the middle. "We don't have to talk about it," I told him. "I just thought you might want to."

A brief silence fell across the room, only the sound of the squeaking floor audible for a few seconds. Then, suddenly, he stopped mopping, his feet frozen to one spot. "It's the anniversary," he said quietly, leaving me to wonder for a heartbeat what he was talking about. "A whole year, to the day, since he died."

Of course. How could I have forgotten? All I could manage to force out was a quiet "Oh."

"Yeah. Hard to believe it's been that long, really." He took a deep breath, his brow creasing in deep thought. "I was going to go up to the cemetery after work," he said, "but I don't know. I haven't been there since the day of the funeral. There's just something about that place... like, it almost brings back bad memories, you know? If I visit, I'm scared I won't see just Dad. I'll see sick Dad, the one who was in the hospital for so long. And that's not how I want to remember him. Not in so much pain."

"I understand," I told him. Because I did. I'd never experienced such a thing myself, but I could feel the words deeper than just the voice that was speaking them. My mum and dad were taken so suddenly I didn't have a chance to remember them as anything other themselves. They weren't riddled with sickness, their last moments spent in agony that was unbearable to watch. One moment they were here. The next, gone.

I wasn't sure which option was the better.

"I want to be able to say I can feel him here, or something cliché like that," Daniel said, gesturing toward the empty shop, its half-cleaned tiles gleaming beneath the soles of our shoes. "But I can't. So I thought maybe... maybe it's time to face my fears and go up there."

"If you feel ready, you'll be able do it," I assured him softly. "It'll be okay. I promise."

"Yeah. Well." He shrugged. "We'll see about that one."

I wanted to move closer, but some kind of intangible force stopped me before I could take a step. "It won't be as bad as you think. The fact that you're considering it has got to count for something, right? Maybe you're not so scared after all."

"It seems like it should work out like that, doesn't it?" he said. "But I am scared. I'm scared as hell."

"I know, but once you face up to this... you won't be. You'll be okay."

"God, I hope so." He lifted the mop, going back to the cleaning, but I could tell he was deep in thought about something. And, sure enough, before he'd even completed one swipe of the mop, he stopped again. "Hey, Flo?"

I looked up. "Yeah?"

"Look, this is probably a really long shot," he began with a sigh, "and you don't have to. Like, at all. If you don't want to you can just say no and I swear I won't–"

"Daniel."

"You really don't have to. I was just wondering if maybe... maybe you'd come with me?"

It wasn't what I'd been expecting. I had imagined Daniel's visit to the cemetery would be a private affair: a situation in which my input was limited to mere words of encouragement and understanding. But here he was, blinking back at me with sheepishness and blatant hope written all over his face. It was a lot to ask, and he obviously knew this, but there was something about his hesitance to even talk about the matter that made me wonder how on earth he'd cope alone.

"Yeah," I breathed. "I mean, if that's what you want. I'll go with you."

Relief flooded his face immediately, and I could've sworn I heard him release a breath he'd been holding. "That's what I want," he told me, more sure of himself than I'd heard all day. "I'm just not sure I can handle it alone."

"Well, that's okay." A smile small tugged at the corners of my lips. "Because you don't have to."

On any other day, it took no more than half an hour past closing to clear up the shop completely, readying it for another day of hardcore ice cream serving. Today, however, we seemed to subconsciously drag it out longer; Daniel seemed to take extra care scrubbing every tile of the floor until the overhead lights produced something of a burnished glare, triple-checking every box of stock in the back room, even organising the drawer that held the ice cream scoops twice over. His nerves shadowed every action; I could see them in the way he fiddled constantly with the pocket of his apron, touched the keys in his pocket like some sort of ritual, and kept shifting his weight from the ball of one foot to the other, even when standing still.

It must've been about quarter to seven when we finally slipped out the main door, following the path around to the back street where his car was parked. I climbed wordlessly into the passenger seat, the quietness between us lasting only for a minute before Daniel twisted the dial on the radio. Playing was a catchy pop song I vaguely recognised, its upbeat tempo much too peppy for the situation. Still, it had to be better than the nervous silence it took the place of, stretched with anticipation of what was to come.

I didn't know how far away the cemetery was, but we ended up driving right out of town, past the touristy signs that read You are now leaving Walden-on-Sea! as if this was something of a significance. Stone buildings and vast stretches of greenery whipped past the windows, moving at a pace too fast to be focused on. At least fifteen minutes must've sped by before the buildings started to become closer together, the fields sparser, and countryside began its gradual transformation into suburbia. At this point the car began to slow down, and Daniel kept looking around, on the lookout for a turning he seemed to have forgotten the location of.

Once he found it, however, everything seemed to happen in the blink of an eye. We pulled into the car park and into a bay just as the radio lost signal, its popular tunes reduced to nothing more than buzzing static. Daniel shut off the engine, pulling his key from the ignition, and for a moment we sat there, staring ahead at the first symmetrical section of gravestones whilst shrouded by heavy silence.

I swallowed, working up the nerve to ask the question. "You okay?"

There was a definite hesitation, but he nodded nonetheless. "Yeah. I think so."

The car door rattled as he climbed out, me following suit a few seconds afterward. The cemetery's entrance loomed before us, and I could feel Daniel's palpable apprehensiveness as he appeared beside me. It seemed to require an odd amount of concentration for him to put one foot in front of the other, and we only managed a measly few steps before he came to an abrupt halt beside me, shaking his head.

"I can't," he said, sounding suddenly panicked. "God, Flo, I honestly thought I could but–"

Without thinking, I reached over and took his hand in mine, giving it a reassuring squeeze. "You're fine," I told him gently. "You can do this. All you have to do is stay calm."

His grip on my hand remained tight and desperate for a few long seconds, but eventually I felt him exhale, the muscles in his fingers relaxing considerably.

"You ready?"

The nod I received looked like it had taken all of his effort, but at least the expression of sheer panic had disappeared. This, I had to take as a good sign. The stone archway that made up the entrance gave way to a vast stretch of land, which came into view as we passed through. It was then that I took in the place in its entirety: the rows and rows of gravestones, sectioned off into even areas. The degrees of care varied hugely between plots; while some sat pruned to the tiniest perfection, fresh flowers serving as decoration, others lay overrun by weeds and the shrivelled remains of cut flowers, forgotten by everybody who had once cared.

"It's towards the back," Daniel informed me, nodding towards the far left corner. "I remember."

He did almost perfectly, too; for someone who hadn't visited the place in almost a year, he was able to navigate as easily through the labyrinth of headstones as if there was some sort of beacon guiding him in the right direction. However, his determined marching pace rapidly deteriorated as we weaved through, and by the time we reached the outermost section of the cemetery the length of his steps was painfully small. In fact, they were so tiny that when he finally did crawl to a halt in front of one particular plot, it took me a while to notice that he'd stopped at all.

"Here," he croaked, his voice raw. "It's this one."

It was tidy – or at least it was in comparison to its next door neighbour, which was swamped by weeds growing as tall as the headstone. Obviously well-looked after, I presumed this was down to Daniel's mum, who appeared to visit with sufficient frequency to keep the plants trimmed and fresh flowers beneath the engraved stone. I took a tentative step closer, moving closer to Daniel and slipping my hand into his.

In loving memory of John Bolton, it read, letters inscribed into the marble, a dear husband and father. Taken from our lives, but never our hearts.

I could already feel a lump rising in my throat, looking on at the sight before me, and dread coursed through my bloodstream as I anticipated Daniel's reaction. However, when I finally dared to glance over, I was taken by surprise. Instead of being met by a face crumpled by sadness, tears already streaming down his cheeks, Daniel was managing to remain remarkably calm.

He slowly untangled our intertwined fingers, letting his arm drop to his side, and stepped closer.

"Hey, Dad," he started, his voice low. "It's me."

Grass sunk underfoot as he approached the headstone, finally getting close enough to run a hand over its curved top. "I know I haven't visited... well, at all, really, but it's been tough. I just couldn't face up to it." He bent over to set down the potted plant he'd brought beneath the stone: an array of bright flowers, colour in a ceramic pot. "I brought you something."

Silence consumed the space between us; it seemed strange, though I didn't know what else I had been expecting. It wasn't like the conversation was ever going to be anything more than one-sided. Not here.

"I remember how you always used to tell me to man up and just do it," he said quietly, the tips of his fingers caressing the smooth stone. "I used to wimp out of things a lot. I didn't today. It took me a while, but... I got here."

The earlier breeze had dropped, leaving just the sunshine, poking its way through gaps in the clouds, to warm our backs. Looking around, all I could see for miles was row after row of gravestones. Each a chunk of marble, a few words engraved as a personalisation. They were all so painfully uniform, and I was suddenly struck by the desperate question of how on earth this was possible: to represent everything that a person is, was and could've been on something so small and insignificant. I don't know why it hadn't occurred to me sooner, but it did just then: that every single one of those stones was a human being. Someone with enough hopes, dreams and thoughts to last them a lifetime, and every other little thing that pieced together to make a whole. We were surrounded by hundreds of them, some simply forgotten, as if it were that easy to disregard someone gone forever.

I didn't understand how it could be done. And suddenly it was so overwhelming that I found myself having to make a conscious effort to hold myself together. Not now. Not here. It wasn't the place to crumble.

"Oh, and guess what, Dad?" Daniel was saying now, a smile so heartbreakingly sad playing at the corners of his mouth. It almost hurt to look, but at the same time I couldn't bear to turn away. "We had our first one-k day at the shop today. You always wanted one of those, didn't you? You always said it was going to happen someday. And it did. One thousand pounds, in one day. God, you would've been so proud."

He was trying so hard to hold it together, I could tell. But his voice was wavering, his expression shaking at the edges as the grief pulled it apart. It was then that he sunk to the floor, kneeling before the gravestone, staring straight into the letters carved into its surface.

"I'm trying so hard for you, Dad," he said, battling to stop his voice from cracking. "I'm taking care of the shop almost by myself. It's difficult, but I know you loved that place. I know how much work you put into it. It's yours. And that's... that's what makes it worth it."

He took a deep breath, making his best effort to stay calm, but even with distance between us I could hear its shakiness.

"I really hope you're not too worried about us," he continued, his shoulders trembling. "We're doing okay. Mum and Erin have even been getting on. Sometimes it's harder than others, but we're managing. We're battling through. At least... I'm trying to. I just want to make you proud, Dad. I'm sorry if I can't handle it sometimes."

I realised I was crying then, tears sliding slowly down my cheeks and coating them with an all too familiar layer of dampness. Word-lessly, I moved closer to Daniel, sinking down beside him. He had his head ducked, pressing the palms of his hands to his face, but looked up when he felt the presence of my outstretched hand.

It took him a moment, his blurred eyes adjusting to the sight of it, before our fingers were once again woven together. Fitting together like the pieces of a puzzle, as they always seemed to.

"There's something else I have to tell you, Dad," he said then, squeezing my hand tighter. "There's... there's this girl. I met her recently, and she's not like anybody else I've ever known. I still can't quite believe my luck when I think about it."

I blinked at him, the movement of my eyelid sending another tear over the brink. "Daniel–"

But he shook his head, not letting me finish. "I just have to tell somebody about her. She's so smart. Unbelievably beautiful. She has a heart of gold, and she's nice to everyone. She has the cutest freckles I've ever seen and can draw like nobody else. I could go on about her for hours, really, but I don't know anybody who has the patience to listen. But the thing is... she gets me, Dad. She's the most unbelievable person I've ever met, and she's sitting here with me right now."

The result was a bizarre rush of what seemed like every possible feeling; it was like I wanted to burst into a fresh round of tears, cry with laughter and squeal at the top of my lungs, all at the same time. Even so, I couldn't bring myself to do any of those things. I just let Daniel continue squeezing my hand as the tears flowed from both of us, trying to keep my head above the wave of overwhelming emotion that was threatening to pull me under.

"I know you said to be careful," Daniel said, his voice low and raw, the words catching in his throat, "when it came to this. I remember that. But the thing is... I've found her, Dad. The one you always talked about. The one you said I'd find eventually. I found her. In the beautiful, crazy phenomenon that is Florence Kennedy."

By now, I was past being able to hold back the sobs; they racked my body as furiously as the boy's beside me. Forcing out coherent words seemed near enough impossible, but I swallowed, resolving to try anyway.

"Hey," I sniffed eventually, glancing over at Daniel through a misty glaze of unshed tears, "can I... can I say something?"

This didn't seem to be what he was expecting; a brief look of surprise crossed his features before he nodded, forcing out a breathy "Yeah."

I inhaled deeply, making a far-fetched attempt to compose myself. Said task was difficult when I'd been reduced to a snivelling mess, complete with sore eyes and make-up running wild across my face, but I tried my best. This was my sole chance to do what I had in mind, and I wasn't about to waste it.

"Hi, Mr Bolton," I began gently, swallowing hard. "I know we didn't get the chance to meet properly... and it's awful, because from what I've heard, you sound like the most wonderful person. I wish more than anything I could've had the opportunity. Daniel thinks so much of you, it's crazy. I just wish I could've gotten here a little sooner.

"I just wanted to let you know how lucky you are to have a son like him. I haven't known him for long, but I can see how hard the past year's been – on him and everyone. And yet he's managed to stay so strong. Certainly stronger than I have." The tears were brimming, threatening a reappearance, but I willed my voice to stay together. "He's done such an amazing job in the shop, and I know how much he wishes you could be there to see it." I gulped. "God knows I don't deserve somebody like him, but I just want you to know this: I swear, I'll take care of him. I'll be there because I know you can't. The thing is, I know I can't even come close to being good enough for your son, but I'm going to try my damn hardest to come the closest I can."

I was crying again by the time the last word passed my lips, and moments later, I felt Daniel's arms envelope me, pulling me into him. Accepting the invitation readily, I wrapped my own arms around his torso and pressed myself into his side.

"Don't you ever say that," he told me, clinging to my body so tightly I wondered if we'd ever be able to separate. Surely if we stayed like this for long enough we'd become permanently moulded, the boundaries where one of us ended and the other started indistinguishable. "Promise me you won't say that again. You are good enough, and God knows if anyone's undeserving here it's got to be me. Just don't think like that. Please."

"Your dad would be so proud of you," I mumbled into his chest, my salty tears seeping into the front of his T-shirt. "I really mean that."

I felt his hand move towards my back, beginning to rub through the fabric in slow, soothing circles. Almost immediately my tensed muscles relaxed, lending me even closer into his side. "Thank you," he said simply, his voice thick. "I just... I can't thank you enough for coming here today."

"You're welcome," was all I managed to whisper back.

And there in the cemetery, enclosed by the warmth of each other's arms, we sat looking on at the gravestone until the soft orange glow marking the beginning of sunset began to edge its way into the sky. We watched the sun sink gradually below the horizon, each fraction disappearing one by one, until there was nothing left but darkness and the kiss I felt Daniel plant on the top of my head.

That night, when I'd slipped past Gram's questions and retreated to my room, I was overcome by an odd feeling of inspiration, the pressing compulsion to create. So much so that I headed straight for the desk by the window, laying my watercolours and brushes and pencils and everything else in a semi-circular formation around the sheets of paper. I collapsed into the chair, pulling my feet underneath me.

And when my pencil made contact with paper, the strokes came more easily than they ever had before. They didn't need long before they started taking shape: rough lines right across the paper that arranged themselves in a way I'd never thought I could come up with. They were lines, then an outline, and before long the foundations of an entire picture stretching right across the page.

The watery shades added colour, pale skin hues and a feathery white texture. Soft-edged moonlight streamed through the window, dancing across the page, reducing my pencil to a sharp-edged shadow.

It took form so quickly; an hour of solid work later, when my paintbrush finally clattered onto the wooden tabletop, a weight felt like it had been lifted from my shoulders.

Gingerly, I lifted the paper up to the light, and there they were: two figures, one female and the other male, stood amongst a layer of wispy clouds. Clad in white, golden halos atop their heads like crowns, they looked subtly downward. To anyone else, they were just two angels. Angels with glistening wing tips and their hands enveloped in each other's. Merely beautiful.

To me, though, they were specific. I knew the messy brown locks of the male too well, the striking brown eyes of the female like I'd been looking into them for years. To me, they were more.

The angels with two daughters.

18

— ◦ —

CHAPTER 18

The following morning, for the second time in the past three days, I found myself woken by the sound of a pounding electronic drumbeat. The first occasion had been bearable; burying my head under the pillow had adequately muffled the sound to allow me to drift back off.

Today, however, was a different story. The artificial rhythm had been cranked up several notches on the stereo, and no matter how hard I tried to ignore it, sleep was fast becoming a wistful fantasy.

I suppose seven a.m. wasn't totally unreasonable – not when you took into account the peculiar hours of the night Gram was often known to clatter around at – but I would've been a lot happier with a couple of extra hours in bed. Accepting the fact it was more likely I'd fly to the moon today, I yanked back the duvet and headed downstairs to investigate.

The noise increased exponentially in volume as I made my way down the stairs, layers of other obnoxious instruments combining with the drumbeat to make the overall effect significantly more awful. I was guided by the cacophony to the kitchen, where I found Gram. She was perched in her favourite corner spot, her easel angled towards the window, giving her a wide hilltop view of the

Walden coastline. What was causing the racket, I discovered, was the ancient stereo on the dining table: through it pounded some kind of hardcore techno music that would've sounded more at home in some shifty underground nightclub.

"Uh, Gram?" Unsurprisingly, she didn't look up; I could barely hear myself over the pulsating beat. "Gram?"

She glanced upward, looking slightly dazed, having been yanked from her artistic state of mind. "Yes?"

"What are you doing?"

Gram blinked, looking down through her thick glasses at the canvas balanced on her easel. "I'm painting," she answered simply, going back to dabbing enthusiastically with her brush.

"But what about the," I paused, searching for a better adjective and coming up short, "... music?"

"Oh, that." A dismissive flick of her brush sent a splatter of miniscule blue droplets across the floor tiles. "Just a couple of old CDs I found. I like it, don't you? I find it very... relaxing."

There was absolutely nothing relaxing about the pounding bass assaulting my eardrums at that particular moment, but Gram did look kind of at peace, even humming absently to herself as she worked. She'd been at it non-stop for the last week or so, in a last minute hurry to get all her pieces finished in time for her opening exhibit at the local gallery. One of her friends had connections down at Walden Arts, and after putting in a good word for her, a representative had been down to the cottage for a look at Gram's paintings and, as simple as that, she'd landed a spot for an entire collection.

"You know, I saw some of the drawings you keep in your bedroom," she'd told me when she first announced the news. "They're very good. I could put in a word for you at the gallery too, if you're interested."

But before she'd even finished her sentence, I was vehemently shaking my head. "No, thanks," I said. "I mean, it's nice of you and everything, but…"

My drawings were the equivalent of my diary; that was the problem. This was where Gram and I differed: while she liked to display her work on every wall, in plain sight of anybody who was interested, I never hung up anything my pencil had touched. My reasoning was this: if you wouldn't paste the pages of your diary on the wall, why do the same with pictures? I'd feel too exposed if I did, like my darkest secrets had been scrawled on the walls for public viewing. There were some things that were just meant to be kept to yourself.

Gram's array of artwork, on the other hand, was the backbone of her cottage. You could never predict where one was going to pop up next – since I'd moved in, recent additions had included a small, abstract watercolour to the left of my bedroom door, one that resembled a pile of leaves propped up on the telly, and a chalk sketch of a mug of hot tea in the downstairs loo. They were her pride and joy, and the place would be nothing more than an empty shell without them dotted around the place.

"I just…" My voice trailed off. It was much easier to justify it in my head; out loud, the words didn't come so freely. "It's embarrassing," was what I settled for eventually, though even to my own ears it sounded weak.

Still, Gram hadn't pursued the matter, instead focusing all her attention on her own collection, which was developing at an extreme rate. With a week until the opening exhibition at the gallery, it was all systems go, and she was working full-time on the finishing touches.

The thing was, I didn't have a clue what any of them looked like. Every time I approached, she'd usher me away, claiming she wanted it to be a surprise on the opening night.

It was looking like a big deal; she'd even invited Nora, Lenny and Summer to drive down to Walden. They, along with what seemed like the rest of the entire town, were all set to be packed into the gallery that night.

But I was proud of her. I could see how pleased she was in herself; the sparkle that appeared in her eye when she was painting something particularly good was second to none.

"So," I said, raising my voice enough to be heard over the continuous techno din, "do I at least get to see this one? Surely just one painting won't spoil the exhibit?"

She paused, her brush poised in midair, considering my proposition. "Well," she said eventually, pushing her glasses further up her nose. "I suppose one look won't hurt. This one's almost finished, anyway."

Spurred on by a boost of energy unusual for such an early hour, I bounded towards Gram's easel, eager to see what she'd been pouring concentrated hard work into for days straight. My gaze fell upon the canvas, and as the sight of the picture met my eyes, I wasn't disappointed.

It was a bright oil paint representation of what I recognised easily as the Walden seafront. I wasn't sure what surprised me more: the fact that for once I could actually tell what Gram had painted, or that I was able to identify the location so quickly. The scene was painted with such intricate detail I wondered how on earth it was possible for each stroke of paint to capture Walden's image so perfectly. Though I wouldn't admit it, the first thing I'd noticed was the edge of the scene: the delicately painted cliff, which I knew hid a beautifully secret beach only a handful of people knew about.

The backdrop of the night I'd never forget.

"It's beautiful," I breathed earnestly.

"Thanks, honey," she said, but her eyes hadn't left the painting. I noticed then that she had a second brush tucked behind her ear; its blue end was coming dangerously close to adding a splash of colour to her grey curls. "I've been working on this one for a while, but I think it's worth it."

"Definitely," I agreed, still finding myself entranced by the image, although I couldn't quite put my finger on why. "And I can't wait to see the other pieces."

She smiled. "Only a week to go!"

I was genuinely happy for her. Really. Just because the thought of my artwork going on display to the general public was enough to turn my stomach, it didn't mean that was the case for everybody else.

"Well, now that I'm almost done with this..." She reached over, snatching up the remote control that was lying on the window sill and pointed it at the stereo. Almost immediately, the deafening – though I used the term loosely – song vanished from the air, leaving in its place a rather welcome and blissful quietness that fell across the room like a warm blanket.

Thank God, I praised internally, but I didn't have the heart to say it out loud.

Instead, I stifled a yawn. "Well, I guess I should make myself breakfast."

My intention had been to go for the first choice I laid eyes on, but once I'd started across the kitchen and pulled open the overhead cupboard door, all that stared back at me was an empty space. No boxes of cereal, muffins or even gross protein shakes in sight. So I moved across the counter, aiming for the bread bin, deciding toast was the next best option. Which, of course, led to further disappointment when I noticed that was empty too. The theme was recurring in the fridge, all bar half a packet of ham and a single mini Babybel, neither of which I could really salvage.

"Um, Gram?"

I turned around to look at her; she'd gone back to her easel, gazing out of the window and adding the tiniest splashes of colour to her painting wherever she saw fit. Upon hearing my voice, she glanced up a second time. "Hmm?"

"The kitchen," I said, gesturing aimlessly toward my surroundings. "You know there's meant to be food in here, right?"

For a moment she just stared blankly back at me, as if I'd started speaking a foreign language. Then, arriving abruptly back on the planet with an almost audible thud, realisation dawned. "Ah, yes..." She scratched the back of her neck sheepishly. "I guess I've been concentrating so hard on making sure all of this is ready... well, it kind of slipped my mind to go shopping this week."

"Oh." My eyes darted back to the fridge once more, just to double check something hadn't miraculously materialized there in the past ten seconds. "So there's nothing to eat."

"No, not really..." She smiled apologetically. "Sorry. I should really go shopping. I guess I could leave this and maybe pop down–"

"It's okay," I cut in. "Look, don't worry about it. I'll go for you and let you carry on with your painting."

"Oh, honey, are you sure? I mean, I know you've probably got better things to do than go round running errands for me. There are only a few weeks left of summer, after all."

"It's fine," I assured her with a smile. "I've got it. Just write me a list, okay?"

As I made my way down to the supermarket, the morning sun was rising over Walden, brightening the cloudless sky. There was something almost tangibly clearer about the day, which was reflected in the weather; it was almost as if the visit to the cemetery had lifted a huge weight from not only Daniel's shoulders, but the rest of the town too.

The shop was quiet as I pushed through the door, only the lazy beat of a pop song pulsing through the overhead speakers to serve as a soundtrack. Grabbing a basket from the stand by the door, I offered the sole cashier a polite smile as I ducked past, heading straight for the cereal aisle.

I could've done with something more sizeable than the basket, I realised, as it started to fill up considerably after the first three items had been dumped inside. The stock level of Gram's cupboard was so alarmingly low that not only did I wonder what on earth we'd been living on for the past three days, I realised I would've been better equipped with an entire trolley to accommodate the constituents of her shopping list.

As I rounded the corner into the next aisle, I was so completely lost in my thoughts that I only narrowly avoided a head-on collision with someone coming in the opposite direction. Thankfully, I managed to swerve at the last second, only brushing elbows with the stranger as we ducked past each other.

"Sorr—"

My apology was cut short, however, when I got a proper look at the person I'd almost slammed into; it didn't take long to recognise the bright purple hair, which looked positively fluorescent under the glare of the supermarket lighting. "Erin?"

It was her, but it was a significantly more dishevelled version of the Erin I was used to seeing. With her hair dragged back into a messy ponytail, eyes less striking without their ring of liner, and her body swallowed whole by a baggy sweatshirt, she was a lot less put together than normal. It took a moment for my presence to even register with her, and she stared blankly back at me for a beat before realising exactly who I was.

"Oh, God." Her voice was a groan as she ran a self-conscious hand through her hair. "We had to bump into each other here, didn't we?"

"I..." For a moment I was confused, but realisation kicked in when my gaze wandered toward her basket, where two boxes of Tampax sat on top of her other items. Combine that with her sweatpants and half-hearted ponytail, the final piece of the puzzle wasn't too difficult to figure out. "Oh. Right. Sorry about that one."

"S'okay. Better you than Jay, I suppose. You'll just have to deal with the fact that I look utterly stunning at this time of morning."

"I'll try not to be too overwhelmed." The corners of my mouth were curling into a slight smile. "Believe me, I wouldn't even be out at this time if Gram hadn't woke me up with her crazy music on full blast. And then there's the fact that she's been so wrapped up working on her exhibition pieces that it slipped her mind to go shopping. Honestly, it was either this or starve."

"Oh, yeah," Erin said, leaning on the shelf beside her, which was stacked high with Digestive biscuits. "I heard about that thing. It's next week, right? At the gallery."

"Uh huh. She's really excited about it. It's just... everything's a little crazy at the minute. Paintings everywhere."

"Oh, I can imagine. I gathered it was kind of a big deal from the way people have been talking about it."

"Apparently so. She's even invited Nora and Lenny down to Walden to see it. They're staying with us for a couple of days. I'm just keeping my fingers crossed that Summer's crying might have progressively quieter since I last saw her, or I'm not going to get a wink of sleep."

Erin nodded, grinning. "Oh, I'm definitely coming. I'm dying to see this cute little niece of yours."

"Yeah, well, half of me's kind of worried she's going to have dreadlocks when I see her. You never know what to expect with Lenny."

At this, she couldn't refrain from giggling, pressing a hand to her mouth. "Now that's something I'd like to see."

An amused quietness settled between us as the image was left to fester in our minds. However, once the smile began to fade from Erin's bare face, I could feel the silence twisting before us, beginning its transformation into quiet imminence. She didn't even have to say anything; we both knew what was coming.

"So," she said slowly, "yesterday, huh?"

I didn't even blink; the thought sprung to the front of my mind straight away. "Um... yeah."

"He finally worked up the courage to visit," she said quietly. "You know, he's been afraid of that ever since the funeral. The thought of visiting the grave... it terrified him. And he got over it. You must've had a lot to do with it."

"Oh, I don't..." I trailed off, not really knowing how to go about it. "I mean, he was already planning on going. I just agreed to come with him. It wasn't really me at all."

"Flo," she deadpanned. "He was scared stiff of that place. He never would've been able to do it alone. He's my twin brother – trust me, I know him better than he thinks. He might've got there, but he wouldn't have made it all the way. You being there... you must've done an amazing job."

"He's... he's okay now, right?" I queried tentatively.

The words had barely escaped me before she began nodding profusely. "Oh, yeah. He's better than okay. In fact, he's better than I've seen him in ages. Today... I don't know. It's almost like I was talking to a completely different person. He just seems so much more... at peace, you know? Like he finally got closure from yesterday. It seemed like it was exactly what he needed."

"Oh." My sigh was full of relief; I'd been worried maybe the visit might've made things worse, surfacing new emotions that risked sending Daniel's progress on a downward spiral. "That's good."

"Yeah," she breathed, managing a small smile. "It is."

With the two of us lost in brief thought, a beat of silence passed between us, only broken when Erin looked up at me. "You know, you two are like some cheesy romance story," she said, smirking. "Sappy, lovey-dovey, all that crap. I mean, I'd never dream of reading anything of the sort, but actually seeing you guys..."

I could feel my cheeks warming, but I don't think she noticed. She was too busy pondering her thoughts, searching for the words to get across what was running through her mind. "All I can really say is... thank God you came here, Flo." An almost pensive smile appeared on her face, translating more than her voice ever could. "Just... thank God."

I couldn't really come up with a suitable response to that, wondering what on earth would be a reasonable reply, but Erin cut in again before the silence could grow too awkward.

"Jesus, did you hear that too? I can't believe how pathetic that just sounded," she said, slapping a palm across her face. "I swear, it's this crazy PMS. I have no idea what I'm talking about half the time. You know what? I'm going home, crawling into bed and eating Ben and Jerry's for the rest of the day. There's nothing else for it."

I laughed then, grateful that the tone of conversation had twisted towards something infinitely less serious. "Sounds like a plan. Have fun."

"Oh, definitely," she said, shifting the weight of the basket hooked on her arm. "Once I get my hot water bottle, the party will really get started. Anyway, see you later."

And as she vanished down the aisle, nothing more than a flash of purple hair and tracksuit bottoms, I found myself smiling gently after her, overcome by a sudden rush of affection for not only Erin, but the entire group of friends I'd been accepted into in Walden. They now made up a vast chunk of my life, and though it hadn't been more than a few weeks, I was left wondering how on earth I'd managed without them.

I was one of them now.

And I didn't ever want to let that go.

19

—— • ——

CHAPTER 19

A week later, and suddenly the date of Gram's exhibit had drawn so close that I began to wonder what consuming entity the days had vanished into. The final few days had, as predicted, reduced her to a bundle of pent-up energy, and the techno music had been going strong for as many as six straight hours a day. I hardly noticed it now; it was almost like I was building up some kind of immunity to the electronic beat, so that the constant vibration of my bedroom walls had become just background noise. In fact, it seemed stranger now to awaken to a quietness throughout the cottage, silence like gentle waves breaking on the shore, instead of the daily tsunami of obnoxiously loud music.

Today, a Thursday, was the final day before the opening. Gram was rushing around so wildly, ten different paintbrushes clutched in her fist at any given time, that I was kind of scared to venture any further than the bottom stair. So instead, when Daniel had showed up at the front door to hang out as planned, we'd come to a mutual decision that retreating upstairs and leaving her to it was probably safest.

"Hey," he said later, when the both of us were settled sideways on my bed. He was beside me, close enough to let our arms brush with every movement, our legs somehow still tangled together whilst dangling off the end of the frame. "It's today your sister's coming down to Walden, right?"

The anticipation of seeing Nora again was growing; I nodded a little more forcefully than I should've. Though I'd adjusted to life without her, the passive consciousness of her absence was always there, like I was missing an unessential but noticeable part of myself. "I'm not sure when she said they were aiming to get here, though."

"I'm sure you'll know about it when she does," he commented, a smile playing at the edges of his lips. "She was with you on the day you first came into the shop, right? The, uh... heavily pregnant one?"

The memory, at least, had some comedic value; I couldn't help but think of Nora in her third trimester, and how ridiculous she'd looked having to waddle everywhere she went. "Yeah. That's her. Except she's not so heavily pregnant anymore."

"Oh, yeah." He chuckled. "Right."

Daniel shifted in his spot, whilst I tried not to dwell on the way the skin-to-skin contact sent tingles coursing through my every nerve. "I can't believe you remember that," I said. "That first day in the ice cream shop. The day we first met."

"Are you joking? How could I forget?" The smirk was already materialising across his face. "I chased you all the way down the street to give you your change."

The initial details of the scene emerged slowly, the rest of it following soon after in one big rush: a tidal wave crashing across my mind. The summer that now lay behind us seemed to have stretched into forever; surely it had to have been close to years long, rather than a mere few weeks? It felt impossible that it wasn't longer since I'd met Daniel on that first day in Walden, impossible that it had only taken us this long to fast-forward through everything we'd been through. A laugh bubbled up inside me before I had the chance to stop it. "Oh, I remember."

"Of course you do," he replied easily. "I mean, you were so blown away by my breathtaking good looks that you let your ice cream melt all over your hand."

I opened my mouth, hoping a witty retort would form in my throat somewhere in the process, but the hot flush of embarrassment beat me to it, creeping up my neck and spreading rapidly across my freckled cheeks. Instead, I settled for ducking my head, letting a curtain of brown curls shield my face.

"You don't need to be embarrassed." He reached over and placed a finger under my chin, slowly forcing me to meet his hazel-eyed gaze. "Look, I'll even tell you a secret."

The blush only intensified when he leaned in, his face so close I could feel his warm breath tickling my ear. "I thought you were pretty too."

The simple sentence sent my heart into a fluttering frenzy, my face breaking out into a smile, but I swatted him away. "You are so just saying that," I countered. "You felt sorry for me because I was hopelessly awkward and incapable of social interaction."

"Well..." His pause was drawn-out, a false display of deep thought. "There was that too."

I took the opportunity to shove him playfully, my hand colliding with his upper arm a little harder than I had intended. My attack obviously caught him off guard because he fell sideways, landing onto a cushion of soft duvet, before losing his balance completely and rolling off the edge of the bed with a spectacular display of clumsiness. For a moment, I just stared back at his newfound position on the floor, his arms sprawled awkwardly around him. The shock rendered me motionless, but the laughter pushed through its barrier eventually. I was giggling like an idiot, unable to control myself as Daniel let out a low groan and pulled himself into a sitting position.

"Okay, that was brutal," he said, rubbing exaggeratedly at his head. "I didn't realise I had such a violent girlfriend."

Girlfriend. Such a simple, ten-letter word. Yet it was able to send a jolt of excitement through me, coupled with a subsequent burst of happiness that seemed to spread through my every fibre. It hadn't been officially discussed, but it seemed like he'd taken our considerably couple-like behaviour over the past week as sufficient permission. Not only had he been holding my hand at every available opportunity, we'd exchanged a fair few kisses – although they tended to lean towards gentle pecks goodbye rather than any heated snogs. Still, it wasn't as if I minded. Just being with Daniel was almost as if someone had flicked a switch for constant sunshine over my world, no matter how stubbornly overcast the weather remained outside.

"Sorry," I said. My hand rose to cover my mouth, but I was failing miserably at letting the giggles subside.

"Well, I guess I can forgive you," he sighed. "I mean, I—" The next statement was cut suddenly short, his attention drawn towards something he seemed to have spotted under my bed. "Hey, what's this?"

I couldn't see exactly what he was so intrigued by, but it didn't take me long to realise once he'd stuck his hand under the bed, it surfacing with the corner of a large sheet of paper held between his fingers. The onset of recognition was almost instantaneous; a tsunami-like wave of dread crashed over my insides, forcing my heart to the pit of my stomach.

"Oh my God," Daniel was exclaiming, while I leapt to my feet at lightning speed.

"Don't look at that!" I cried a little too forcefully, prising the picture from his hands. Still, it wasn't like that would do much; he'd already seen it, and the damage was done.

"Holy shit, Flo, did you draw that?"

He was staring down at the sheet in my hands – the one that hadn't seen daylight since I'd drawn it a week ago – with almost entrancement. It was too big to slip inside my sketchbook, the usual repository for anything my pencil had touched. Instead, intending for it to remain strictly unseen, it had ended up beneath the frame of my bed: a place I was sure nobody would be looking. "It's amazing."

"It's nothing," I insisted. More than anything I wanted to turn away, move the angels somewhere out of sight, but seeing them out in the open for a second time had rendered me strangely motion-less. I couldn't move my feet even if I wanted to, and as a result, the pair of us stayed staring down at the drawing as if it were physically impossible to tear our eyes away.

"It's... it's..." He seemed to be struggling to find the right word. "Jesus Christ, why is something like that under your bed?"

"I... I don't know."

But I did know. Those two-dimensional figures were the closest thing I had to my mum and dad, regardless of the fact they were composed of little more than pencil strokes. That drawing came into being in a moment of weakness: a moment when I felt so compelled to create that I thought my head might explode if I didn't pour the contents of my mind onto the page. I didn't need it on display; my innermost thoughts were meant to stay just that, locked away under my outer expression. Not for everyone to see.

Daniel wasn't the whole world, but he may as well have been.

"Holy shit," he said again, the rest of his vocabulary seeming to have floated out of his left ear. "Why isn't this in a gallery or something? You know, it's easily good enough to be. I've never seen anything like it."

"I don't—"

"Hey, what about the place your gran's having her exhibition at? Surely she could put in a good word for you or something down there? I mean, they're not exactly going to turn something like this down, are they? It's unfrickingbelievable."

"No," I interjected, a little too quickly. Daniel's brow was already creasing, a questioning frown weighing down his features. To him, I suppose, it was simple. I had a talent for drawing, and I should want people to see that. But the pictures meant more than that; their sentimental values ran much deeper. It just wasn't something that translated as easily into any words, let alone spoken ones. "I mean, that'd be way too embarrassing. I just couldn't..."

He looked down at me, his speckled eyes wide and unblinking, at a distance I could paint them from. "You really don't see it, do you?" he asked softly, and I was struck by the odd thought that if his voice were an object, it'd be a warm blanket on a cold day.

My eyes trailed upward to meet his. "See what?"

"How amazing you are." His hands moved to enclose my own at the picture's edges, our skin brushing. We were standing much too close now, so close that one of us really should've moved away, but neither seemed to really want to. "I don't know how you don't see this incredible talent, Flo, but I promise you: it's there."

Even in the circumstances, the corners of my lips were curling, the sincerity of Daniel's expression folding my face into a smile. "Thank you."

"Just as long as you know that. Even if you still refuse to show it to anybody else. Which, I'll add, is a very bad idea. I'm telling you, you could have filthy rich art dealers lining up to get a load of this picture, and you're probably missing out on being a millionaire right now—"

"Daniel," I cut in softly, grinning.

He stopped long enough to blink back at me. "Yeah?"

"Shut up and kiss me, will you?"

For a moment he just stared back at me, evidently taken aback by my newfound boldness. It didn't take him long, though, to regain his composure, obeying my instructions without need for any further encouragement. He leaned in to meet me halfway, and soon enough our lips were once again connected, sending a tingling mixture of nerves and excitement through every inch of me. My legs seemed to weaken, as if the bone had spontaneously turned to jelly, about the same time as my fingers lost all grip on the sheet of paper. It fluttered to the floor beside me as I felt Daniel's hands snaking around my waist, tugging me gently closer, and I found my subconscious hooking my arms around his neck.

I was getting better at this kissing thing, I concluded. At least now it felt considerably easier than the awkward fumble on the beach some weeks ago, which I had to take as a good sign. My lips seemed now capable of matching Daniel's without a great deal of thought, although the action was still enough to reduce me to a jittery mess, with a heart rate similar to that after running a marathon. But there was something about this kiss, right now, that was different; it was considerably more heated, and after a while I found myself debating the merits of risking oxygen deprivation just so I wouldn't have to break away.

The decision was made for me, however, when the sound of the door banging open, swinging with so much force it collided with the wall behind it, jolted us apart like a shot of electricity.

"Oh shit, sorry," a familiar loud voice echoed through the room, sending my already excitable heart into overdrive. "Probably should've knocked."

"Nora?"

Daniel was hastily removing his hands from the small of my back; my arms dropped back to my sides soon afterwards, but it was obvious to even the most naïve onlooker what we'd been doing. Even Summer, cradled in Nora's arms, probably could've made a pretty educated guess.

And anyway, even if mine and Daniel's extreme proximity had been miraculously overlooked, the way my cheeks had burst into flames was enough of a second giveaway to mean we were never going to avoid what happened next.

"Oh. My. God." Nora was already gushing. She barged right across the threshold, deeming herself evidently too important to wait for an invitation. "Wait, are you guys official now?"

"I..."

The sound of my voice prompted her eyes to swivel specifically toward me. "Why didn't you tell me?" she whined, the words already spilling from her lips so fast I could barely keep up. "Come on, I completely missed the opportunity to act like the embarrassing parent. You know, I could reel off a ten-minute-long speech about using protection from the top of my head. You've got to admit that's pretty impressive. Although I suppose I could manage to squeeze that in sometime while I'm here..."

"Nora," I cut her off, wondering if there was a metaphorical fire extinguisher around to cool my burning cheeks. "Please stop talking."

"So how long has this been going on?" Completely ignoring my request, she continued, barely pausing to inhale. My last hope was that she'd run out of oxygen at some point and be forced to stop to breathe. "Because I swear, Flo, if it's been any longer than a week and you haven't even thought to pick up the phone and tell me you've got a ridiculously cute boyfriend, we're going to have some problems."

"Hi, I'm Daniel." Nora's rambling was mercifully cut off by a third voice; I looked over to see he'd taken a step towards her, offering an extended hand to match his expertly charming smile. The conversation didn't seem to have fazed him in the slightest, although I did wonder if part of the reason behind his grin was my sister's choice of adjective. "We met before. At the ice cream shop?"

"Of course!" Her attention diverted from embarrassing me, she was now shaking his hand enthusiastically, while still somehow managing to cradle Summer. "I mean, I'm pretty sure I weigh a lot less now this thing's out of me, but yeah, it's me."

"Summer, right?" he asked, peering down at the baby in her arms.

Distracted by the shock of Nora's arrival, it occurred to me that I'd completely forgotten to even acknowledge the fact she was accompanied by my little niece. She was swaddled in a badly tie-dyed blanket – clearly one of Lenny's bright ideas – and I wondered whether it was my imagination, or if she really had grown about three times her size since the last time I'd seen her. Tufts of dark hair already stuck out from the top of her head, seemingly a paternal donation, but the wide blue eyes that gazed up at her onlookers were unmistakably my sister's.

"Yeah," she said. "Well, Summer Moonbeam, to be precise. We finally decided on a middle name."

I inhaled so sharply I almost choked on air. "Moonbeam?"

"Uh huh." She was nodding fervently, her blonde ponytail bouncing up and down. "It's sweet, isn't it? I was a bit wary of Lenny having free reign on picking the middle name, especially considering some of the suggestions he was coming up with before she was born. But then he mentioned Moonbeam, and I thought it was actually pretty cute. Original, don't you think?"

"Yeah," I murmured, and then, under my breath, "that's one word for it."

But she seemed oblivious to my apprehensiveness, shifting the newborn in her arms and readjusting the brightly-coloured blanket around the edges. Summer, on the other hand, didn't seem happy with the new arrangement; her face was already crinkling in agitation, preparing her lungs for a full-blown crying fit.

And when the noise broke, I couldn't say I'd heard anything like it.

"Oh, sweetie," Nora cooed, though there was absolutely nothing 'sweet' about the noise that was emanating from her daughter's mouth. "Look, let's go find Daddy, okay? He's downstairs somewhere. He's probably got your dummy as well."

With a fleeting call of "We'll have to catch up later, okay?", she was turning to leave as swiftly as she'd arrived. She hugged the screaming Summer closer to her chest as she set off for the staircase, leaving the door wide open in the process of her exit.

"Well," I said, once I was sure she'd gotten far enough away to clear the edge of earshot, "that was arguably one of the most awkward experiences of my life."

"I think she's funny." I felt Daniel's presence behind me, his arms finding their way around my waist and tugging me slightly backwards, my back pressing against his strong torso.

"Yeah, well. You weren't the one she was intent on embarrassing into the next century."

"True." He leaned in, placing his lips so close to my ear that an involuntary shiver of electricity was sent jolting through my body, all the way to the ground. "But it's worth it to see you blush."

I prised myself from his gentle grip, spinning around to face him. "You're just saying that," I said, but a grin I couldn't keep at bay was creeping onto my face. "You get some kind of sick pleasure from my discomfort, don't you?"

"Well... that too."

For a second time, I moved in for a playful shove, but Daniel's brain seemed to be one step ahead of mine. Before my hands could even make contact, I found myself caught up in his arms, held against his front with only the sound of our steady breathing for company. We stared back at each other for what felt like an eternity, suddenly very aware of how close we were.

"You think she's downstairs?" Daniel asked softly, his voice gently edging through the quiet room.

I paused, listening intently for any audible sign of Nora hovering on the landing. "I think we're safe."

The corners of his lips curled into the slightest smile. "Good."

This breathy answer was my cue, it seemed, to let my eyes flutter closed, preparing myself for what was about to happen. With my heart hammering in my chest, I forced the tension from my muscles, and let myself relax into the fact it was happening again.

This time, uninterrupted.

20

CHAPTER 20

Nora was on a mission.

It wasn't a military agenda, nor did the fate of the earth rest on her shoulders, but the look on her face could've fooled anyone. No, as she stood in front of my wardrobe, sifting through the hangers and their respective outfits with lightning speed, Nora was focused on one thing and one thing only: finding me something to wear.

"You didn't even think about it?" she was asking, as her fingers lingered on the fabric of a printed vest top. "Not at all?"

"Well…" I said sheepishly, from my seat on my bed across the room. "I thought since you'd be here, you could pick me out something… you know, like you used to?"

It was partly true. However, another reason distinctly tainted with truth was that I'd been so caught up in spending the past day and a half with Daniel, goofing off by ourselves in order to keep us out of Gram's way, that I hadn't even spared a thought on matters such as what I was going to wear to her long-awaited exhibit. And so, when Nora had bounded into my room late afternoon today, asking if she could borrow that gold necklace of mine she'd always liked, she'd been horrified to find me standing in front of my wardrobe without the faintest clue.

"You know, there's always my jeans," I offered. "It's not like a formal event or anything. They could work."

But all I got by way of response was a dismissive one-handed wave. "We can find something better," she told me. "Something that will make Daniel do a double-take."

"Oh, no." I got to my feet warily, stepping closer to where my older sister was standing. "Is that what all this is about?"

But she was barely listening; moments later, her moving hands froze on a particular hanger. Wasting no time, she unhooked it from the rail, holding it out in front of her so that the airy fabric floated gently in the incoming breeze from the window. "This," she said simply, her eyes skimming up and down her choice. "This is what we're looking for."

It took me a while to even recognise; I couldn't recall the last time I'd worn the dainty cream-coloured dress she was holding out, if at all. Its thick straps and sweetheart neckline flowed into an airy skirt, the entire fabric decorated by a bold floral print.

"I didn't even know I owned that," I said truthfully.

"Well, maybe you should start looking a bit harder," Nora said, tossing me the hanger. "It wouldn't surprise me if you've got a stash of Prada handbags in the back of there you don't even know about."

"That'd be nice," I murmured, but most of my attention was captured by the dress. It did look like it might be sort of flattering, which was something of a miracle when it came to my plain figure. But I was tall enough to get away without heels, and I could always do something with my hair...

"Come on, then, try it on," Nora egged me on. "I want to see how it looks."

I did as she said, wriggling out of my jeans and pulling the dress over my head right there on the spot. And when I'd tugged it over my hips, Nora stepping in to assist with the zipper at the back, I wondered why I heard a sharp intake of breath when I spun around to face her again.

"What?" I asked, frowning. "Why are you looking at me like that?"

"God, Flo," she said. There was a strange expression painted across her features – one I couldn't quite fathom. "You look so pretty."

I went to shrug off the compliment, but the feeling of Nora's hands on my shoulders stopped me, and I realised she was steering me towards the mirror on the wardrobe door. I thought it was a bit strange – I'd only pulled on a dress, after all – but the moment my eyes landed on the reflection that blinked back at me, the reasoning behind Nora's reaction became the slightest bit clearer.

It was flattering, but even more than I'd thought so whilst it was on the hanger. Though I could definitely have lived with another couple of centimetres around the waist to breathe more comfortably, the fit was fine – even giving the illusion that I had slightly more boob than what may have been true. And even though the effect may not have been as striking as it was to Nora, I knew what she was talking about: with soft curls framing my freckled face, five-foot-eight above the ground in a delicate dress, I did feel... pretty.

"Daniel won't be able to take his eyes off you if you wear that," she commented with a smirk.

"Shut up," I told her, but I was smiling too.

There was a slight pause, and the way that Nora continued looking at me, an expression of knowing curling her lips at the edges, indicated that the tone of conversation was becoming more serious. "You really, really like him, don't you?" she asked.

It took a moment for the words to form on my lips; they'd been buzzing around in my head for so long the journey out was a delayed process. "Yeah," I breathed eventually, it almost tasting sweet on my tongue. "I mean, I know I don't really know anything, but... I think it could be it, you know?" I shook my head. "Maybe I'm just crazy. I don't know."

"You're not crazy." Her voice was equally as quiet, the background noise of the room seeming to have dropped into negative figures. "I mean, looking at you two... you rarely see anything like it. The way you seem to get each other. I don't think it's so crazy at all."

"Yeah?"

"Yeah. You know, I never expected for you to be so... at home here in Walden. I was worried you'd have trouble settling in. But seeing you here now... well, it's like it's more your home than our flat ever was."

And though it hadn't really occurred properly to me before, it did then. Nora was right; when I thought of our old apartment, in the smelly block whose stairs seemed to get steeper with every climb, just down the street from the multiplex cinema, it seemed years away. And, if I was back there, I knew I'd be forever yearning for the faint noise of the ocean from my window, the sleepy summer evenings spent effortlessly wandering around the town I'd come to know so well, and the friends like no other.

I was here now. And, finally, I was home.

Gram, it seemed, had turned into some sort of local celebrity overnight.

I had guessed the opening of her exhibition would be big news amongst her circle of friends, but, as evident by the sight of the gallery when I stepped inside that evening, I had underestimated the diameter of said circle. What seemed like the entire population of Walden was crammed into the Picture Perfect gallery – and that was half an hour before the event's official start. The news had spread like wildfire, meaning Nora and I had to elbow our way through a mildly dense throng before we could even get inside the door.

As soon as I felt the blast of air conditioning on my face, indicating we were properly inside the building, the gradual onset of self-consciousness began to work its way in. My legs felt exposed, the length of the dress seeming suddenly much shorter than it had stood in front of my bedroom mirror. And even with a cardigan over my shoulders, the neckline of the dress left too much of my collarbone on show – especially with my hair pulled back into a bun of Nora's handiwork.

I swallowed, forcing myself to conquer the fear that people were looking. They weren't, really. Of course, they were much too taken with the selection of artwork lining the gallery walls to pay me a slither of attention.

And that was the way I wanted it to stay.

"Relax," I heard Nora say beside me. Either she'd read my mind, or just my nervous energy. "You look fine."

It was only then, less conscious of myself, that I really took notice of the array of paintings dotted around the room. Each was surrounded by their own mini-crowd, the hordes of admiring compliments bouncing right off the canvas. I couldn't see the minor details from here, but their main features were clear enough. They were all of Walden; that was the first thing that occurred to me. Each separate image took the form of something I now recognised easily, though wouldn't have been able to place several weeks previously.

But these weren't ordinary representations of the town outside the door; instead, each had been painted with the colours of a palette that had been enhanced in brightness, so the whole collection shone in glorious Technicolor. The effect was striking.

"Wow," I heard Nora breathe beside me, echoing my own thoughts. "She did a good job, didn't she?"

"Yeah." My focus was scattered, eyes unsuccessfully trying to take in every sight at once. "She really did."

Though my first instinct was to get as close as possible to each painting, to take in their every detail like only an artist would, the anticipation of everything seemed to be having an effect on my bladder. There was a toilet sign towards the back of the room, and I leaned in towards Nora.

"I'll be back in a sec," I told her. "Just heading to the loo."

"'Kay. I'll catch up with you in a bit; I've got to see where Lenny's got to with Summer. He's probably having trouble with the car seat again."

With the agreement sealed to find her again as soon as possible – apparently she was dying to meet my new friends, a situation that could really only end in embarrassment on my end – I wove my way through the crowd, heading for the corridor at the back of the room. The ladies' was the first door on the right, and the cool air I was greeted with as I stepped inside was more welcome than I'd expected. The sheer volume of people packed into the gallery's small space was sending the temperature soaring, and I was beginning to wonder why I'd even bothered with a cardigan in the first place.

Once the foremost matter was taken care of, I found myself standing in front of the mirror above the sink, staring blankly at my reflection. It was almost surreal; the girl that blinked back at me, with soft curls pulled together neatly on the top of her head, and muddy brown eyes that seemed brighter than usual, did not register as me. I wasn't used to seeing myself like this: preened and delicate and, for lack of a better word, pretty.

And for once, as I studied my reflection, I found no trace of the broken lines of my past, the slightly mismatching shards that constituted my insides. For three years I'd remained convinced they were visible to everybody, impossible to conceal with even the thickest make-up or the blankest expression, but standing there, I realised this wasn't the case.

I was okay.

My thoughts were interrupted when the sound of the door clattering open echoed throughout the room, startling me slightly. I whirled around to face whoever had joined me, the flicker of recognition only kicking in when I caught sight of the cropped brunette style and kohl-rimmed eyes.

"Collette," I said.

"Oh, Flo! Hi," she responded easily, once my presence had registered. As soon as it did, her eyes dropped to my outfit, preparing to deliver her wordless opinion. Except this time it wasn't so wordless. "Wow. I love the dress. You made an effort, didn't you?"

"Well, I..." I trailed off. "It was just something Nora picked out, really."

"Still. Looks great." She smiled genuinely.

"Thanks. And you too, of course." She looked utterly striking, but was there ever a time when she didn't? Even alone in her room that evening a week ago, when she'd crumpled under the pressure like a piece of paper, the word 'mess' hadn't seemed anywhere near fitting for Collette. It was as if her make-up had run in dainty, symmetrical lines down her face – she wasn't the unattractive, red-nosed crier I was. Tonight, in a flowing maxi dress that grazed the tip of shoes, she was at her usual standard, and I knew she'd receive almost as much attention as Gram's artwork itself.

She shrugged off my compliment, laughing as if I'd made a joke, but there was something in the way she strode over to the adjacent mirror I couldn't help but pick up on. Maybe it was how she seemed to have stood up a little straighter, or that tiny twinkle in her eye, as if injected by a minor dose of confidence that somehow made all the difference.

"You know, your gram's amazing for doing all of this," she said, rummaging inside her handbag until she finally presented a coral-coloured lipstick. "Those paintings out there are crazy good. She's really talented."

"I know."

"I mean," she continued, "it must be good if my parents have turned out. They don't make the effort for just anybody."

I looked back over at her as I washed my hands, wondering if the question on the tip of my tongue lay in safe territory. "Did Beth...?"

Surprisingly, though, Collette didn't even flinch at the mention of her sister's name. It was almost as if she'd blocked her out completely, erecting up a firm mental wall between herself and the girl at the heart of her problems. "She's gone," she answered, quickly and simply. "She left the other evening. Packed her bags and set off on a flight to Italy the same night, taking Angelo with her. She's gone for the rest of the summer. Maybe even indefinitely."

"Oh," I said. I shouldn't have been surprised, really; the behaviour was nothing but typical of Beth. "That's..."

"A relief," Collette finished for me, lowering the lipstick and puckering in the mirror. "Yeah. Things are definitely a lot easier around the house without her there trying to cause trouble. And she'll be having the time of her life over there. Probably planning some extravagant Italian wedding."

"Well, that's not all bad," I told her. "I mean, it's an excuse for a holiday if you get an invitation, right?"

"Yeah." The ghost of a smile was curling the corners of her lips: something I hadn't expected to see whilst the topic of conversation revolved around her older sister. "I think I can probably cope with that."

When Collette and I made our way out of the loos, into the stuffy warmth of the gallery showroom, it didn't take me long to spot our group of friends amongst the crowd. Preoccupied with searching to see if Daniel's head was hidden somewhere amongst Freya's blonde and Erin's startling violet, I almost didn't notice who they happened to be with – or, more specifically, whose baby carrier the four of them were bent over.

"Oh God," I murmured. I was already doing the mental calculation; in exactly how many minutes I'd spent with Collette, how many opportunities would Nora have had to say something to embarrass me? The answer wasn't really something I wanted to think too hard about. "They've already found Nora and Lenny."

"Your sister?" Collette asked, to which I nodded.

By that time, we'd already reached the group, receiving something of an enthusiastic greeting from all six of them. Almost immediately Erin straightened up, pushing a strand of hair from her face and looking over at me.

"Flo," she started. "Why didn't you tell me you had the most adorable niece ever?"

"I... sorry?"

"Hey," she said, only seeming to really notice my appearance at that moment. "Nice dress. If that one's not for my brother, I don't know what is."

"I don't—" I started to protest, but in my peripheral vision I could already see Jay and Scott smirking and knew there was absolutely no point in trying to convince anyone otherwise. "Where is Daniel, anyway?"

"Missing your lover?" Jay started puckering exaggeratedly then, inching in closer toward me. I rolled my eyes, shoving his arm playfully, but all he did was laugh at my meek attempt at retaliation.

Erin shrugged. "Haven't got the foggiest, to be honest. He disappeared off as soon as we got here. I didn't even get a chance to ask him where he was going."

"I saw him talking to your gram earlier," Jay chipped in, "but I didn't get the chance to speak to them, and I haven't seen either of them since."

"Maybe he's just helping her out," Scott suggested. Somehow, he'd end up stood tactfully next to Collette, his eyes sneaking over in her direction every so often. It wasn't exactly the most inconspicuous of moves, but she seemed oblivious anyway.

Suddenly, as if wanting to provide her own input to the discussion, our ears were met by the sound of a mild whimpering emanating from Summer's carrier. This, however, didn't last for more than a few seconds; once that marker had passed, the whining promptly became full-blown, ear-splitting wailing.

Summer's lungs must've been tiny, but boy, could they make some noise.

"You've got the changing bag, haven't you?" Nora was saying to Lenny, shifting the baby carrier hooked onto her forearm. Though her voice was a normal volume, it was a wonder he could hear a word she was saying; Summer's screaming was almost blocking out any other noise within a twenty-metre radius.

"Yeah, it's right here," Lenny said, sliding the bag off his shoulder. "You want me to get it?"

"It's alright, I'll come with you. I think we might need moral sup-port on this one."

And with that, they were off – scuttling in the direction of the loos while Nora shot apologetic looks at the people who were now staring. The noise diminished as increasing distance found its way between them and us, but Summer's cries were in no way hushed even when they'd disappeared around the corner, out of sight.

"Still think she's the most adorable niece ever?" I challenged Erin.

"Well, not ever..." she said, scrunching up her nose. "I mean, top ten... maybe?"

"Yeah, I thought so."

Our conversation was interrupted at that point, cut short by loud screeching feedback from a microphone elsewhere in the room. Following suit and clamping hands over my ears to block out the noise, my attention swivelled with everybody else's to the front of the gallery.

The feedback dried up and I released my hands just as my eyes locked onto Gram, positioned at the front of the room. She stood in front of a large white sheet, covering something mounted on the wall behind that was obviously about to be revealed. Of course, it was the centrepiece of her collection – the thing she'd waited months to unveil to the Walden public. It had been so secretive that even I didn't have the faintest clue what lay under the white fabric, and we'd been living under the same roof since the beginning of the summer.

"Evening, everybody," she began, her voice projected around the room.

She was such a small woman – at least five inches shorter than me, and petite all round – but standing there, at the head of the showcase she'd been working on for months on end, she looked stronger and more confident than I'd ever seen her before. Her tiny frame seemed somehow above the rest of the crowd, even though in reality, a great deal of the guests could pat her on the head with ease. My best guess was that it had something to do with the fact she was surrounded by the peak of her pride and joy, showered with nothing but solid praise, that added inches to her height.

It was remarkable.

"First things first – I want to thank you all for being here tonight. It means so much to me that you've all turned out to show your support, and to see everything come together like this... well, it's really something."

A ripple of assent went through the attentive crowd, filling a pause before Gram started speaking again.

"Now, you've probably all worked out that the main theme of my collection is Walden-on-Sea. This very town has been my home for over ten years now, and I have to say this: in that time, it's become my favourite place in the world. There's just this whole community of people who are among the most welcoming I've ever met, and I've never felt so at home anywhere else. So much so that when I pick up a paintbrush, I can't imagine myself capturing anything in paint and canvas other than this town.

"See, I know you're all expecting something spectacular under this sheet. On that one, I won't disappoint. It's just… well, it's not what you think. Put it that way."

"What is she talking about?" Erin leaned in to murmur, as a wave of similar questioning swept through various points of the gallery audience. "Do you know what's under there?"

"No clue," I whispered back. "The whole thing's been top secret business."

"I'll make a confession – on this one, I had a bit of help. And so, to help me with this whole 'grand unveiling' business," Gram continued, "I've enlisted some help. Daniel?"

It was then that the guy in question stepped forward, approaching the covered spectacle and smiling as he did so. He looked as he always did; there was that half-smile always curling his upper lip, the hair that was never quite cooperative enough to stay put in a neat style, the hazel eyes that seemed bright underneath the gallery spotlights. He seemed to be scanning the crowd, looking for someone in particular.

It didn't click that it was me until his gaze locked on my own, and he shot me a heart-melting grin that proved much more difficult to gather the composure to return.

"There's something different about this one. In fact, technically, you could say that it's not even a part of this collection at all. But to me, it is. Because while this particular piece may not seem like it fits in alongside all the others, it's perhaps the most important one of all."

What was going on? I wasn't able to make it out. The words that spilled from Gram's moving lips were cryptic; I was sure I couldn't have been the only one in the room lacking the faintest hint as to what she was talking about. Even in Daniel's gaze I could spot a look of knowing, something above the confusion of the rest of the audience, that I couldn't put my finger on. All I could do was smile back at him in response and hope things were about to become clearer.

"At the start of the summer, my granddaughter, Flo, came to live with me. See, at first, she may not have thought that Walden was the place for her. I could tell that. But in the short time that she's been here, I've watched her grow to love the place. And that's something that makes me happier than you could ever imagine.

"So, while I was working on this collection, I couldn't help thinking it felt... incomplete. There was something missing, even if I couldn't quite put my finger on it. It took me longer than it should've to figure out – I even had to have a little bit of help, and that's where Daniel here comes in. Without him, I don't think I would've even come up with this at all. But I came to realise that my vision of Walden-on-Sea had changed. After this summer, I can't imagine the place without Flo – so what would a collection of it be if it didn't contain at least an essence of her?"

By now, everybody was looking at me; that much I could figure out from the stone-cold effect their gazes were having, even if I refused to look directly back myself. My eyes remained glued to the front of the room, flickering between Gram and Daniel with some sort of painful regularity. But I couldn't help myself: suddenly the pieces of the puzzle were coming together, aligning themselves automatically into shapes that would allow them all to fit. I could see them about to click into place, and all I could do was pray desperately that my inkling was mistaken. There had to be one tiny fault, something that would stop it all coming together in the way it looked like it was going to.

"And so, I present to you the final piece of the collection," Gram said. She gestured towards Daniel, who shot me one last smile before beginning to pull away the sheet from what it was concealing. "The final touch. The essence of Flo."

And then it happened.

The sinking dread that had coursed through my veins with Gram's every word moulded into one in that moment – the resultant effect was a storming wave of horror that swept over me with such force I almost stumbled physically backwards. It was like the action of removing the sheet happened in ultra-slow motion; I could see every miniscule shift of fabric, all coming together in a movement that left me completely and utterly exposed.

There they were: the angels, right in front of me.

Blown up on a canvas twice their original size, they were in plain sight for everybody to see. There was nothing between them and us – nothing to stop anyone from picking up on each soft brunette curl of the female's locks, nothing to stop people noticing the individual freckles on the male's nose and the care with which they'd been painted. Every little detail was there, replicated perfectly on their journey from my head to huge, public canvas.

I couldn't breathe.

My lungs refused to fill up with air; my chest refused to go through the motions to get the air there in the first place. I was drowning, somehow drowning, stood in the middle of a room that contained not a trace of water.

This couldn't be happening. How could this be happening? Those angels were supposed to be under my bed, safely shielded from the prying eyes of anybody but me. But somehow – somehow – they'd ended up beneath the eyes of almost everybody in Walden, uncovered and ultimately exposed. I could feel the tangible scrutiny of the dozens of pairs of eyes all around me, tainting the image, twisting it into something that wasn't meant to be. The angels were morphing right before me, and for the first time, I had no control over it.

I wasn't sure I even had control over my thoughts anymore.

"Holy crap." The words were whispered from somewhere beside me; I couldn't bring myself to distinguish who exactly the voice belonged to. "That's amazing."

But I couldn't hear it. The words were audible, but they had no meaning; my brain refused to process them into a form I could understand. The only thing I could think over the roaring in my ears was that I needed to get out. I needed to be out of there, and I needed it with such stinging desperation that it felt as if my life depended on it.

I spun on my heel and began shoving my way through the crowd, unconcerned by the trivial matters of who exactly I was pushing. The stares of the crowd were burning holes into my back, my front, every single inch of me, but all that mattered was putting one foot in front of the other and making my way towards the gallery's exit. Those double doors were the only things that stood between overwhelming terror and a chance at relief. I hadn't wanted something so desperately in years.

Voices were shouting my name somewhere behind me; perhaps the most prominent was the male's I recognised even over the commotion as belonging to Daniel. By now, I was outside, the feeling of cold air on my skin a total shock to the senses. I barely made it a few steps before I wobbled, my emotional control faltering the same time as my balance did.

The tears were already streaming down my face when I felt the hand on my shoulder, forcing me to turn around. Through a blurred haze of tears, I could make out the fragmented features of Daniel's face, looking down at me with the utmost confusion and concern.

"Flo," he began, but the sound of my name spoken by his voice was sufficient to shock me back to reality.

His touch was repulsive, and I recoiled, a throbbing in my head now accompanying the tears. "No," I snapped. "Get away from me."

"Flo, listen—"

"No!" I yelled, much too loudly. "For God's sake, Daniel, just leave me alone!"

And this time, even I heard the finality in my tone.

21

CHAPTER 21

My first instinct was to run away; in a fight-or-flight situation, the latter was always the safest option. At least that was the way it'd been for me.

Like when I was in primary school, on the first day back after the summer holidays. My class was given the task to draw a picture of My Summer: relatively simple, designed to ease us back into addition and fractions. While the other kids scrawled messily in crayon, depicting basic scenes of sandcastles and ice creams in five minutes so they could get to playtime early, I poured my seven-year-old heart and soul into that picture. The memory was as vivid as if it had happened yesterday. The sloping yellow sands, choppy waves, the way the clouds weren't just blobs in the sky but wispy strips blending into blue: they were all permanently imprinted in my brain. I'd shone with pride the moment the teacher had pronounced it best in the class, pinning it on the classroom wall for everybody to see.

No one else had been bothered. It was only Joey Granger who was jealous, and he was the sole reason I turned up to school the following day to find my pride and joy scribbled all over in thick, black crayon, tarnished forever.

When the teacher had asked me if I knew what happened, I ached to dob him in. But Joey was the toughest kid in our class, with eyes that held permanent threats. He could pound me into a pulp on the playground, and that terrified me into obeying his every silent order. So instead of passing the blame, I'd mumbled something about not seeing anything and ran away at the first opportunity.

That night, I went home and cried, but at least I'd avoided a beating from Joey.

The situation I found myself in now, I thought, was no exception. Yet somehow, standing on the deserted Walden seafront in an angry face-off with Daniel, I found myself frozen to the spot, rendered completely incapable of movement. My brain was too jumbled to focus on anything but the raw pain pulsing through my veins, slicing my heart into sharp, wounded segments. I wanted to run, to put as much distance as I could between myself and the source of my discomfort, but I'd momentarily forgotten how to move my limbs.

Helpless.

The broken features of my teary vision swam before my eyes, but the contours of Daniel's face remained clear.

He took a single step forward; the movement was enough to shock me into stumbling backward, an automatic impulse to keep a constant space between us. There was something he wanted to say; I could see the words he held back reflected in his eyes. Those eyes, whose hazel colour swum amongst hurt and misunderstanding, blinking back at me with a sincerity that almost melted a fraction of my anger.

Almost.

"Flo," he coaxed, gentle. His tone was tiptoeing towards me slowly, approaching as if I were a wild animal he didn't want to startle. "What's the matter?"

But the question sent a fresh jolt of irritation through me, reigniting whatever his eyes had dissipated.

"What's the matter? What's the matter?" I yelled, much louder than necessary. "What do you think is the matter, Daniel? What the hell was that?"

"It..." he trailed off, disarmed by my anger. "I thought you'd be happy when you found out."

"Happy?"

An overwhelming urge was rising through me, folding in on itself and pressing against my throat. I wanted to scream at the top of my lungs – or maybe it'd be more satisfying to fall to my knees and sob. However, despite my trembling legs, I didn't do either, staring instead into the melting eyes of the boy opposite me.

"Yeah," he whispered. "I mean, I know that you'd never have had the confidence to do anything like that yourself, and I don't know... I thought you'd be happy once your incredible talent was recognised."

"Happy?" I repeated again, the word foreign on my tongue. "How can you...? I mean, how could I... I thought..." I was stumbling over myself now, the message malfunctioning somewhere on its journey from my head to the bitter evening air. "I thought you understood."

This shouldn't be happening. Not here. Not now. Not on the street I'd walked up and down countless times, on so many occasions that even the intricate cracks of the pavement were familiar to me. Not on the night of Gram's exhibition, when everything was meant to be about her.

I shouldn't have been crying, but I was way past the stage of being in control of my emotions.

"You, of all people, should've known. You've been through this. I thought we got each other, or at least that's what you said, wasn't it?"

The memory, once a gateway to feelings of such elation: it was now cruel to replay. Evidently, it was having a similar effect on Daniel; his mouth kept opening and closing, struggling to decide upon a suitable response to my cutting tone. But did anything count as suitable here? Could anything be right when everything had gone so, so wrong?

"And now that freaking picture's on display for the whole of Walden to see, I mean—"

"What are you talking about? It was just a picture, Flo."

"They were my parents!"

The ensuing silence was deafening. My throat felt raw and exposed as the words finally dislodged themselves, tunnelling out into the salty air. I didn't know why I'd felt the compulsion to shout it so loudly, but it had certainly put a stop to the conversation. Daniel's features were twisted with despair and painful realisation, ceasing all hope of speech. Even the waves, metres down from us on the beach, seemed spontaneously quieter, shrinking in volume to make room for the aftermath of my colossal confession.

There'd been no way for Daniel to know, of course. Anybody who hadn't known my mum and dad personally wouldn't have had any means to recognise the personal features of each figure. Even for Gram, who had known them, the identities weren't obvious; it was only when you got really close, close enough to take in each glowing feature aligned carefully on the angels' faces, that you could really latch onto their symbolic meaning.

To Daniel, they'd just been two faceless people: figments of a drawing from which only the quality of the work had been picked up on. He'd stumbled across it accidentally, been impressed, and formed one half of the heads that came together on the idea for Gram's final showcase piece.

But the pair were convinced I was merely embarrassed by my talent; they had no idea that the reservations about what transferred from my pencil to the page ran much, much deeper.

"Flo…" His mouth was open, frozen in its small o shape. "I didn't know."

"It doesn't matter." He took another step forward, but I mirrored his movement in reverse, as if his presence had a repulsive effect of its own. A humourless smile creased my crumpled expression. "It's done now, isn't it? It's not like it matters."

I wasn't fooling anyone. It did matter, and the way the foundations of my world were crumbling beneath me was adequate proof.

Maybe to other people it wouldn't be such a big deal. Maybe to people who didn't pour their innermost secrets into pencil strokes on paper. Maybe to people who hadn't lost their parents to someone else's stupid, drunk mistake three years ago.

It just so happened I wasn't one of those people.

"Flo, listen." By now, Daniel's voice was verging on desperation. "I've made a massive mistake. Probably one of the biggest mistakes of my life. We both know that. I never should have gone ahead and done this without your permission. I just thought… Well, I don't know what I thought. But you have to understand that I'm so, so sorry. Please. You have to understand."

"No," I said. "I don't."

The wind had picked up, nipping at my bare skin with a biting chill that brought me out in goose-bumps. I shivered, the broken shards of my insides feeling like ice.

"I made a huge mistake."

"Yes. You did." My eyes fluttered shut, willing the impeding wave of tears to stay back for just a little while longer. "But there are some mistakes that can't be undone."

I turned to leave, wetness already brimming between my eyelids, but only managed a few steps before I felt a hard encircle my arm. The gesture only angered me further, and I snatched myself away, recoiling from the effect of the skin-to-skin contact. Where it had previously sent my nerves into a tingling frenzy, I now wanted nothing more than to shrink away, repulsed by the thought of somebody that could misunderstand me to such an extent.

"Don't touch me," I snapped.

"Please don't do this."

"Don't do what?" More fuel was thrown in the fire, the biting tone back in my voice. "You want me to forgive you on the spot and go back in there, acting like nothing happened? Is that what you want?"

"I just—"

"That picture was the closest thing I had to my parents," I cut him off viciously. "Do you even understand that? See, I thought you did, but then you go and do something like this..."

"It's—"

"This isn't something you can just take back. All those people in there have seen it now, and that's not something you can undo. You know, that was the first painting of my mum and dad I'd done since they died. The first time I had the courage to draw their faces again.

It was one of the most personal and private things I'd ever created, and now it's on display to the public."

"I know," Daniel said, his voice wavering. "I know that now, and I'm so, so sorry."

"Yeah, well," I cut in, cracking on the second syllable, "there are some things that sorry doesn't make up for."

I turned around at that point, my steps slow and shaky but in the right direction. I wasn't looking at Daniel, but I didn't need to be to see his lost, hopeless expression swimming in front of my eyes.

When Gram's cul-de-sac came into view an eternity later, my eyes were no drier than they had been when I'd set off. The sobs still furiously racked my body, only intensifying every time my mind wandered back to what had happened with Daniel. The subsequent despair and panic left me shaking; it was a wonder I was able to hold my hand still long enough to shove the key into the front door.

Once safely inside the eerie stillness of the cottage, I closed the door and sunk back against it, overcome by a strange feeling of relief. Maybe it was the knowledge that I was finally behind closed doors, shielded from the prying eyes of the rest of Walden by several layers of brick and wall plaster. It didn't matter that I'd heard nothing but awestruck comments in my swift departure from the gallery; no matter how wonderful anybody thought the painting was, it carried with it the feeling that the innermost regions of my head were under a beaming spotlight, and that would never be a comfortable one.

The relief, however, was incredibly short-lived. Seconds later it paled in comparison to the soul-crushing agony that dominated when it occurred to me once again exactly what had just happened. Not only had my worst fears become a horrible, twisted reality, it was the guy I'd thought could've been the one that was responsible.

A huge, gaping hole now sat between Daniel and I, and I was teetering on the very edge, the unconsolidated rocks crumbling beneath my feet. It was only a matter of time before I was swallowed whole myself.

It took all of my energy to drag my heavy limbs up the stairs, but I managed it eventually. Once confined by the four walls that made up my bedroom, I collapsed face-first onto the bed, burying my face in the thick fabric of the duvet and succumbing once more to the ferocity of my sobbing.

I seemed to have left all perception of time back at the gallery; I had no idea how long I stayed there, motionless, before the sound of keys jangling in the front door found its way up the stairs.

Footsteps shuffling on linoleum. The sound of a door closing. My name being called.

It was Nora, her concerned version of my name bouncing off the mismatching furnishings to reach me. The sound of her boots on the staircase followed shortly afterward, their pace slowing noticeably once they got to the door of my room. Tentatively, she pushed it open; I heard the long, slow creak louder than anything else.

She didn't say a word for what felt like a long time, not until I felt the mattress sink under her weight.

"Flo." Her tone was gentle, understanding. Above all, familiar.

But I didn't move. The tears were still seeping onto the duvet beneath my face, blackening its fabric with watered-down mascara. Nora's hand moved to my arm. "Please, Flo. Talk to me."

Something hit me then. I couldn't be sure of exactly what it was, nor why it occurred to me right at that moment, but suddenly the only thing I could think about was how much I missed my sister and her safe, perpetual reassurance. I wanted nothing more than to relive the feeling of being enveloped in Nora's arms, having her stroke my hair, being told by her soothing gentle voice that everything was going to be okay. She'd been the mum I hadn't had for the past three years, and right then, I realised I needed her more than ever.

"Oh, sweetie." She pulled me into her arms the moment I sat up, her free hand moving to rub circles on my back. The sobbing intensified then; I was overcome by a feeling of weakness that being cradled in my sister's arms had induced.

I'd been kidding myself when I thought I could manage. How on earth could I ever have thought I'd be okay without Nora?

I might've thought I'd found someone like her. Someone who could fill the gap that our separation had left. But tonight had only proved me wrong, and now I realised it: the only thing that was ever going to stay constant in my life was her. Nothing else could be relied upon.

It was all as unstable as a sandcastle; it could fool you into thinking that it was strong, especially in that moment when it emerges looking deceivably perfect. It could look like the best sandcastle in the world, cemented together and indestructible. But in reality, all it takes is a gust of wind just a fraction too strong. Someone's footsteps just a little too close. The tiniest change can send it crumbling.

"Everything's all wrong," I sobbed. She was rocking me back and forth now: slow, soothing motions designed for the comfort of a small child. "Everything."

"Shh." She pulled me even tighter, so close that I was inhaling nothing but her sweet floral perfume. "It's just been a rough night, that's all."

"I thought it was all okay. But it's not. Nothing's okay."

"I know it hurts, sweetie." Her hand moved up to my head, high enough to stroke her fingers through my hair, the constant motion extracting some of the tension from my muscles. "I know it does. It was Mum and Dad, wasn't it? I recognised them the moment I saw it."

"Everyone saw it."

"I know they did, Flo, but really, it's not what you think. Nobody saw what it really meant. All they could see was your talent."

"It doesn't matter. They still... I just can't..."

"Flo..."

"I thought he was it," I forced out, squeezing my eyes together in an unsuccessful attempt to keep the tears at bay. Without even saying Daniel's name, the stinging hopelessness was there: the constant, plaguing thought that things would never be the same between us again. "I thought I'd really found what I was looking for. But then something like this had to go and happen..."

"It's okay."

"Why do things like this always have to happen to me? What have I done to deserve this?"

"Nothing. You've done nothing wrong, you hear me? I know it seems bad right now, but you have to remember that it's just been a bit of a rough night. Everything seems worse right now while you're all worked up. Once you lie down, get some sleep, it won't feel as bad. I promise you, honey. Just try to calm down and sleep."

"I can't." At least not with such buzzing going on in my head, the despair ricocheting right off the insides of my skull. "I can't."

"It's going to be okay," she repeated. The words had become a mantra; I'd heard them countless times before. So much so that I wouldn't have been surprised if they were permanently imprinted somewhere inside my head. "It's what I always say, isn't it? I said it all those times before. And it was. It all turned out okay. We got through it. And you'll get through this too; I've got no doubt about that one."

"How can you know?" I whispered.

"I just do," she answered simply, wiping away a stray tear from my cheek with her thumb. "You know, you're so strong. I'm beginning to wonder if there's anything you can't handle."

I knew she was only really saying it to make me feel better. Still, there was no denying that her words offered comfort of some sort, lifting my spirits a fraction of a centimetre. At any rate, the tears had dried up when Nora's grip finally loosened from around me, which I had to take as a good sign. I sat motionless on the bed while she dabbed at my face with a make-up wipe, removing all traces of the salty tears that had sent everything awry. I obeyed when she handed me my toothbrush, sat still while she brushed my curls out of their tight bun. By the time she retrieved my pyjamas from the foot of the bed, I was in a state of mind to dress myself, and there was an almost tangible sense of relief at the feeling of my familiar, soft nightie against my skin.

"You're going to be okay, Flo," Nora repeated again. I'd moved into bed now, cocooned in the sheets. She lay beside me, our arms wrapped around each other in a way we hadn't needed for months. "I promise."

And in that moment, I knew it: while I might not have had much else, I'd always have the older sister I needed so desperately. I'd never completely outgrow her reassurance; there'd always be points when she was the only person I could turn to. Really, though, it was inevitable after going through what we had. The resulting bond was stronger than anything else.

No matter where either of us ended up, there'd always be an invisible thread tying us together, keeping us tethered to home. That much, I could count on.

22

CHAPTER 22

I stumbled through the next few days in a state of insentient numbness.

It was a peculiar feeling: not like anything I'd ever experienced before. Usually, in situations of such hopelessness, I bared the brunt of my emotions for days on end, the stinging plague of thoughts a mental torture. It had never happened quite like this before. I'd never been left in such a strange state of lethargy, finding it difficult to work up the energy to care about what was going on around me. Instead of sobbing until my eyes were raw, as I had done on the first evening, I found myself curled up in bed for hours and hours, my attention span too short to occupy myself for any length of time. The only trips I made out of my room were essential.

Even Nora's departure hadn't affected me as badly as I thought it would. I'd been upset, of course, that my main source of comfort was relocating one hundred and fifty miles away yet again, but the event of her packing up her belongings and setting back off for London was much less distressing than I'd anticipated.

"It's going to be okay, Flo," she'd said, as Lenny piled their suitcases into the boot of the waiting taxi. "This'll all blow over, and everything will turn out fine."

The smile I managed as she pressed her lips to my forehead was weak; even her heavy perfume failed to evoke a significant emotion from the depths of my head.

The thing was, it would've been nice to fool myself into believing my sister's reassurances, but I just couldn't bring myself to do it anymore. What had gone down the night of Gram's exhibition was not something that could just 'blow over', as much as I wanted to believe it. Daniel and I together, let alone as we had been, was now nothing more than a faraway memory, as well as an unattainable future.

My relationship with Gram was only marginally better; while the words we exchanged were civil, they were undeniably limited – there had been no more pressing matters to discuss than "Dinner will be ready around six, is that okay?", and my answers remained clipped. She was aware of what a tragic mistake she'd made, the glaze of guilt visible in her eyes every time she looked in my direction. Still, she seemed to sense that I was not in a place to accept apologies – and at least that way, it saved both of us from the awkwardness of trying to talk something out that ran much too deep.

Here I was, suddenly closing in on the three day marker of mooching aimlessly around my room, trapped in my weary, unfeeling state of mind. It had been much too long since I'd endured actual social interaction – or, at least, social interaction that was more than stilted questions and pauses tinged with heartache, of which I could gain my fair share just by walking downstairs.

But then again, no way of spending the past three days could've prepared me for the moment, several afternoons later, that the tornado otherwise known as Erin Bolton came barging into my room uninvited.

When the door swung open with enough force to send it bouncing off the wall, I sat up in bed like a shot.

"There you are!" she declared, her voice an echoing foghorn in the quiet room. "Jesus Christ, I was beginning to wonder if you'd packed your bags and fled the country."

"Erin," I started, still in a daze, "how on earth did you get in here?"

"Your gran let me in, stupid. And I don't blame her! I imagine she's worried about you holed up in your bedroom like this, refusing to speak to anybody. What's the deal with that, anyway? Are you planning on becoming a hermit, or something?"

I groaned, letting my head fall back onto the pillow. "I don't want to see anybody."

"Well, yeah, I gathered that one from the way you haven't gotten out of bed for three days," Erin stated. She approached the bed, staring disapprovingly down at my curled-up form. "This isn't still about what happened at the gallery the other night, is it?"

"I don't want to talk about it."

"Okay, fine. I never said we had to." She shrugged dismissively. "That's not why I came here, anyway."

"It's not?"

"Nope. The real reason I came up here was to make sure you drag yourself out of bed for the bonfire party tonight."

The first few moments left me failing to grasp what she was talking about. A vague recollection had been triggered in my head, but it was only something that had been mentioned fleetingly somewhere over the course of the summer. Of course, at the time, I'd been much too caught up in the present to dwell on it, reassured by the notion that the rest of the summer seemed to stretch out forever in front of us.

And yet somehow, it had caught up with us. Sneaking around behind our back until we were hit by the realisation that we had less than a week left. After that, it'd be over. Nothing but a memory.

"The what?"

"The bonfire party," she repeated. "It's a kind of tradition we have here – we have it every year, down on the beach. An end-of-summer, can't-believe-it's-almost-September type thing. You have to be there. It's just a rule."

"Well, I won't be." I pulled the duvet closer towards my face, burying my nose in its thick fabric. The sensation offered more than just warmth; I felt infinitely less exposed, shielded from Erin's disapproving expression. "Sorry. You guys will have fun without me."

"Oh, no. You don't get out that easy."

I should've known she wouldn't let me off that easily. This time, she went much further, taking hold of the edges of the cover and tugging it right off the bed. It landed in a crumpled heap at her feet, her towering form standing triumphantly before it.

"Erin."

"Flo."

"Erin."

"Flo."

"Seriously," I said, pulling my knees up to my chest on the now bare mattress. "I'm not going. Just go to the party and enjoy yourself. You're wasting your time here."

But I hadn't even got halfway through my sentence before she started shaking her head. "Uh uh. You're going, Flo, even if I have to dress you myself and drag you kicking and screaming down to the beach."

It was intended to be a figure of speech, but this was Erin, and I had a feeling I should've been taking her threat a lot more literally.

She stepped even closer, sinking down onto the mattress beside me, the old springs creaking slightly under the weight of both of us. "Listen. I don't know exactly what went down between you and Daniel. That's your business. But this bonfire's a big deal to us. We do it every year, and everyone has to be there. It just wouldn't be the same if you weren't."

"I don't want to."

"No, you don't want to see Daniel," she corrected me. "And trust me on this one, Flo: you don't need to be worried about that. He's been moping around the house just as much as you – except he's probably even worse. You should've seen him down at the shop. He could barely scoop ice cream. I'd say it was pathetic, but... well, it obviously hit you two pretty hard. I can't really judge."

"I just..." I could feel myself struggling to find the right words. "I just couldn't believe he'd do something like that."

"Well, yeah. In hindsight, it was a pretty dick-ish move on his part. At least, it was to go ahead and do that without even talking to you about it first. But the thing is, Flo... he knows how badly he's screwed up. Trust me on that one. He can't stop beating himself up about it."

I didn't really know what to make of it. While the knowledge seemed to have struck a chord of sympathy in a small portion of my heart, the other refused to release its tight hold on the anger and betrayal that coursed through me with every beat. It wouldn't let me forget the moment of horror when that sheet was pulled back: the feeling of ensuing terror once I realised everything had gone so terribly wrong.

What was I doing, anyway? Why was I even allowing myself to feel the tiniest slither of compassion towards the guy that had caused all this in the first place? Without the decisions that Daniel had made, the situation would be entirely different; we'd still be together, I wouldn't be here right now, having this argument with Erin, and the groundbreaking earthquake that had shattered our very foundations would never have occurred.

It was because of him. I couldn't let myself forget that.

"I know you're upset," Erin continued, "but this party is exactly what you need. Staying cooped up in your bedroom until school starts isn't going to solve anything; it'll just make everything worse."

She was talking sense. I knew that much, but that didn't make it any easier to stomach the thought of attending a beach party with Daniel himself.

She was right, though.

"Okay," I said eventually. "Okay, okay."

The smile that lit up her features was luminously genuine; I could almost feel her happiness seeping in, ebbing away at my aura of hopelessness. It was strange, but suddenly I found myself struck by the impossible urge to reach out and snatch back what had been shifted. An almost attachment seemed to have formed between myself and that familiar way of thinking; in the past few days, the lines that marked the end of me and the start of my wallowing air of self-pity had become increasingly difficult to distinguish.

I couldn't determine whether it was a relief or a discomfort to have it slowly dissipating before my eyes.

"See, I knew I could make you see sense," she told me, grinning. Then, it began to fade, her expression falling into one more serious. "Look, don't worry about my brother, okay? He's just as hung up as you on this whole mess, but you two will work something out eventually. I know you will," she added, when I went to interject. "But it won't just be the two of you there. We're all going. And you'll have fun, I promise."

It was only a pause later, a sudden afterthought, that she added, "Hey, I know it's no consolation, but, well... I feel like I should tell you. Honestly, that painting was the best thing I'd ever seen in that gallery."

"No, it isn't any consolation," I told her. "But thank you."

Erin and I were about halfway between the Walden seafront and the towering cliff at the cove's entrance when the inevitable wave of nauseating nervousness hit.

It was only then that the realisation properly hit home – the realisation that I was making a huge mistake. What was I thinking, getting myself into a situation like this? Launching myself right into the firing line of an awkward face-off with Daniel, which was the one thing I'd spent the past few days trying desperately to avoid?

And yet I found myself almost there, minutes away from edging past the cliff outcrop and into the cove where it had all started.

"What am I doing?" I asked aloud, stopping in my tracks.

Erin came to an abrupt halt a few steps in front of me, pivoting to shoot me a look. "You're coming with me to the bonfire party. Have you been unconscious for the past few hours or something?"

"I can't do this," I told her, shaking my head fervently. "I can't. Do you realise how awkward this is going to be? I don't know why I thought it could ever be a good idea."

Suddenly, she'd taken two steps towards me, her hands clamping down on my shoulders. I wobbled on the spot, my balance mysteriously faltering, before realising she was physically shaking me.

"Listen to me," she commanded, her voice strong and calm: exactly what I needed. "You're coming with me to this party, you're going to enjoy yourself, and above all, you're going to stop giving a shit about what my brother will be doing. Understand me?"

The words seemed impossible, yet in Erin's confident tone, not so much.

"Okay," I breathed eventually. "Okay, okay, okay."

It would have to be done sooner or later, I knew. The act of avoiding Daniel completely couldn't be kept up forever, especially in a town as miniscule as Walden. Eventually, I'd have to swallow my reservations and face him for the first time since the argument. It just so happened that, thanks to Erin, that eventually had come a lot sooner than I'd anticipated.

I forced my feet to move, each step a rigorous and exhausting motion commanded individually by my conscious mind. We trekked slowly over the rounded pebbles of Walden beach, towards the chalky cliff that, to any other person, looked like it marked the end of the territory. But, of course, we were more clued up on the geography of the place, familiar enough to know that Walden concealed its own secrets. As we ducked past the jagged edge, emerging a few seconds later on the other side, I realised there was no going back.

The cove was unchanged from the night of our previous visit; the memory was so vivid I wouldn't have been surprised if it was engraved on the inside of my skull. Coarse sandy grains curved with the shape of the cliff, eventually giving way to the frothy waves that crept up the irregularities of the shingle. But this time it was bathed in the last rays of sunshine, illuminated by a lazy orange glow instead of silver-edged moonlight.

Another difference was that the place harboured considerably less peace than it had done before. Several metres up from the tide mark sat a huge bonfire, blazing healthily, its flames seeming eerily close to singeing the sky itself. Positioned in a semi-circle around it were several large logs, serving as seats for the figures milling around in the area. As we approached, the steady, thumping bass of a dance tune originating from a portable sound system set down on the sand increased in volume.

My legs were becoming exponentially more jelly-like with every step, but I pushed myself to continue onward, somewhat reassured by the bubble of Erin's usual confidence at my side. Moments later, we were noticed by one of the tallest of the figures, which later turned out to be Jay. He came bounding towards us, enthusiasm radiating his mere presence.

"Hi!" he greeted us. His hair was as spiky as ever, raked through with what had to be an extra dollop of gel. I wondered momentarily if I was the only one who experienced the urge to physically rinse out his hair myself whilst I was around him, before my attention refocused on the primary matter. Which was, of course, my crippling anxiety about the prospect of the evening ahead. "You made it!"

"Told you I'd get her here, didn't I?" Erin said, smirking triumphantly. "You know I always deliver."

"Should've believed you on that one," Jay said. He paused, his eyes dropping for the shortest of moments to Erin's overall appearance. "Hey, you look great."

In the periphery of my vision, I could've sworn I noticed a slight pink tinge forming on Erin's cheeks: a stark contrast against the vibrance of her hair. "Thanks," she replied, her tone remarkably level, considering. "You don't look so bad yourself. Although jeez, have you broken out an extra bucket of gel for that hairstyle tonight?"

"Hey! You don't insult my hair, and I don't insult yours. I thought we had a deal."

"Fat chance. Life wouldn't be worth living if I didn't get to make a comment about it every time I saw you."

"Alright, alright," he said, but he was grinning. It took a great deal of self-restraint to hold back from yelling "Get it over with and snog already!", forcing the both of their heads together until my demand was met. However, I was soon distracted once more by the uncomfortable lurch of my heart once Jay hooked his thumb behind him, gesturing to the rest of the party. "Anyway, come on. We're just getting started here."

As we drew closer to the bonfire, more of the group came into view; Collette was perched on one of the logs, Scott beside her. I could tell he was trying hard to play it cool, but his attempt was rather unsuccessful; every time there was a break in the conversation, giving him opportunity to respond, he was reduced to a flustered mess. Even from here I could see the red flush across his face.

And then, of course, he was there. In an ideal world, I would have spared barely a fraction of my attention on the guy sat several spaces away from the others, staring emptily into the fire. But this was situation was far from ideal, and I found it difficult to tear myself away. His hair was dishevelled, the waves even more unruly than usual, his overall air tired and weary. There was a can in his hand, and every so often he'd take a sip, but even from my position I could tell he was hardly present.

That was, of course, until he looked up.

Our eyes met from numerous paces away, locking onto each other's with startling abruptness. It seemed sickeningly cliché, but in that moment I was struck by the sensation that our entire surroundings had ceased to exist, leaving just the both of us staring at each other in the middle of a painfully empty space. I could feel my heart pounding in my chest, its beats erratically frantic, my head reeling in a state of equal frenzy.

And then, suddenly, everybody else was back. They were there again, along with the cove, the hazy orange sky, the wisps of smoke from the bonfire forcing their way down my throat.

In that moment, the awkwardness hit like a slap in the face.

I could feel it, and so could everyone else.

After what felt like several years, an acceptable level of self-control was attained to allow myself to pull my eyes away, forcing my rigid legs to let me take a seat on the furthest log. My movement seemed to alleviate a significant chunk of the tension, and I breathed a silent sigh of relief as Erin plonked herself down beside me.

Daniel was still upset; anybody with eyes could see that well enough. Though his desperation for forgiveness seemed to be much less severe, I could tell the longer term feelings had buried themselves somewhere in the subsurface. His eyes, speckled with uneven colour and unidentifiable emotion, gave too much away.

I expected that, of course. Erin had warned me that Daniel had spent much of the last few days in the same way that I had done. But his wallowing in regret didn't justify his actions, nor did it erase them by any means. The damage was done, and this unspoken truth was known amongst all of us.

"Jesus, I can't believe we're here already," Collette said, her level tone shattering the silence that had descended. "The end of summer party. Has it really been all that time?"

"Tell me about it," Erin chipped in. "I don't even want to think about the fact that we'll be back at school next week."

Her statement predictably sent multiple resounding groans through the rest of the group; the mention of school was obviously a sore subject. Perhaps it was only Daniel and I that remained quiet, our thoughts too complicated to be included with the mass reaction of the group.

"Hey, that's not the attitude for the annual bonfire party, and you know it," Jay scolded. "This is a tribute to the summer gone. It's not quite over yet."

"A pretty good one, you know."

"One of the best."

"And Flo's first summer here."

The voice came as such a shock that all our heads seemed to whip round at the exact same moment. Milliseconds later, Daniel found himself under the scrutiny of six pairs of eyes, and I watched him shrink under their intensity. It was difficult to tell whether he regretted speaking up.

"Yeah," Jay agreed, more quietly. "It's been one hell of a ride. But you know, Flo, I think we can officially call you one of us now."

Despite myself, the declaration, and its subsequent agreement, ignited a momentary spark of joy somewhere inside me. It didn't matter that it was extinguished moments later by the suffocating tension; it was the fact it had been there in the first place that counted.

"Amen to that," Erin agreed. Then, she glanced over at Jay, her head ducking towards the cooler set down on the rocks nearby. "Now, enough with the serious stuff. I think we've had enough of that for a while. Pass me a drink, please, will you?"

A can of beer was passed in her direction before Jay took a look at me. "You want one, too, Flo?"

A beat's pause left me considering. The automatic declination was already on the tip of my tongue: a habit I'd perfected in an attempt to remain sensible. But then I noticed something: at the very corner of my vision, I could see Daniel eyeing me, almost as if he was convinced he knew what my response would be. As if I was that predictable.

As if someone who really knew me would make a mistake such as his.

It was that look in his eyes, the one that seemed to silently boast about how well he could work me out, that changed my mind.

"Yeah, okay," I told Jay eventually, swallowing over my previous response. "I will have one."

Little did I know, that decision was the first of the mistakes I'd make that night.

23

— • —

CHAPTER 23

There was a reason I didn't drink.

Maybe it was because the burning taste of alcohol always made me mildly nauseous. Maybe it was the loss of dignity associated with staggering around, drunk out of your head. Maybe it was that I didn't like the thought of lending part of my conscious brain to the drink, succumbing to only partial control of my actions.

There was definitely a reason. But on that particular night, I couldn't remember what it was no matter how hard I tried.

I hadn't intended to go overboard. When the first can of beer had been passed over, I'd already consciously decided to limit myself to just a couple. But somewhere over the course of the evening, Jay had presented the bottles of vodka he'd stashed away in the cooler, and my previous resolve had been washed down with the shots.

It was a bad choice, but I wasn't thinking about that. All I was aware of was that each dose of alcohol made the situation with Daniel just that little bit easier to bear, and for that reason, I found myself continuing.

However, drinking only formed part of the mistake. Getting involved with the game of Truth or Dare Jay was adamant we had to play made up the rest of it.

"Collette!" he declared, as the empty vodka bottle came to a halt with its lid facing the brunette. Sitting with her legs pulled beneath her, she held a plastic cup in one hand. The other five of us made up the rest of the circle, the bonfire still blazing healthily somewhere behind us. "Pick your victim."

Now, we were getting into the swing of the game; the questions had begun to progress from the tame – "What's the most embarrassing thing you've ever done?" – toward more explicit varieties. I watched as Collette's dainty fingers flicked the bottle into its second spin, it later coming to a stop in front of the game's most eager participant.

"Oh, look at that," she drawled, shooting a smirk in Jay's direction. "Come on then, big boy: truth or dare?"

"Truth."

She groaned. "Come on, man up. I thought you were a shoe-in for a dare."

"All in good time," he shot back, confidence reaching new heights with its alcohol fuel. "This is just a warm-up."

"Okay, okay. Fine." I looked on as she paused, evidently wishing to take time over concocting a suitable question. It was a difficult decision; it had to be something that'd induce just the right amount of embarrassment and squirming. "Tell us, then, Jay. If you're such a big ladies' man, how many girls have you slept with?"

This, for some reason, shut him up. Unnerved by the bluntness of Collette's question, he seemed to be struggling to settle upon any response from his usual stockpile of witty comebacks. Instead, his mouth began opening and closing in what could only be described as pure goldfish fashion. "Well, I mean... there was just... you know—"

"Come on," Collette taunted, "you're not feeling shy, are you?"

"Yeah, come on," Daniel coaxed. Though still under the influence of a couple of beers, Daniel had to be the most sober of all of us. The small dose of alcohol had alleviated a fraction of his depressive mood, acting as a solvent for not only that, but also the underlying tension between us. "We all want to know."

"I—"

"Unless..." Collette said, smirking. "Unless you're a... virgin?"

The rest of us were attempting – rather unsuccessfully – to hold back our laughter; his bumbling reaction had already made the answer pretty clear.

"Fine, I am!" he burst out eventually. "I'm a virgin! I've never had sex with a girl! There! Are you happy?"

The few seconds that ensued were weighted by silence, but also short-lived; moments later we all simultaneously burst into laughter. Maybe it was the alcohol talking, but my bubbling giggles refused to subside, leaving me in hysterics alongside the rest of them.

"You can all stop laughing right now! It doesn't mean I'm not a ladies' man!" he protested vehemently. "Just because a girl hasn't wanted to sleep with me yet doesn't mean I'm not a player!"

"The biggest flirt in Walden is a virgin," Collette repeated, the words forced out between bouts of fresh laughter. "That's gold."

"Come on, guys. It's not that funny."

"No, it's not." Erin's composed, level tone attracted collective attention for a heartbeat; she found herself on the receiving end of five questioning looks. Then, straight afterward, she came to her senses, bursting into her original uproarious laughter once more. "It's hilarious!"

Had any one of us been sober, we probably wouldn't have found ourselves laughing so uncontrollably. But unfortunately for Jay, this was far from the case.

"Alright, alright," he muttered, ducking his head in an attempt to keep his darkening cheeks from view. "Moving on."

His hand moved to spin the bottle again, the rest of us calming down enough to turn our attention to its haphazard rotation across the uneven shingle. This time, it rolled to a stop in front of the gangly figure sandwiched between Collette and Jay.

Scott let out a triumphant victory cry before leaning in to select his prey with a second spin of the bottle.

Collette.

I half-expected him to get flustered, seeing as this was usually achievable for him with a mere look in her direction, but the alcohol seemed to have significantly diluted his crush-related nerves. I guessed it had that effect. "Truth or dare?" he asked.

She considered it for a moment, before bringing her cup to her lips and taking another swig. "Oh, fuck it. Dare."

At this point, I watched Jay nudge his friend, leaning over to whisper something in his ear with an unnervingly knowing smirk. When he drew back, Scott paused for a moment before laughing out loud. "Yeah, okay, I've got one," he announced.

"Oh, God," Collette murmured. "I'm not sure I even want to hear this one, judging by the look on Jay's face."

"I dare you to kiss Flo."

"Wait, what?" Predictably, my surprise was poorly contained. Incredulity had my eyes darting rapidly back and forth, pausing not long enough to focus on either one of them.

"Oh, right – nothing like a bit of girl-on-girl action for your amusement, eh, Jay?" she joked, the sarcasm dripping from her tone. Receiving only a self-satisfied smirk from him in return, smugness oozing from his very demeanour, her attention swivelled towards me. "Come on, then, Flo, let's give him a good show."

"Why do I have to be dragged into this?" I complained. "The bottle didn't even land on me."

Scott shrugged offhandedly. "No rules against it."

Despite my objections, the alcohol coursing through my bloodstream was making the prospect slightly less ridiculous than it was likely to have felt in sobriety. It was only a stupid game of Truth or Dare. It wasn't like any of this was serious, anyway. What was the worst that could happen? The likelihood was that everyone around us would be embarrassing themselves one way or another this evening.

"Screw it," I said, though I wasn't entirely sure the voice belonged to myself. "I'm not a chicken."

It was funny; I'd always thought I was. The alcohol seemed to disagree.

I found myself angling towards Collette anyway, the action co-ordinated by a less conscious part of my brain. Looking over her smirking expression, at the features I'd come to recognise easily over my summer in Walden, I could only think of how weird this was going to be. The only person I'd ever kissed was Daniel, and there were no prizes for guessing this was about to be totally different.

Even from this distance, I could smell Collette's overpoweringly sweet fragrance, and it occurred to me that I'd never thought I'd be kissing someone wearing just as much perfume as me.

Daniel's raised-eyebrow expression was the last thing I noticed before we started leaning in.

It couldn't have lasted more than two seconds, but that was more than enough time for me to establish it was one of the weirdest things I'd ever experienced. It was much too crazy to feel anything but incredibly awkward.

And altogether there was a bit too much lip gloss.

At any rate, the short-lived spectacle was enough to satisfy Jay and the others, whose hoots of laughter started up the moment we broke apart. "Is it hot in here or what?" he yelled.

"Did that satisfy your little fantasy?" Collette asked sweetly. "Don't go having too many wet dreams about it."

"Can't make any promises, I'm afraid."

"Oh, and before you ask: no, there were no sparks, and no, Flo and I will not be entering a lesbian relationship any time soon. Right, Flo?"

"Yeah," I chipped in, "sorry to disappoint."

"You know, I'm just glad I didn't roped into that one," Erin commented. "I mean, you're nice and everything, Col, but I don't want to snog you."

"Don't speak too soon, Erin," Jay told her. His warning was punctuated by a mischievous wink, at which she rolled her eyes. "The game's just getting started."

His words were true, but I'd almost allowed myself to get a little too settled into the situation. Listening to the crazy anecdotes and watching the outlandish antics unfold was nothing short of hilarious from the sidelines, especially with the buzz of alcohol in my system. Nevertheless, I still experienced a beat of shock once the bottle was spun again, coming to an unanticipated half with its open top pointing directly at me.

But even so, holding the responsibility for dishing out the next dare was a largely better position than the receiving end.

I forced a smile as I took the bottle in my hand for another spin, but as it circled wildly amongst the group, all I could think with every pound of my heart was not Daniel, not Daniel, not Daniel. I might've been drunk to the delicate point bordering on the edge of sense, but I'd been left with enough to know that having him on the other end of the next round was not a desirable scenario.

Thankfully, the laws of physics seemed to have been compassionate towards my silent prayer, selecting my victim as Jay instead.

"This is rigged!" he exclaimed, frowning.

"It's your bottle," I pointed out with a shrug. "We're just going by what it says. Truth or dare?"

"You know what? I think I'm warmed up enough." His statement sent a mild ripple of suppressed giggles pooling out across the circle. "Dare."

This moment here was my chance. I knew that after what had happened earlier, Jay would be willing to redeem himself from previous embarrassment with any crazy dare I put forth. Whatever I chose, it had to be something good. I wasn't about to let an opportunity such as this one slip through my fingers.

I took another sip from my cup for inspiration, wincing as the sting of the drink burned its way down my throat. I was beginning to gain accustom to the sensation by now, but the acrid bitterness preceded its numbing mental effects. Tonight I was already past sensible; there was no going back.

Glancing around the circle, I came face-to-face with five expectant expressions, all eagerly waiting to hear what I would come up with.

And when my eyes locked onto the violet vibrance of one person in particular, I realised exactly what power lay in my hands.

"Okay, Jay. I dare you to kiss the prettiest girl here."

His surprise was evident in the way his head snapped towards me; clearly, this hadn't been what he was expecting. I could almost see the feigned confusion about to tumble from his lips; I cut him off before he got the chance.

"You heard me," I said, smirking. "Go on, Jay, take your pick."

"I…" He caught sight of my raised eyebrows, which seemed to shut him up. "Okay. Fine. I'll do it."

But he didn't make any attempt to move. It was difficult to keep the amusement from leaking into my tone. "Go on, then."

He paused a moment longer than necessary, rising to his feet with exaggerated – yet seemingly false – confidence. It took no more than a few steps to approach where the three of us sat, forming a huddled line along one of the logs. To an outsider, it might've looked like Jay was mulling carefully over his decision, but even with my increasingly fuzzy head, I knew there was no doubt about who he'd choose.

"What are you doing, dumb arse?" Erin said. "Collette's sitting over there."

Jay looked confused. "What?"

"Were you not listening? Flo dared you to kiss the prettiest girl here… and Collette's over there."

"I know," he said. "I wasn't aiming for Collette. I might be drunk, but I'm not that drunk."

"Are you sure?"

But their conversation had been deemed over at this point; Jay's answer was instead conveyed by his subsequent action. Leaning forward, and allowing Erin only the tiniest slither of time to comprehend what was going on, he pressed his lips against hers.

It looked like he'd intended to go in for a simple peck, but somewhere in the midst of those few seconds, the plan seemed to change. At first, Erin was frozen with surprise, her cold rigidity evident even to us. But then something kicked in, the release of a shot of adrenalin from somewhere inside her brain, and she leaned inward, lending herself into the kiss.

When she reached up to cup his cheeks with her hands, holding him in his exact position, the swelling astonishment throughout the rest of us became almost tangible.

I felt like an intruder on the moment when they finally broke apart, their lips leaving each other with reluctant speed. Staring back at each other, eyes widened with surprise, Erin suddenly realised her position, letting her arms drop back to her sides with a sense of startling urgency. Jay cleared his throat, moving to retreat back to his seat with a slightly dazed grin. His typical self-assurance had almost completely evaporated; he, along with everybody else who'd unintentionally played witness, could tell he'd just strode into stark new territory.

None of us were quite sure what to make of it.

The stunned silence was eventually shattered by none other than Erin herself, moments later. "Is it my turn?" she asked, avoiding anybody's gaze but the floor's. The dancing light of the bonfire cast enough illumination across her face to mean her reddening cheeks were visible, and I was sure I wasn't the only one who could detect the note of squeakiness in her voice.

The following few rounds of the game passed relatively uneventfully; that was, compared to the earlier happenings of the evening. Still, there was no denying that Scott and Jay's shirtless rendition of The Ketchup Song provided thorough entertainment, and then there was the fact that Collette almost talked Jay into kissing Daniel. They both chickened out at the last minute.

I'd lost track of how many drinks I'd downed by that point, but my mind was beginning to feel unnervingly foggy, and the beach had developed a tendency to tip alarmingly if I moved my head too quickly.

Somehow, I'd managed to avoid the receiving end of a dare through ten whole rounds, though my escapade with Collette had to count as paying my dues. But I should've known that my luck was running thin, and sooner or later I would be faced with the prospect of being asked the infamous question.

In the next round, I was right.

"Truth or dare?"

"Uh..." My gaze trailed around the group, as quickly as my reeling head would allow. Half of me ached to pick truth, to wriggle easily away from the insanity of another dare, but the obvious stopped me. The moment permission slipped from my lips, I'd become fresh meat for a plague of Daniel-centric questions. Even in my far-from-sober state, where the awkwardness had been pleasantly numbed, I wasn't in a place to handle that. "Dare."

"Looks like we've got a daredevil on our hands," Scott taunted, grinning. "Well, let's see how well you can live up to that title. I dare you... to go swimming."

"What?"

"Swimming," he repeated, hooking his thumb behind him, as if the threatening crash of the waves wasn't obvious enough in itself. "In there."

"Are you crazy?"

The interruption originated from a voice opposite me. Daniel was looking over at his friend, brow creased in an expression of pure disbelief. "She's pissed out of her mind, and you want her to go swimming? Do you have any idea how stupid that is?"

"She doesn't have to swim," Jay pointed out. "It doesn't get deep out there for ages. She could stay near the shore."

"She is not swimming." Daniel's tone was adamant; the severity of it surprised us all. Though he was easily classed as the sober one of the group, no one had elected him decision-maker. "Just quit being stupid and pick another dare. One that's not about to get someone killed."

Scott seemed to have shrunk under the weight of Daniel's fierce warning. "Alright, man, calm down..."

Yet the conversation had sparked a sudden anger in me: an inner fire in me that was fuelled by something more volatile than alcohol. Maybe it was the sky-high emotions of the past few days all being thrown into one, spontaneously combusting upon impact. "Who made you the boss of me?" I shot at Daniel, my tongue lashing. "You certainly don't get to make my decisions for me."

"Look, Flo, just calm down," Erin started. "It was a stupid dare, anyway..."

"I'm fine," I insisted. Scrambling clumsily to my feet, I did my best to ignore the way the ground wobbled beneath me, the sloping gradient of the beach seeming much steeper than usual. "You want me to go swimming? Fine. I'm not a chicken. I'm going swimming."

"Flo, don't be an idiot," I heard someone cut in, but I was past listening. Wriggling out of my shorts, I was drunk past the point of caring about stripping in front of my friends. I pulled my shirt over my head, feeling much less exposed than I should've in nothing but my underwear, I set off at a marching pace towards the shore.

Multiple people stumbled to their feet somewhere behind me, but my gaze remained locked on my destination: the waves creeping harmlessly up the shingle bank on the foreshore. The darkening sky made up their backdrop, the first few hints of glittering stars already scattered across the deep blue blanket. With each staggering step the echo of Daniel's voice replayed over in my head: his stubborn tone, as if he had the right to determine what I could and couldn't do. Even from here, I could see the waves weren't that high. They looked calm, even. It wasn't as if I was going to swim out of my depth. I was drunk, but not that stupid. I didn't need to go any further than waist-deep, a point at which I could prove them wrong. Then I'd wade back, no harm done.

There was no need for an overreaction.

"Flo!"

My name was being shouted from further up the bank, but it wasn't anything that I hadn't expected. Of course, they were scared I was going to do something stupid. But they didn't need to be.

The cutting chill of the water came as a shock when it first rushed over my bare feet; it was almost enough to stop me in my tracks. But the pressing urgency succeeded the surprise; if I could just get this over with, I'd prove I wasn't a chicken. That a few shots weren't going to put my life in danger. That Daniel didn't have the power he'd like over me.

There must've been some sort of dip in the sea bed, because the water got much deeper much quicker than I had anticipated. I continued against the resistance of the current against my legs, the feeling likened to the peculiar prospect of wading through treacle. I couldn't have been more than ten metres in before I felt the water lapping above the waistline of my underwear, only my top half visible from above.

I allowed myself to turn around: slow, controlled movements to ensure my balance didn't falter. Back on the shore, there was a platoon of vaguely-outlined figures, all staring out to sea. I wasn't close enough for their expressions of concern to be visible, but I didn't need to be.

The resultant rush of triumph was suddenly comical; I found myself laughing out loud with the absurdity of standing in the ocean in my undergarments at such a ridiculous hour. The others had been stupid to worry. There was absolutely nothing dangerous about this. In fact, it was kind of fun.

As long as I stayed in my depth, everything would be fine.

At least, it would've been if I hadn't had my back turned to the approaching wave: the curved-top ridge of water that stood much, much taller than the others. The ghost of a strangled scream escaped my lips before I was dragged backwards by its strong current, the water curling like arms around my waist, my entire sense of balance collapsing under the force of the moving water.

There was no chance to yell. No chance to cry out for help.

Not even a chance to gulp down a last lungful of air.

24

CHAPTER 24

The water had a personality. It wasn't just a large mass of liquid, but a ferocious, personified monster. Its twisted watery claws wrapped around the contours of my body, their grip fluid and yet eerily vice-like. I struggled desperately against its hold, but the moving force was overpowering; my flailing limbs had close to no effect on the current dragging me backward.

My head plunged beneath the surface, the movement too sudden to allow time for a desperate breath. Bubbles erupted from my open mouth as the salt stung my eyes, their rapid back-and-forth movement a despairing attempt to gain some sense of direction. But the water was much too uniform; it held no distinguishable features, nothing to assist in determining which way was up and which down. For all I knew, I could've already been spun around and turned on my head three times over.

I thrashed hopelessly, but my balance was lacking even inland, let alone amongst the swirling torrent of the incoming waves. No matter how hard I tried, my furious kicking failed to propel me upwards, leaving me powerless against the ocean.

That was it. I'd drown here. A stupid drunken decision, enough to kill.

It wouldn't have been the first time.

I was on the brink of consciousness, floundering on the border between awareness and ignorance, when I felt the arms encircle my waist. Initially, they seemed just another extension of the water's deadly current, yet another force to drag me in the wrong direction. There were a few seconds of delay before I noticed the stark differences between the two: the way these felt significantly less fluid, their strength and stability a perfect imitation of muscle.

Just when I'd come to accept the fact that it was all over, I felt myself being yanked upward, and my hazy head broke the surface of the water.

My burning lungs felt the oxygen first, gulping huge doses to make up for what they'd lost. Drifting between various states of consciousness, I became aware of the stronger force as it moved me along. I vaguely noticed a pressure on my stomach; it felt as if I'd been hooked over somebody's shoulder. The only water I could feel now was lapping at my ankles, its level retreating further with every step forward.

Then, suddenly, it had disappeared; even the tip of my toes had been removed from the water, finding themselves instead amongst bitingly cold air. Miraculously, the monster had retreated.

Either that, or I'd been rescued.

My back met a hard, rocky surface as I slipped further away from consciousness; there were other things going on around me, I was sure, but I couldn't work them out. It was as if my whole body had been sucked of its entire energy supply, a lifeless shell left behind in its place. I was alive, I knew, but by how narrowly I wasn't sure.

Drifting. That was the only way to describe it, the only word suitable for my state of mind. Not conscious enough to hold awareness of my surroundings, to interact with them in the way I was supposed to, yet somehow not quite gone. Present enough to reassure myself I was still alive.

I hadn't drowned. I was alive.

"Flo! Oh God, please tell me you can hear me. Please, Flo. Wake up."

The voice startled me; amidst the fogginess of my head, it was clearer than anything else. So clear, in fact, that I found myself able to latch right onto its tone, hang off the sound of every syllable, guiding myself back into the delicate state of reality.

"Please. Come on, please, wake up. You have to!"

At that moment, my eyes fluttered open. Vision returned to me all at once, revealing Daniel's crumpled expression bent over mine, our noses mere inches away from brushing. The freckles, bizarrely, were one of the first things I noticed: a collective mass of detail across the slope of his nose that tugged me back into familiarity. For the first few seconds, all I could do was stare at him, taking in the outline of his facial features through blinking, widened eyes. The words of his desperate begging had died in his throat, leaving the two of us in silence as he gazed disbelievingly back.

I pulled my body upwards, into a more upright position, my actions slow and controlled to ease my swimming head.

I was going to say something, but all at once the tension shattered and what could only be described as a breathy cry of relief escaped Daniel's lips. Before I could respond, I was enveloped by the same strong pair of arms, pulling me into his chest. With my face pressed against his shirt, my own arms wooden with surprise, the result was something of a swaying motion: a desperate, thankful hug.

"Thank God," I heard him breathe, his whispery voice close to my ear. "Thank God, thank God, thank God."

He seemed unconcerned by my lack of response, the only thing mattering was that he held my sopping form in the circle of his arms. "Oh, Jesus, I thought I'd lost you."

The phrase was the trigger; my heart, paralysed with shock, suddenly thawed, along with the rest of my body. Without thinking, I felt myself collapse into his grip, the physical reassurance too long overdue. My arms moved up towards his back, pressing myself closer into him. The salty water was dripping from every inch of me – from the ends of long, straggly strands of hair, my sodden clothing, which had at some point been pulled back on me, the curve of my face – but here, I was suddenly warm, my previous anger at his every fibre of being miraculously dulled into a warm, glowing heat.

"Flo," he started. "I'm so, so sorry."

I knew I should've said something, but my head was reeling at an incomprehensible speed, and not just from the alcohol. The words were instead a jumbled mix of letters in my head, the string that usually wove them together tangled worse than my iPod earphones. I couldn't find it in myself to do anything more than remain still in Daniel's arms.

"I just... I don't know what I would've done if I'd lost you," he whispered. "It doesn't even bear thinking about."

He pulled me closer, if that was even possible.

"I'm sorry," he repeated. "I've said it too many times, I know. But what I did was the biggest mistake I'd ever made in my life. I haven't stopped thinking about it since it happened. It's been torturing me non-stop."

The fabric of his clothing was warm: heavenly warm. It was all I could think about as I buried my nose deeper into it, trying to hide from the ferocious shivering racking my body.

"Please... I just want you to know that if I could take it back, I would in a heartbeat. Without a doubt. I just can't stand the thought of you being mad at me. I know you have every right to be, but... I just can't take it. It's too much."

Though my hopelessly frazzled brain could barely keep up with the rhythm of his words, the heartfelt apology shone through. Even when it did finally muddle its way through their meaning, figuring out what exactly to do with them was a whole other matter. At present, I wanted nothing more than to snuggle closer to Daniel, to forgive him for everything he'd done just so that I could stay caught up in his reassuring hug. To stay enclosed in that safe little bubble, protected from the atrocities of the outside world.

It was what I wanted. I just wasn't sure if my judgement was impaired by a combination of the alcohol, crippling shock of almost drowning and my emotional vulnerability.

"Please," he said again, his head ducking further, until I could feel his warm breath on the skin of my ear. "I need you to give me a second chance."

It hit me then: the startling obvious, staring me right in the face. "You saved my life," I whispered.

"Of course I did," he answered, seeming surprised by my sudden realisation. "What did you think I was going to do? Stand there and watch you drown?"

"I don't know..."

"I couldn't take it if I lost you," he said, his grip tightening, holding me close as if scared of the consequences of letting go. "You're the most important thing in my life. Honestly, I..." He paused, searching for the words inside the depths of his mind.

They weren't what I was expecting.

"I love you."

My surprise had me pulling back, but the envelope of Daniel's arms allowed only a limited range of movement. I didn't know what on earth I was about to say in response; my lips were acting entirely of their own accord as they parted. "I..."

"Look, I know it's crazy because you probably hate my guts right now," he stammered, the gaps between each word vanishing so they came as one continuous stream. "And you have every right to. I understand that. I just have to tell you. I honestly don't know how I would've gotten through this summer without you. You're everything I was looking for. I just didn't realise it until you were already gone."

Brown met hazel as I stared, utterly dumbstruck, back at him, searching the region behind his eyes for the faintest hint of exaggeration. All I could spot, however, was a huge, swallowing vat of sincerity.

"Florence Kennedy," he whispered, "I love you. So, so much."

I was meant to do something. That much I could work out from the silence, tugging at and stretching the mental space between us, each second pulling Daniel's confession further and further away. The moment was dissipating right before my eyes, crumbling into its constituents, threatening to pass completely if I didn't reach out and grab it.

I'd been determined to hate Daniel for what he'd done. The extent of his misunderstanding had been cruelly felt on my part, and I hadn't expected to be able to forget that any time soon. Yet here, frail and shivering, my face mere inches away from his own, I found myself melting under the warmth of his honesty. There was just something about the look in his eyes that told me he meant every word; the mistake was fiercely imprinted into his memory.

He truly was sorry, and in that moment, I was a goner.

And, swallowing, I found myself saying, "I love you too."

The space, both physical and mental, snapped into nonexistence as I fell back into the cradle of Daniel's chest. Our position shifted unexpectedly as his arms retracted from around me; I was confused until I felt the soft fabric of his jacket draped over my shoulders. It wasn't enough to stop the shivering completely, but at least it acted as a barrier against the wind whistling around us, making the biting chill that little bit less severe.

"You could do with a foil blanket, or something," he said quietly, the smile evident through his tone. "But I don't think that was one of the things Jay had stashed away in the cooler."

I found myself laughing: the type of light, carefree laughter that rose through my body like helium being pumped into a balloon.

"I'm sorry," I mumbled eventually, when it died away and I leant further into Daniel's hug, "for being stupid."

"What are you talking about?"

"Going swimming was a really stupid idea," I told him. "I was just caught up in the moment. Hopelessly drunk. I still am. I should've listened to you."

"Shh, don't be silly. We all do things we regret. Believe me, I know," he assured me. "But what matters is that things have worked out in the end. That's all we can focus on. The past is the past; it's right now that counts. Right?"

And in that very moment, right there, I realised it was true. My head might've been hopelessly scrambled, thoughts swirling and churning every which way inside, but I came to my senses long enough to ponder over Daniel's words. The past was fixed, set permanently in stone. No matter how long you spent wishing things could be different, they never would be. The only power than lay in hand was that of the present, and consequently the future: fresh clay, ready to be shaped and moulded at our fingertips.

We couldn't change what had already happened. Not the events of three days ago, or those of three years. But we were here, clinging to each other beneath the darkening night sky, and before us the endless possibilities stretched.

And as he planted the gentlest of kisses on my forehead, I breathed an audible sigh of relief.

"Daniel?" I murmured several minutes later, breaking into the moment of the hug that seemed to be stretching into forever.

He shifted above me. "Yeah?"

"Do you think... maybe... you could take me home?"

"Oh." He softened. "Yeah. Of course."

Slowly emerging from the bubble of the moment, Daniel rose to his feet first to help me up. I wobbled a little initially, my legs unsteady under the weight of my trembling body, but his arms met my waist before my balance even had a chance to falter. With his support I moved forward, grateful that the reeling of my head seemed to be subsiding slightly with each step.

The others were gathered some distance away from us along the beach, evidently having sensed that it was better to leave us to our time alone. Their collective expression of concern, however, turned to one of breathtaking relief when they noticed me up and walking, relatively unharmed from my experience.

Under the spotlight of their attention, I couldn't help but feel ashamed. Even mild intoxication was no excuse for my dangerous stupidity. But I managed a smile, which, thankfully, was reflected back.

Trekking along the Walden coastline towards the town took longer than I expected, but Daniel remained remarkably patient. I seemed to stumble over every pebble out of place on the beach, almost falling flat on my face several times. Yet on every occasion I was steadied immediately, caught and pulled back into position by the guy at my side, upright as if I'd never tripped at all.

What must've been at least half an hour had crawled by when we finally reached the trailing road up to Gram's cul-de-sac; when the roof of her cottage finally came into view, I exhaled with content. The night had been a long one, and now I wanted nothing more than to crawl underneath the warm covers of my bed and sleep off the short-term effects. There was sure to be hell to pay in the form of a hangover in the morning, but I'd have to deal with that later.

Daniel held onto my hand as we made our way towards the front door of the cottage, fumbling himself around in my bag for the key. I thought he would leave me at the door, plant a kiss on my forehead and depart with the promise of calling me in the morning, but he surpassed my expectations. Moving inside the eerily empty kitchen, darkness pooled in the corners of the room, he closed the door behind us and set my bag down on the counter.

He refused to leave until I'd taken a hot shower, emerging from the bathroom in long pyjama bottoms and my comfiest T-shirt. As I climbed into bed, relishing the sensation of fabric against skin when my feet slipped between the mattress and the duvet, he bent over to brush his lips softly against my forehead.

His tone was comforting, forging a path across to me in the darkness. "Goodnight."

But as he tried to untwine his fingers from mine, I found myself struck by an inexplicable sense of longing; it might've been a rush of drunken emotion, but I couldn't bring myself to watch Daniel leave. Not after I'd only just got him back.

"Wait," I said suddenly.

He stopped in his tracks, peering at me curiously. "What?" he asked. "Do you need something else?"

"Stay with me?" I burst out, the ends of the words running into one another to form a garbled rush. Taking hold of his hand once more, I linked our fingers, wishing there was some way I could live without ever having to break them apart. It was ridiculous, I knew, that drunken thought. Still, that didn't stop it from running across my mind. "I don't want you to go."

His gaze swept over me briefly, melting slightly when it met my pleading expression. But just as the impulsive response was about to leave his lips, he changed his mind, a shake of his head replacing earlier words. "Flo, you've had too much to drink," he said, matter-of-factly. "I'm not going to take advantage of you like that."

I, too, shook my head, though the vigorous action sent the room momentarily toppling to one side. "I don't mean like that," I told him. "I just... I need you. Like that other night."

The very moment was being replayed in his head too, I could tell. The thoughtful glaze across his eyes served as a giveaway that he was back there again, staring back at me in the foggy darkness of his landing, hardly present. The combined memory seemed almost powerful enough to send us both back in time.

"Flo," he said eventually. "What will your gram think when she wakes up and finds me in your room with you?"

"She's not here," I whispered. "She's staying with a friend for the night, out of town. It's for some art conference she's going to."

He looked at me for what felt like an incredibly long moment – so much so that I began to wonder if the part of my brain responsible for timekeeping had failed, leaving me frozen in a snapshot of time. "Nothing has to happen," I breathed. "I just really need you here."

He considered it for a moment longer, before finally moving forward, squeezing my palm with his own.

"In that case," he said slowly, just as my heart melted, "I'm not going anywhere."

25

CHAPTER 25

"What is this? A burger or a piece of charcoal?"

Collette stared briefly down at her plate before glancing over at Jay, a look of incredulity written upon her face. I suppose she did have a point – the circular, blackened mess that currently sat atop her burger bun could not in any universe have passed as meat. But, then again, that was what she got by appointing Jay – who clearly had no idea how to work Collette's family's fancy grill – Head of Barbequing Operations.

I had to admit: the expensive contraption did have an unusual amount of complicated dials and levers for something whose job was, essentially, to heat food. That was the main reason behind his struggle; no matter how hard he tried, he just couldn't seem to work out the correct orientation of each knob and button to make the barbecue function as just that. Yet I couldn't imagine any of us would've done a better job.

"That was my best one," he pouted, looking hurt. "I thought it was at least an improvement on Scott's."

The guy himself chipped in at this point, a mildly disgusted expression directed towards the head chef. "I think I'm chewing on a piece of coal."

The six of us were sprawled on a huge picnic blanket on Collette's lawn, basking lazily in the late afternoon sun. Though we did our best not to dwell on the thought, the obvious continued to stare us right in the face: it was the last day of the summer, and school was due to start the next day. The prospect no longer scared me witless, but even knowing that I'd be enduring my last year of sixth form with those who'd become my new best friends didn't compensate the fact that it was still school.

And whether in London or Walden, it still put an abrupt stop to the placid summer days I'd grown increasingly used to over the past two months.

"I'll do you another one if you want to risk it. Just bear in mind that it might turn out even worse."

"On second thought," Collette interjected quickly, finishing her burger with its top bun, "I'll just slather it in ketchup."

"You know, it's really your fault for having such a complicated barbecue," Jay said, pointing his spatula in her direction. Slung from his neck was an apron – which would've looked okay, had it not been bright pink and embellished with the sequinned words Kiss the cook. Collette had claimed it had been the only one she could find, but I had a feeling she hadn't exactly exhausted her options. "I've got no idea how to work this thing."

"Yeah, we guessed that one, mate," Daniel cut in. He'd managed to stomach one of Jay's offerings – a blackened, crunchy piece that had been a sausage in its previous life – but only by drowning his entire plate in half a bottle of ketchup and mustard.

I was pulling up the rear with only half a burger stomached; I hadn't quite got used to the feeling of clamping through a smoky charcoal layer with each bite. But Jay's effort was valiant, and since none of us could make a better attempt ourselves, we kept quiet.

"So," he said, gesturing back towards the grill, "anyone up for seconds?"

The subsequent disagreement was so sudden and vehement that it was almost funny; Jay seemed to take a step back on his bombardment with fervent declinations. We'd originally been hungry, but just one taste of his awful cooking had been enough to suppress our appetites.

There was a banging sound as Collette began aggressively pounding the bottom of the ketchup bottle, but to no avail: the contents of her plate remained as dry and blackened as ever. She groaned. "Who used up the last of this?"

"That'd be me." Erin glanced down at her own plate. "I needed an ocean to cover up the taste of this."

"Yeah, I don't blame you." Straightening out her legs, she began to pull herself into a standing position. "There's probably another bottle in the kit—"

"I'm the chef, I've got it!" Jay chirped, unusually helpful. He scrambled to his feet before Collette even had the chance to move; within a matter of seconds he'd already bounded across the lawn, his pace carrying him towards the back of the house with peculiar speed.

My voice was the one that broke the ensuing silence. "Well, that was weird."

"Jesus, he's not usually that eager, is he?" Collette said, frowning as she plonked back down onto the ground. "I say we should be wary."

Expecting him to return with the same bizarre urgency, we were instead surprised to find that he still hadn't emerged from the kitchen several minutes later. It was getting to the point that we were considering sending out a search party that he poked his head around the back door, his attention directed primarily in Erin's direction.

"Hey," he called, "could you come in here for a second? I need some... help."

She frowned, muttering something along the lines of, "What does he want me for?", but her bemusement didn't stop her from gathering herself to her feet. "Does he think I have ketchup-locating superpowers or something? It's Collette's kitchen."

"Somehow I don't think ketchup's what he's looking for," Collette commented with a smirk, but by this point Erin had already cleared the edge of earshot, disappearing past the threshold. "It's pretty obvious what those two are going to be doing in there."

Daniel made a face. "I don't want to think about that. You know that's my sister, right?"

"Oh, I know," she answered amusedly, "but just because you don't want to talk about it doesn't mean it's not happening as we speak."

I was sure Daniel was about to respond with a suitably witty remark, but he was robbed of the chance; the moment his lips parted, the words about to spill from them, he was cut off by a particular something.

And that 'something' happened to be a cold stream of water, jetting right over the lawn like a shot, right into the faces of its unsuspecting victims. Which, of course, happened to be us.

My head whipped around the moment the water collided with my skin, effectively drenching my entire face and seeping down into the upper layers of my clothing. Eyes searching the vicinity for the source of the surprise, they hit the jackpot once they landed upon the pair stood at the back door, brandishing bright plastic – and incredibly vicious-looking – water guns.

"You have got to be joking," Collette exclaimed, but I could've sworn I noticed the edges of her lips curling upwards at the sight.

Jay, unmistakably the mastermind of the operation, raised his gun. At some point preceding the commotion he'd shed his pink apron, the end result being an overall more intimidating appearance. An effect, I found, that intensified when I found myself his gun's locked target. "This is war!" came his loud declaration.

And then, suddenly, they were running towards us, their pounding footsteps on the lawn so rapid it barely gave us a chance to scramble haphazardly to our feet. I heard the click of a plastic trigger and suddenly the water was flying through the air again, splattering my back with an uncomfortable cold dampness that seeped right through to my skin.

Amongst the kerfuffle, a hand grabbed my own, and I looked over to see Daniel glancing expectantly at me. "What do you say – allies?"

As if he needed to ask, I thought, as he ducked out of the way of Jay's latest shot and yanked me forward in the process.

"Come on!" he called over his shoulder. "I know a good place to hide."

I stumbled dazedly after him, my sense of awareness compromised amongst the disorder as we sprinted to avoid the incoming streams of water. Even underneath the warmth of the afternoon sun,

Jay's source was obviously the cold tap, the sensation too much of a shock to the senses to be anything near pleasant.

The brief time slot in which Jay and Erin's guns were pointed in directions other than ourselves allowed us an opportunity to leg it around the side of the house, ducking past the corner and stopping, breathless, to lean against the rear wall of Collette's garage. The scratchy brick rubbed at my back as I pressed up against it, trying to remove myself from the radar of our attackers.

"I think we're safe," Daniel whispered after a few seconds, and we both let out a breath of relief.

"Trust Jay to declare a water fight," I whispered back.

"Yeah, well. That's what you get when you combine his immaturity and the last day of the summer."

The last day of summer. His words, unpleasantly expectant, hung in the air between us. It was almost as if they themselves were visible, the string of letters suddenly much more than that: something tangible that I could reach out and grab hold of. If I wanted to.

It had been hanging over us for days now, folding the final days in on themselves at an unnerving pace, the obvious prospect niggling at the back of everybody's heads. Yet somehow, spoken from Daniel's lips, it seemed much more real. The inexplicable sense of finality to his tone was felt through my every fibre of being.

"It really is the last day, isn't it?" I murmured quietly.

"Uh huh."

I wasn't leaving Walden, nor moving anywhere away from my new friends, but it was impossible to shake off the feeling that it was like the end of an era. At the start of the summer, I'd been a whole other person. Convinced that coping without Nora was impossible, that belief had been imprinted into every region of my brain. And yet here, months later, the knowledge that my sister resided over a hundred miles away no longer terrified me. Not when I only had to move a few inches to find Daniel.

And then there was the fact that things had finally been patched up with Gram. When she'd returned from the conference, I hadn't been able to stop myself from running at her, enclosing her in a hug and apologising for the cold shoulder of the past few days. Her own apologies had come in full force, too, and some hours later we came to a mutual reconciliation that stitched the last piece of my life in Walden back into place.

"So, tell me the verdict," he cut in, his voice considerably cheerier. "Summer in London or Walden? Which one comes out top?"

The resulting urge tugged my lips into a smile that spread across my face. "Come on," I teased gently, "you know there's no competition there."

He was grinning too. "No?"

"Oh, no. London, without a doubt," I told him. "The guys are cuter. More eye candy."

I resisted the impulse to laugh out loud as his eyebrows raised, looking down at me with a mildly amused expression. "You're sure about that one?"

"Positive."

It looked like he'd been intending to make a sarcastic remark, maybe even duck down to kiss me in an attempt to sway my answer, but I wasn't given the opportunity to find out. The interruption came quickly, and initially I froze against the garage wall, preparing for an ambush by Erin and Jay. Seconds passed, but I didn't find myself staring down the barrel of a water gun. The pair had made an appearance, but not in the way I'd expected.

Their voices, carried from somewhere around the corner of the wall we were pressed up against, were easily heard. I dared to sneak a peek, peering around the edge of the building to see them having completely abandoned their weapons in favour of holding the other's hand.

"Well, that got rid of them," Jay said breezily.

"You were right," Erin answered with a laugh. "Your methods might be childish, but I have to admit they're effective."

"Didn't I tell you? You should listen to me more often."

"Yeah, alright. Don't push your luck."

He laughed too, but the carefree sound ebbed away when he leant in to kiss her, weaving his hands onto the small of her back. Her response was nothing short of enthusiastically, and I noticed how she threw her arms up to link them behind his neck, the ends of her vibrant hair brushing his hands with the upward tilt of her head.

I recoiled back against the wall, shooting a glance at a bemused Daniel. "Don't look now unless you want to catch your sister in one intense snogging session."

Unfortunately, the consequential surprise was served with a shot of impulsiveness, and, completely disregarding my warning, he poked his head around the corner too. Needless to say, Jay chose the wrong moment to back Erin up against the wall, letting her fingers tangle themselves in his hair, as demonstrated by Daniel's startled and slightly grimacing expression when he looked back to me.

"I shouldn't have looked, should I?"

"I did warn you," I told him simply.

He groaned. "Brilliant. That one's going to be burned in my head for a while." Slumping back against the wall, his attention seemed to catch on an object beside him. Had the arrival of inspiration been any more noticeable, I could've sworn I'd have been able to see a bulb blink to life above his head. "Hey, I've got an idea."

"What?" I craned my neck to see exactly what he was peering at, but as soon as my gaze latched onto it, I realised his proposal immediately. "Would that not be completely and utterly evil?"

He shrugged. "They started it. We're the ones already dripping wet."

His argument, brief as it was, served as sufficient conviction. I didn't even need instruction to grab the other side of the bucket as we held it under the garden tap, watching the water level creep slowly up the plastic sides. It wasn't until it reached a few inches below the rim that Daniel shut off the tap, silencing the quiet splashing.

"We need to be quick about this," he told me. Though his tone was serious, the mischievous smirk could not be kept from either one of our faces. "Leg it out there, and then right over their heads."

"Got it," I affirmed. "Though I imagine they'll both be too absorbed in each other to even notice what's going on."

He grimaced. "Let's get this over with quickly, then. Ready?"

I nodded.

"Three, two, one... go!"

The snapshot effect came into action from that moment on, and every one that followed: the first footstep out of our hiding spot; the weight of the slippery bucket in our hands; the raw muscle exertion of lifting it above our heads. It all came as individual bursts, each conscious moment seeming oddly clean-cut from the last. It was Daniel's expression, shaking under the pressure of holding back laughter, that was the last thing I noticed before we hitched the bucket up all the way, angling it forwards so the water came sloshing out in one giant burst, all over our victims' heads.

They jolted apart immediately, the immediate drench freezing them right out of the motions of their kiss. Erin's arms snapped back to her sides immediately, while Jay leaped away from her, widening the gap between them until it stretched at least two feet. It was at this moment that the dam broke, and mine and Daniel's laughter erupted into the air, rapidly evolving from suppressed giggles to uncontrollable hysteria.

"You two!" Erin said, her finger drifting between the both of us.

"Come on, man, you completely ruined my hair!" Jay complained, running a hand through his now sopping mane and examining it with revulsion.

"That's what you get for starting a water fight," I told them.

"And also for bringing my sister around the side of the house to snog her," Daniel chipped in.

To this, Jay could only muster a sheepish smile. "Well, I mean…"

He didn't get to finish. The third and final unexpected event of the afternoon was about to commence, and that came in the form of the shocking sensation of a huge sheet of water crashing down on us from above. Not only effectively silencing the entire group, I was soaked in seconds, the squelching feeling of dampness felt everywhere from the strands of my hair down to the gaps between my toes. The effect was felt across the other three in the vicinity – though Jay and Erin had already been more than sufficiently drenched a minute ago, this time Daniel's hair was also plastered to the sides of his head, eyes closed as water continued to stream down his face.

"What the…?" My thoughts were voiced by Erin's exclamation as we all looked upwards, attempting to investigate the source of the water. In hindsight, we should've known.

Standing directly above us, leaning over the railing of the master bedroom's balcony, were the missing two members of our party. Each held either end of a huge plastic tub – the one that obviously, a few moments ago, had contained the same water that was now seeping through the fabric of my T-shirt. Scott perhaps wore the widest grin of the pair; even from my position on the ground, I could see that it almost stretched ear-to-ear. Even so, Collette came in a close second, the hair scraped away from her face in a neat ponytail meaning her own grin was that much more visible.

"You guys are novices!" she shouted down, her voice carried easily by the afternoon breeze. Which, thanks to the bucket of water stored between the fibres of my clothing, now felt considerably cooler on my skin. "That's how you win a water fight!"

"Bow down to your superiors!" Scott called, winking at Collette.

There was a heartbeat's pause: a moment in which I watched as she gazed back at him, the smile yet to slip from her features. It happened suddenly – had I blinked, I was sure I would've missed it. The empty plastic container clattered, discarded, to the floor beside them, and in the space of a few seconds Collette had took a leap at the guy opposite her, throwing her arms around his neck and pressing their lips into contact.

At first he seemed stunned, his surprise evident in the way he stumbled slightly backward with the unexpected momentum. Still, it didn't take long for him to recover, eventually lending himself into the kiss he'd been waiting for.

And there, beneath the sunshine on that warm afternoon, as the last piece of the puzzle seemed to finally click into place, I couldn't stop myself from smiling.

"So," Scott yelled down several moments later, "who's up for ice cream?"

26

— ⚬ —

EPILOGUE

"**O**pen the door! It's the police!"

There was somebody outside the house – and not just there, either; it sounded like the caller was trying to batter the door down with their bare fist. Two rooms away, where I stood in front of the living room mirror, the commotion was as loud as if I was standing right beside it.

Despite their insistence, however, I was certain enough the person had no real legal authority. For one thing, I was sure a real policeman wouldn't sound like they were having trouble keeping a straight face, nor would they have had a voice that sounded exactly like the guy I happened to be dating.

"Ma'am, if you don't open this door right now, I'm going to have to arrest you!"

Rolling my eyes, I set down the hairbrush and made my way into the hallway. It was only luck the rest of the family were out; Daniel had left for Flo's thirty minutes ago, and Mum wasn't due back from her ballroom dancing class (as ridiculous as that sounded) for at least another hour. As I'd been expecting, the glass of the front door was obscured by a distinctly Jay-shaped silhouette, though that still wasn't enough to prepare me for the sight faced when I finally pulled the door open.

Leaning against one of the porch posts (in a way that was supposed to look casual, but ended up completely failing), he was dressed head-to-toe in police get-up, swinging a pair of fake handcuffs from his finger. The shirt and trousers looked entirely too tight, like he'd squeezed into a size too small, and a policeman's cap lay skewed on his head.

"Oh, God."

Once the door was open wide enough, his eyes dropped to my own outfit, lingering there just a little too long. All of a sudden, I became all too conscious of my equally ridiculous costume: the red corset-style top that was tight in not only the right places, but the rest of them too; the star-print skirt I'd been convinced was missing several inches of fabric when it'd been delivered; the crown-shaped headpiece that ended up wonky no matter how many hair grips I fastened it with.

Thankfully, the place we were both headed not only accepted a dress code this stupid, but actually welcomed it. Collette had made it clear anybody who didn't make an effort with the fancy dress theme would pay the price, especially as her guest list now stretched to friends from school, and not just those in Walden.

"Wonder Woman," he addressed me, in a way that suggested he was enjoying himself way too much, "I'm afraid I'm going to have to arrest you. Anything you see can and will be held against you."

He straightened up, starting to broach the distance between us. However, once he got close enough, reaching over to place his hands on the small of my back, I ducked out of the way.

"Hey!" When I twisted back around, he was fake pouting. "What gives?"

"I may have agreed to go out with you all those months ago, Jay," I told him, "but that doesn't mean the offer can't be revoked if you keep using lines like that."

"Aw, come on. That was my best one."

"In that case, I'm in for a really long night." I shook my head, though I couldn't quite contain my smile. "Come on in, then, while I finish getting ready."

I stepped aside to let him across the threshold, shutting the door behind the pair of us. The clutch bag I'd been planning to take was strung over the arm of the sofa, so I grabbed it on the way to the kitchen: a space that seemed strangely empty in the absence of my other two family members. Jay, of course, didn't hesitate to make himself at home; he hopped right up onto the worktop as I began rummaging in a drawer for my keys.

"What time did Collette say this thing started, anyway?"

"Uh..." I pushed aside what had to be a dozen takeaway leaflets, horded by Daniel, in the hope of laying my hands on what I was looking for. "I think she said people were going to start getting there around nine, but she wanted us there early."

"I'm guessing the ever-eager Flaniel have left already?"

At this, I found myself grinning; the rest of us had taken to combining my brother and his girlfriend's names, joking that they spent so much time together they could no longer be counted as two separate people. Collette had once tried to do the same with Jay and

I, but after finding herself on the receiving end of two death glares, the term Jerin hadn't caught on.

"Of course. He left about half an hour ago. Aha!" My fingers enclosed cool metal; I'd found the keys. Bumping the drawer closed with my hip, I headed over to the kitchen island and dropped them into the bag. Turning back to Jay, I noticed he seemed momentarily distracted; the meeting of our gazes seemed to jolt him out of it, and I raised an eyebrow.

"Really, now?" I asked, though I was more flattered than I'd ever let on. We might've been an official item for six months now, but that hadn't been enough time to wrap my head around the whole thing, especially since I'd long grown used to his incessant flirting. Having it now directed at me still sometimes caught me off guard.

"Sorry," he said, not sounding apologetic in the slightest. The smirk threatening to tug the corner of his lip upward gave enough away. "Any particular reason why you didn't think to tell me about this outfit before?"

"Gee, I don't know. What reason do you think, Jay?" I couldn't keep my own smile from my face; maybe the effort I'd have to put into maintaining my decency in the skirt that night would be worth the reaction. "Do you need to take a cold shower or something before we leave?"

"Nah, I think I'll be okay."

Shaking my head, my gaze wandered slightly higher than his eyes. Under the bright light of the kitchen, I noticed his hair was almost glistening, raked through with what looked like half a tub of gel. Even his cap, tilting haphazardly on his head, wasn't enough to hide it completely. "Seriously, though. What have I told you about the hair gel? Less is more, remember?"

"And what have I told you?" he asked, jumping down from the counter. "I'm not taking any tips from the girl with purple hair."

We'd ended up too close, his face hovering above mine, and I realised just in time what he was planning to do. Determined not to give him the satisfaction, I ducked away at the last minute, moving before he had time to catch me in his arms.

"Oh, come on. What, are you going to avoid me all night? Don't I get to kiss my girlfriend?"

"Not if you keep insulting my hair, you don't," I told him.

He'd now taken to making a butchered attempt at a puppy dog expression, widening his eyes, though he knew nothing of the sort ever worked on me. "I take it back. I'm sorry."

"You'd better be."

"Anyway, you haven't said a word about my costume. What do you think? Sexy, huh?"

"On account of the fact you and my brother have chosen matching costumes, I am not about to tell you it looks sexy," I said. "And put your hat on straight. At least make an attempt to hide some of that hair gel."

Ignoring my piece of advice, he went on, dangling the handcuffs in front of my face. "These are awesome, though, aren't they? You've got to admit they're a nice touch. And they actually work. Look."

"Jay, I don't need—"

However, he'd already moved toward me, capturing my wrist in his gentle grip. With remarkable timing, he fastened one of the metal rings, and I heard the mechanism click into place. When he raised his hand, I found my own being dragged along with it.

"See!" he said, a little too triumphantly. "Now there's no getting away from me."

"A thought that fills me with dread," I returned jokingly. "We really ought to get a move on, though. You know what Collette's like when we show up late. Especially when she's under the stress of party planning."

"Oh, yeah." Digging his free hand into his trouser pocket, it was a few seconds before he froze, the smile vanishing from his face with unnerving speed. "Um…"

An instant reaction, my heart felt like it turned to lead, dropping to the pit of my stomach. Somehow, even before he'd said it aloud, I knew what was coming. "Jay," I said, with an extreme effort to keep my tone level. "What have you done?"

The sheepish expression was enough to confirm my fears. "Um… I'm not sure, but I think I may have misplaced the key somewhere on the way over here…"

"Jay!"

He winced, almost like he'd been expecting me to hit him – which I may have done, had the movement of my right arm not been compromised. "I could've sworn I put the key in my pocket!" he cried. "It's not my fault these trousers are so damn tight. It must have fallen out on the way over."

"Please tell me there's another key."

"Daniel's got another one," he told me.

"Oh, thank God." I leaned back against the worktop, exhaling a small breath of relief. It wasn't exactly the best case scenario, but at least it meant freedom was only as far away as Collette's party. "You know you're an absolute idiot, don't you?"

"I know, I know." He looked over at me, managing yet another sheepish smile. "How about seeing it as one of my many charms?"

"Until you get me out of this handcuff," I warned him, in a half-serious tone, "there's nothing even remotely charming about you."

"Fair enough." He reached over, picking up my clutch from the countertop and holding it out. "Suppose we better leave for Collette's party now, then?"

"The best idea you've had since you got here." I took the bag from him, looping the chain over my free arm. "Come on, then. Let's go track down what is quite literally the key to freedom."

I had to be thankful for Collette's insistence that we arrive early; it meant we were one of the first guests, and having free run of her house made it a lot easier to find my brother. She looked a little surprised upon opening the door, but any comment she might've been about to make was cut off by my interjection.

"Don't even ask," I warned, as I stepped through the doorway, pulling Jay along with me. "You don't want to know."

True to her own dress code, she looked predictably striking in a fashionable take on a pirate's costume: striped over-the-knee stockings, an eye-patch and matching hat. Her smoky eyes raked over the both of us as we came inside, a silent look of amusement noticeable across her whole face.

"Daniel's here already, right?" Jay asked her, as she closed the door.

"Yeah, he's in the living room with Flo," she replied, unable to keep the impending smirk from creeping onto her face. "But unlike you, he doesn't seem to be handcuffed to his girlfriend."

"Congratulations," I said to Jay over my shoulder, "you're an even bigger idiot than my brother. And that's saying something."

The living room had been set up for a bigger affair than we were used to; Collette's sofas had been pushed back further against the wall, the coffee table nowhere in sight, freeing up a larger space in the centre of the room. The door to the kitchen was wide open, the entire countertop full of packs of plastic cups – not to mention way more bottles than we'd ever need for the guest list she was expecting.

Daniel and Flo were cosied up on one end of the sofa, apparently only seeking to further prove our point about not classing them as separate people. These days, it was odder to see one of them on their own; their relationship had got serious fast, which kind of made mine and Jay's look like child's play in comparison. Still, I'd learned not to let it bother me. I was content with what we had, and we certainly weren't about to turn into Flaniel 2.0.

"Finally got here, then?" Daniel asked, before his eyes dropped to the way our hands were unusually linked. "Is that part of the costume, or…?"

"Please tell me you've got another key to these handcuffs," I said, hoping the desperation on my face was sufficiently evident.

Collette, who'd appeared in the doorway behind us, chose then to speak up. "You mean you've actually lost the key to those things?"

"Correction: Jay lost the key to these things," I said, raising my hand and taking his with it. "Please, Daniel. Do us a favour and pass us the spare."

"Are you joking?" he asked incredulously, an expression I didn't like the look of now written all over his face. Beside him, Flo's was similar, and the sinking feeling in my stomach intensified when I realised the situation had probably required more delicacy than I'd approached it with. "This is the funniest thing I've seen in a long time. You two like spending time together, right? Why don't you see how this works out?"

Disbelieving, I spun around to look for Collette's backup, but my heart sunk once I realised her expression matched Daniel's. "It is kind of funny," she pointed out.

"Come on, guys," Jay pleaded. "Just hand over the key and get us out of this."

Before anyone could further the conversation, the sound of the doorbell rung out across the house, and Collette appeared to spring into action. "That'll be the first of the lot from school," she announced, even though that was obvious in itself. "Party's just getting started. Man the stereo, Daniel."

"On it," he said, extracting himself from Flo, making for the sound system in the corner of the room. On the way, he turned to face Jay and I once more, eyes sweeping the two of us with an expression that only worsened my feeling of dread. "How about I let you have the key at the end of the night?" he asked, holding it up. "I don't know about everyone else, but I kind of want to see how this pans out."

"Stop kidding around," I snapped. "Just hand it over. This isn't funny."

"Actually," he said, as the sound of the front door opening and Collette's greeting travelled through to the living room, "I think it's hilarious. You two have fun."

"I'm going to kill you later," I warned, making to fold my arms over my chest, and realising I couldn't only when Jay let out a small yelp. "Oh. Sorry."

He turned away as the first few people entered the living room – a group of faces I recognised from various classes at school – and left Jay and I standing there, linked together in the most irritating of ways, and apparently with a few hours' suffering ahead of us.

As I looked over at my boyfriend and his stupid wonky police hat, all I could do was shake my head, suddenly at a loss for words.

"Erin."

The sound of his voice, a little too close to my ear, had me looking over. We were squashed up against one end of Collette's sofa, our linked arms splayed awkwardly in front of us, looking on as a group of tipsy partygoers – a group which included Flo and Daniel – carried out a very sloppy version of the Macarena. For the entire time we'd been sat here, I'd found myself staring at the metal contraption linking our wrists, mentally evaluating all the ways I could break it apart by force.

It wasn't that I didn't enjoy Jay's company – most of the time he was a laugh, despite his definite idiotic tendencies – but I was a firm believer in personal space, and this situation didn't exactly go hand-in-hand with that. Maybe Flo and Daniel would've been able to cope, but I was a little less tolerant.

Jay was looking at me with an unusual hesitance, which only had me feeling more wary. "What is it?"

"Don't shout at me."

I raised an eyebrow, but couldn't help feeling a little sorry for him; he looked genuinely apologetic, which had my tough exterior wavering slightly. "I'm not going to shout at you. Well, not unless you're about to cuff my other hand, because I really don't think our relationship could cope with that."

"Don't worry, I've learnt my lesson," he assured me, "but I feel like this is going to go down equally badly."

I sighed, but held my gaze all the same. "I can handle it. Just tell me."

He leaned in a little closer. "I have to go to the toilet."

I couldn't help letting out an exasperated groan; I clapped my free hand to my forehead. "You've got to be joking."

"I'm sorry, okay? You're going to have to come with me."

"Funnily enough, I gathered that part," I said, looking over at him, my expression caught somewhere in the midst of disbelief. "Well, I suppose it was inevitable at some point. Let's get this over with."

As we both gathered ourselves to our feet, skirting round the group still overly enthusiastically doing the Macarena, I heard Jay's voice behind me. "You know, we could always just consider this as taking our relationship to the next level," he said, the smile audible in his tone.

"This was a level I kind of hoped we'd never have to get to."

Collette's hallway was a lot quieter than the living room. It wasn't a wild party by any means, and she appeared to have kept the number of unknown plus-ones to a minimum, so the house was far from breaking point. Thankfully, the door to the downstairs bathroom was open, and the absence of a queue only meant less people to have to explain our situation to (something we'd already had to do dozens of times that evening).

"How are we going to do this?" I asked, as we approached the bathroom. "Is there any way I can stand outside the door?"

"I'm not on a lead," Jay pointed out. "These handcuffs are too short. It's never going to reach. You're going to have to come in with me."

"I've never hated my brother so much as I do at this moment," I muttered scathingly, thinking of how much I wanted to punch him. He was going to have some serious payback coming to him when we finally got out of this trap. If he and Flo ever got themselves into a similar mess, as unlikely as that was, they could stay like it forever. "Right. Let's get this over with quickly."

"Not like it's anything you haven't seen before," Jay murmured, almost under his breath, as I closed the bathroom door behind him.

I felt my cheeks beginning to flame. "Oh my God. Don't even go there," I warned, as he broke off into loud laughter. Turning on the spot, I fixed my gaze on a random spot amongst the gleaming tiles. "You know how much I hate you right now?"

"Not at all," he returned, in a tone that was far too cheery for the circumstances. "One day, we're going to look back at this and laugh."

"Jay?" I asked, still forcing myself to stare at the wall.

"Yes?"

"Shut up."

"Dance with me."

"No, Jay."

"Come on. Dance with me."

"In case you haven't noticed, we're handcuffed together. We can't."

"That doesn't have to stop us."

"It doesn't have to," I admitted, "but it probably should. We're going to make fools of ourselves if we try."

"Come on." He leaned in closer, nuzzling his head into my shoulder. In hindsight, I probably should've stopped him accepting the shots Daniel had offered us fifteen minutes ago; my brother, still highly amused by the whole thing, seemed committed to making the experience as hilarious as possible. Unfortunately, our perspectives on humour differed; he wasn't the one who had to deal with being attached to Jay, who got even flirtier than usual under the influence. If that was even possible. "You know you want to."

"Do I?"

He shot me a knowing look. "If you get up and dance, maybe later on we can do that thing you—"

I shoved him away as quickly as I could, but he only laughed off my reaction. "Oh my God, Jay. Not here."

"Why? Are you embarrassed?" he drawled, slurring his words a little.

"What do you think?" I murmured, willing my face to return to its normal colour; I only hoped it was dark enough to go unnoticed by anybody else. "Okay, fine. I'll get up and attempt to dance with you if you behave yourself for the rest of the evening."

"What if I don't want to behave myself?" he asked, wiggling his eyebrows in a ridiculous fashion. However, the look I gave him soon wiped the smirk from his face. "Okay, okay. I'll behave. Now come on. Let's dance."

"I'm not drunk enough for this," I groaned, as he gathered himself to his feet and pulled me with him.

"Luckily, I'm drunk enough for the both of us."

And his dancing presented a point that definitely couldn't be argued with; he wasn't exactly talented when sober, let alone under the influence of a little too much alcohol. For a moment, all I could do was stand there watching, my arm getting pulled around in sync with his slightly erratic movements, before he decided I had to take it up to a higher level of participation.

"Come on, Erin."

I quirked an eyebrow. "You know you look absolutely ridiculous, right?"

"You know you're jealous of my out-of-this-world dancing skills, right?" he shot back, with a self-satisfied smile. Then, suddenly, he had both arms around me, pulling me into something that was caught between a hug and a slow dance, despite the track on Collette's stereo being anything but slow.

Eventually, though, I had to give in. Looping my free arm around his neck, and intertwining our fingers as best we could when impaired by a clunky handcuff, I let myself match the rhythm of Jay's jerky movements. The triumphant grin that materialised across his face made it clear he was pleased with his persuasion, and I couldn't help but laugh.

"You know the most ironic thing, though?" I moved to murmur in Jay's ear, as the track melted into the next.

"What's that?"

"We're still better dancers than those two," I said, cocking my head towards Flo and Daniel, who were moving somewhat awkwardly as he tried to twirl her around, "and they're not even handcuffed together."

I heard Jay's laugh straight away, a little too close to my ear, as he pulled me closer. And, in that moment, I realised maybe – just maybe – the night wouldn't turn out to be quite as unbearable as I first thought.

"Collette!"

I elbowed my way through the living room, Jay in tow, and through the open door into the kitchen. There, I found the girl I was looking for: she was leaning up against the countertop, plastic cup in hand, giggling wholeheartedly at something Scott was saying. Her pirate hat had slipped sideways, teetering wonkily on the side of her head, but she didn't seem to have noticed.

"Collette," I said again, and this time she looked over.

"Erin!" she greeted, the corner of her mouth quirking upward when her gaze flickered toward the handcuffs once again. "How's it going?"

It must've been past one; the place seemed significantly sparser as time wore on, and I'd seen a few people drifting towards the front door as parental curfews began to come into force. Jay, whom I was now physically withholding drinks from, despite his determination to consume more alcohol, had now reached slightly inappropriate levels of flirtatiousness, at which point I decided it was best to supervise his journey home.

But before I could do that, of course, I needed to locate my brother.

"Have you seen Daniel?" I asked.

"We don't need Daniel," Jay drawled from behind me, coming up and wrapping his arm around my waist. "Let's stay like this forever."

Resisting the urge to laugh, I shot a look at Collette that I hoped read please help me now. "Um... I think he went home with Flo, actually," she said slowly, wincing as if in preparation for my reaction. "Didn't he give you the key already?"

"No, he didn't," I said through gritted teeth. "You're sure he left?"

"He definitely said they were going back to Flo's," Scott piped up. He too had a plastic cup in one hand, with an oversized buoyancy aid tucked under the other arm: the prop he'd been carrying around all evening, as part of his lifeguard costume. "Didn't mention that he still had the key, though."

"That little shit." I shook my head scathingly. "I swear, when I see him tomorrow..."

My train of thought was interrupted by Jay pulling me even closer, squeezing me a little tighter than necessary, for no particular reason. "Are you trying to get rid of me?" he asked.

"That's exactly what I'm trying to do," I told him, biting back a smile. "You hit the nail right on the head there, Jay." Shaking my head, I glanced between Collette and Scott, who both seemed to be torn between looking amused and sympathetic. "Well, I guess we're going to have to follow him back to Flo's, then, because we need this key…"

"We can't go there!" Jay protested, so forcefully his loud voice had me wincing.

"Why not?"

"They've gone home together," he said, purposely slowly, and not just because of the alcohol. "You know what they're doing."

I couldn't help but grimace. "Shut up. That's my brother. I don't want to think about that."

Still, despite this, I knew Jay had a point – which was nothing short of remarkable, considering the lack of sense he'd been talking most of the evening. As desperate as I may have been for freedom, there was a definite list of things I didn't want to walk in on, and I couldn't guarantee that a trip to Flo's would end well.

"Right, then," I said bracingly, glancing over my shoulder at Jay. "Guess you're sleeping over."

"Result!" he exclaimed, with what was meant to be a surreptitious wink in Scott's direction, but ended up being the least subtle thing I'd ever seen.

His laughter, however, soon dried up once I'd hit him in the arm.

***

"You better be quiet."

"I can be quiet."

I couldn't help but raise an eyebrow. "Are you sure? Because you spent the whole walk home singing Taylor Swift at the top of your lungs."

He grinned sheepishly. "I got it out of my system."

"For everybody's sake, I hope so," I said. "Now shut up. Mum should be asleep, but I'm not about to take any chances."

We were stood on the front doorstep of my house, as we had been for the last two minutes: the entirety of which I'd spent trying to convince Jay of the importance of him shutting up. It was nearing two in the morning, and I wasn't exactly in the mood to try explaining why on earth I was handcuffed to my boyfriend – and with no sign of a key – to my mother.

"Don't worry about it," he told me, in a surprisingly reassuring tone. "We got this."

As it turned out, he was true to his word; once I'd unlocked the front door as quietly as possible, I managed to lead him all the way up the staircase, hissing instructions about exactly which step creaked the loudest. The whole thing kind of felt like a military agenda. However, with each step we surpassed, the tight feeling of anticipation in my chest loosened a little, and I realised we might actually make it unnoticed.

Once inside my room, and with the door safely closed behind us, I couldn't help but let out a sigh of relief.

"Told you, didn't I?"

I smiled; alone in the quietness of my bedroom, the reality of the situation seemed to finally be sinking in. And it was kind of hilarious.

"Yes," I said gently. "I suppose you did."

"After all this, you better be letting me sleep in your bed."

I raised an eyebrow, shooting him an incredulous look. "After all the trouble you've caused me tonight? As if. You can stay on the floor. With any luck, Daniel will be home first thing tomorrow morning."

"Oh, come on, Erin. Just admit it. You've loved this whole thing."

I scoffed. "As if."

He stepped a little closer, looking down to meet my gaze. "You loved it just as much as you love me."

"In other words, not at all?" I offered, with an innocent smile.

Without warning, he had both his hands on the small of my back, dragging me closer until the space between us was verging on nonexistence. He'd taken his cap off somewhere in the evening, so I could see his ridiculously spiked hair up close, which was enough to stop me wanting to run my hands through it. "I beg to differ," he said, too quietly, before leaning in.

We didn't exactly get far on the whole kissing front; with what had to be the worst timing ever, my phone vibrated, making us both jump. With some slightly awkward adjustment, I was able to fish it out of my bra (the costume was nowhere near practical enough to come with pockets), pulling up my newest text onscreen. It came complete with Daniel's name.

Oops, it read. I think I forgot something.

Rolling my eyes, I typed out my one-handed reply as quickly as possible. You think?!

Sorry. I owe you one, Erin. Name your price.

The idea entered my head almost immediately; as it did, I could feel the involuntary smirk creeping onto my face. I think it's your turn to spend a little time in the handcuffs, I tapped out.

With Flo?

Glancing upward, my gaze met Jay's for a split second, who was looking on unknowingly. Actually, I returned, I kind of had somebody else in mind.